D0554174

RENEWALS 458-4574

DATE DUE

MY FATHER'S WAR

THE NEW PRESS INTERNATIONAL FICTION SERIES

Tahar Ben Jelloun *Corruption*
Hector Bianciotti *What the Night Tells the Day*
Bruno Bontempelli *The Traveler's Tree*
Patrick Chamoiseau *Creole Folktales*
Marguerite Duras *The North China Lover*
Tibor Fischer *Under the Frog*
Tibor Fischer *The Thought Gang*
Romesh Gunesekera *Monkfish Moon*
Romesh Gunesekera *Reef*
Abdulrazak Gurnah *Paradise*
Mark Kharitonov *Lines of Fate*
Jaan Kross *Professor Martens' Departure*
Jaan Kross *The Czar's Madman*
Antoine Volodine *Naming the Jungle*

MY FATHER'S WAR

A Novel

Adriaan van Dis

Translated from the Dutch by
Claire Nicolas White

THE NEW PRESS • NEW YORK

Library of Congress Cataloging-in-Publication Data
Dis, Adriaan van.
[Indische duinen. English]
My Father's War: a novel / Adriaan van Dis:
translated from the Dutch by Claire Nicolas White.
p.— cm.
ISBN 1-56584-033-X
1. Indonesia—History—Japanese occupation, 1942–1945—Fiction.
2. Dutch—Indonesia—History—Fiction.
3. World War, 1939–1945—Concentration camps—Indonesia—Fiction.
I. White, Claire Nicolas, 1925– . II. Title.
PT5881.14.I8I513—1996
839.3' 1364—dc20   95-49084
CIP

Originally published as *Indische Duinen* in the Netherlands by J. M. Meulenhoff bv.
Published in the United States by The New Press, New York
Distributed by W. W. Norton & Company, Inc., New York

Established in 1990 as a major alternative to the large, commercial publishing houses,
The New Press is a full-scale nonprofit American book publisher outside of the university presses. The Press is operated editorially in the public interest, rather than for private gain; it is committed to publishing in innovative ways works of educational,
cultural, and community value that, despite their intellectual merits, might not normally be commercially viable. The New Press's editorial offices are located at the City
University of New York.

Book design by Ann Antoshak
Printed in the United States of America

9 8 7 6 5 4 3 2 1

MY FATHER'S WAR

THE GIRLS wanted to see the coast. They could hear excited voices in the hall and a loudspeaker broadcasting over all the decks: Holland in sight. The steam whistle blew, steps tramped on the stairway, seagulls screeched. The girls climbed out of their bunks and pushed the trunk in front of the porthole. The youngest got the first peek, her two sisters lifted her up. She flattened her nose against the pane and said, "Nothing but waves." The glass clouded over.

In the corner of the cabin next to the door their mother was washing herself at the little washstand, the water splashing onto the wooden floor. She took the towel from its hook and looked at herself in the mirror. She sighed. Every morning she rose exhausted, and it was a relief that the mirror steamed over, so that as she dried herself she could not see the deep lines in her face. The cabin was airless, and she went to the porthole to unlatch it. A cold salt breeze blew into the room, and the girls shivered, pulling sweaters on over their pajamas. A gull flew by, lazier than the kind that had been following the ship; it must be a land gull.

"My turn," said the second girl, pushing her mother aside, and stuck her head out the porthole. She looked disappointed. No land was in sight.

"Look down," said the oldest. "Holland is below sea level." She stood on the trunk, legs spread wide, sticking out her bottom and making a telescope with her hands.

There was a knock at the door. A bald man entered, fully dressed, carrying a short military jacket. The youngest ran toward him and threw herself into his arms. She wrapped her legs around his waist, her body bent over backward and her arms outstretched. "Justin, Justin," she cried. "I saw the Dutch sea!"

He laid the child down gently on the bed and cuddled her brown belly. "It's called the North Sea," he said. "In a few hours we'll be in Amsterdam." He kissed the mother and leaned over the second girl, but she drew back.

"Ada," her mother admonished her, "say hello when Justin speaks to you."

"Hello," Ada snarled. Going to the washstand, she began to brush her teeth.

The bald man laughed, shrugged his shoulders, and went to the window. "Come, Jana, you'll catch cold." He put his arm about the oldest girl's hips and drew her to him. "You're looking in the wrong direction. The coast is to starboard."

Against the light the mother could see how skinny Jana's legs were through her pajama bottom.

While the girls dressed, the man pulled an orange ribbon from the pocket of his pants. "Today is a holiday," he said. "It's Princess Juliana's birthday."

The thirtieth of April, how could he remember such things? She no longer counted the days and had no idea how long they had been at sea; even her body ignored the calendar. The mother was nauseous and way overdue. She cut the ribbon into three equal lengths, its stiff fabric crackling in her fingers. Her daughters' hair was too short to hold a bow. Before they had come on board, a nurse had shaved all the children's heads. There had been a scabies epidemic in Palembang.

The girls couldn't wait to see their new country and ran down the corridor, danced impatiently behind slow-moving passengers, and squeezed up the stairs along the banister. They wore sweatpants under their skirts, and their mother insisted they button their new duffel coats and tie the hoods under their chins. She did not trust the Dutch spring, and the children were still recuperating from various illnesses. After Port Said, one epidemic after another had spread on board— measles, scarlet fever, whooping cough. To dress warmly was the best medicine.

Their mother shuffled along after them, holding on to both railings, for climbing stairs was hard on her. Her legs would not obey. When she poked her thighs with a finger in the morning, after washing herself, dents stayed in her skin. She swallowed calcium and vitamins but could not get rid of the edema. Strange, in hard times her resistance had been much greater, but on board, where she could relax, she had lately been too tired to go to the saloons. At night the girls brought her dinner in bed, and Justin kept her company until dark. As soon as the oldest girl fell asleep, he returned to his cabin.

But this time she must go on deck, for she wanted to show her children their first villages. Had they ever seen a stone pier, a lighthouse, floodgates, a black-and-white cow? She shivered, for she had been unable to find a winter coat that fit. The Red Cross had only provided small sizes. On the boat she had cut three jackets out of the coat that had been given to her in Ataka.

The main deck was crowded. Where had all these people suddenly come from? Entire families from the East Indies were huddled against the railing; most of them had never shown their faces in the saloons, and now they were mingling with the Dutch citizens to get a glimpse of this strange country. The mother pitied the women in their sarongs and kabayas. Landing in Holland in those clothes, they were sure to have a hard time, she thought. Even a thick blanket wouldn't be any help.

Justin wrapped his jacket around her shoulders and rubbed her arms to warm them. She leaned against him, but the feel of her bony hips poking him frightened her. She was ashamed. When she had met him in Palembang, she was still strong, even though she was only skin and bones. She had still had the will to fight for survival, but after they left the Mediterranean, the oppressive gray sky sapped the last remnants of her energy. Her eyeteeth were loose, and she found gray hairs on her pillow—no doubt caused by delayed fear, she told herself. How could she possibly have danced all night under a starry sky in Egypt, buoyed by a ship's band that had come aboard in Aden and left them in Port Said, to travel southward on another ship? She had felt safe in his arms, and he was a good leader, but would he also be able to play a role in her life?

The adults crowded along the railing, but to the children the coast remained hidden behind pants and wraps. Justin lifted the youngest onto his shoulders, and the mother wobbled next to him, standing on tiptoe. She was a head taller but couldn't see any more than he, for a fine drizzle colored everything gray. The engines pounded at full speed, the ship turned and rolled less, they could feel the waves in their wake. People pointed. There, over there should be the locks. An Amboinese engineer thought he saw a windmill.

"At the first sight of Holland you may make a wish," said the mother.

"A drawing pad," cried the youngest and, excited, she drummed on Justin's head.

"A secret wish, Saskia, otherwise it won't come true," her mother said. She took a deep breath and stepped forward. "These children have never seen their homeland," she called in a loud voice. "Now it's their turn. Don't rob them of a precious memory." She took Jana and Ada by the hand and, excusing herself over and over, wormed her way through the dense crowd. To her own surprise she could hear the upper-class guttural Dutch accent, which had softened in the East Indies, rise out of her throat, returning automatically now that the land of her birth was in sight. Forgetting how ill she felt, she cleared a stretch of railing with a broad gesture, grabbed several unattended children by the collar, and drew all those who were young and undersized forward. Justin and Saskia followed obediently.

The ship's horn blew, and at that very moment the sun broke out, a tentative sun. There lay the dunes, layers deep, the clouds torn by the light, and the sand turning a golden yellow. No one said a word. Gulls dove toward earth, and the sun made shadows dance over the dunes, a wajang shadow play in the cold. Married couples looked at each other and reached for each other's hand.

"What are those?" asked Saskia.

"Dunes," the mother said. "The dunes of Holland." Her voice quivered.

"They look like cake," said Saskia.

Bystanders laughed and cried all at the same time. A woman cleared her throat and burst into song, "Where the white crests of the dunes glisten in the blazing sun." The crowd joined in, but the girls kept their lips tightly closed, for they were crazy about cake and were making wishes in silence. Justin stared up at the sky to hide the fact that he did not know the words. He too shivered, but with cold rather than emotion. How in heaven's name could people think of a feeble ray of sunlight as blazing?

The ship entered the lock and the water level sank, but the land was sinking even more. Passengers applauded. Men standing on the quay leaned a gangplank against the railing, threw their bags on deck, and jumped aboard just as the gates opened. The Amboinese engineer saluted, and adults crowded around the newcomers. This was a solemn moment, for Holland was coming to welcome them, but the men picked up their bags in silence and did not utter even a single word of greeting.

Now the children took over and began to clamor and shout: Such fat cows, they had never seen such monsters! And so many churches, and flags, all in their honor! And their mother explained, yes, that was a meadow, and that lowland a polder, and that odd-looking barn with the crooked roof was not a barn at all but a haystack, provisions for the cows to eat in winter. She remembered the smells, this land had formed her. You could tell by looking at her, no matter how weak and wasted she was, for she had hands that could turn a calf during birth. Her father had been a gentleman farmer and had been known as the Tough Guy in the village where she was born. She was built like him and could stand a hell of a lot. Amazing how delicate and dainty her daughters looked, amazing that such elegance could be born to a farmer's daughter, the slender fingers, the flat little noses and the almond-shaped eyes—they were splendid daughters. She loved the way they looked, and in this Dutch light they seemed even darker than they had under the tropical sun. Not until now had she seen their *kuliet angsep* in all its glory, they had the golden skin of her husband. Didn't they have any of her own looks? Would they be able to bicycle into the wind or would the frost bite their little bats' ears too sharply? Cod-liver oil, it would be the first thing she'd buy after landing. To survive in Holland, you had to swallow a lot.

And they would manage, for mother and daughters had one thing in common—they adapted easily. They could adjust to anything when necessary. On this princess' birthday they showed their mettle, for the pilot had brought his children on board and they had drawn a hopscotch game on deck, with a heaven and a hell, such as her daughters had never seen in the East Indies, and look how cleverly they had caught on to the rules! Only half an hour in the new land, and already they played the strange games better than those *kaaskoppen*, those little cheeseheads. That's the spirit! And that they inherited from her.

She was afraid nevertheless. Would she herself be able to make it? Uncertainty overwhelmed her. She had no money, no home, her health was failing. What should she do? Hope or resign herself? Nausea rose in her throat. For an instant she thought she was losing consciousness, but Justin supported her.

People were returning to their cabins as they were told to fetch their hand luggage and to wait for further instructions in the dining saloon. Pretty soon they would be stepping ashore. Already they could see the flags hanging from the towers, and pretty soon they would be dealing with the Dutch bureaucracy. The men who had come aboard were distributing forms to be filled in. They were government officials, and their welcome consisted of paperwork. What would she write down—married or formerly married?

The girls walked backward down the stairs. Without the sea breeze the hold was even more airless. Justin disappeared into his own cabin to pick up his duffel bag, and the mother longed to lie down for just a little while. But the halls were noisy and full of commotion, the officials were inspecting the cabins. When the girls came to their own cabin, they saw that their trunk had been broken into. The mother groped for an arm to steady herself and fainted.

There was nothing seriously the matter, the ship's doctor said, the vapors perhaps, an emotional fit, that's all. Some smelling salts and Mother could get up and walk again. Edema, yes, he had noticed that, and he touched her slightly swollen belly. He pulled a stethoscope out of his bag and put the metal cone against her stomach. A smile, another probe, and then a serious expression. "Just step out into the hall for a minute," he told the girls then washed his hands and looked at the papers he was holding. "When did you last see your husband?" he asked.

"At the beginning of forty-two," said the mother.

"And have you had news from him yet?"

"No, the Red Cross is very slow."

"As soon as you get home, you better have a complete checkup."

Home, home, was there a home? To return to the Tough Guy was out of the question. Her father had never forgiven her for leaving for the East Indies at such an early age. He knew her husband and her children only from snapshots. He had never seen them in the flesh. No, she couldn't face it yet. She would keep her distance. She'd rather land in a home for immigrants, use her own wits, even if she had to scrub floors on her knees.

"And where do you plan to go?" asked the official in the dining saloon.

"I have no idea," said the mother.

"Any family?"

"I haven't been able to get in touch with them yet."

"What do you mean? Is there no mail service in the East Indies?"

"I want to file a complaint."

"You can send a free telegram."

"My tea was stolen."

"Let's first see to the list, Madam."

"My trunk was broken into."

"Lady, you're lucky to be admitted to the Netherlands at all." He looked at his papers. "Do you have any preference?"

She did not understand.

"North or south? City or country?"

She turned toward Justin, who was giggling with the girls as they recited the railroad stations from north to south: "Roodeschool, Groningen, Assen, Hoogeveen, Meppel. . . ."

"I don't know," she said.

"There is still room on the coast."

"In the dunes, in the dunes," the girls exclaimed.

"And that business with the tea," the mother said later, after they had been living in the dunes for several weeks. "I minded that more than three and a half years in the prison camp."

1

DEATH IN THE FAMILY

FORTY-SIX years later I stood by my half-sister's deathbed.

Ada was dying, with open eyes. She was seeing something we were unable to, and we saw ourselves mirrored in her tears—mother, brother, sister, son, and husband. Tiny, we swam inside her retina and washed down her cheeks in smudges. Then the light grew dim.

Saskia pressed her sister's mouth closed and tried to raise her lips into a smile; then she lowered the eyelids with a practiced gesture. One could tell that this was not the first time she had closed the eyes of the dying.

The family had been standing around the deathbed since early morning. Ada had not been able to sleep for days, she was caught up in a circle of waking and pain. We did not want her to depart alone. Outside, weeds were waving behind the curtains, the sun had already passed the zenith, and children's voices rose from the summer gardens, but no matter how often I looked away and focused my attention on other sounds, Ada's death rattle bored through everything. Her dying was a tough process.

Her son Aram kept watch, sitting with legs akimbo at the foot of her bed. His fists clutched the railing, his knuckles white, as if he wanted to push his mother away from death. He was still young, only just fourteen, but that day he behaved like a man, strong and self-controlled. Aram pulled back when Saskia put her arm around him, he withdrew his fist when his grand-mother tried to caress him. His body was trembling in protest, the muscles in his neck throbbed, he could no longer control his tears, large drops fell on the blanket, strong and far-reaching, like the first seed of an adolescent. I thought it inappropriate to think of anything as life-giving as seed at this deathbed, but Aram reminded me too much of the days of my own father's dying and of my own growth from boy to manhood.

I was eleven when I lost my father. I did not see him die, my mother thought I was too young to visit the hospital. (As if I had had no experience of death: I had speared porpoises washed ashore onto my stick, and I had fished seagulls paralyzed with tar out of the surf.) Still, I saw my father fight for those final hours, I listened carefully to the stories my mother and the girls told. It is possible to see with one's ears.

My father was a fierce patient. I saw him squirm with pain, he kicked, swept the medicine from his bedside table, and almost choked to death. The nurses had to attach his oxygen mask with tape. My mother referred to the mask as spectacles. I imagined him wearing a pilot's goggles. Goggles to help him breathe.

"He's wearing spectacles on his nose," she said on her return from the hospital. "He says I smell of garlic." We had to take turns smelling her mouth, her hands . . . just mother smell, redolent of the white cream in the jar with the blue lid next to the washstand, fresh as usual. "What he smelled was his own death," the family doctor said later, when he paid a condolence call.

According to the night nurse, my father's last words were, "The sea, the sea." He had pulled off the tape and was suffocating. The oxygen mask lay on his stomach. My mother came too late to take him to the ship.

In my imagination my father changed into a bespectacled sea serpent who could see through walls and blankets, and a few years later, when I masturbated for the first time, he came swimming by at the foot of my bed, hissing with disapproval. My seed smelled of garlic.

Aram's tears fell on my hand. We adults sniffled a little or shed no tears at all. Perhaps it was because of the beauty of Ada's wasted body that sex came to mind. She was lovely, all her curves had turned inward, her bones gave a new outline to her shoulders, arms, and hands, and the skin of her chin had withdrawn into the hollow below her jaw. She was once more a six- or seven-year-old girl from the East Indies, a "child of the camp," as Mother put it.

Saskia spoke encouragingly to her sister, asked her whether she was comfortable, whether she was thirsty, and even though Ada could no longer speak or make any sign with her eyes or lips, Saskia translated her wishes out loud. "Yes, she wants some more to drink." She poured some drops of water into a teaspoon and carefully let the liquid flow onto Ada's teeth. Even her gums were receding, she had teeth like a skeleton's. Saskia bathed her clammy forehead with a washcloth and brought an extra blanket; her sister was growing cold. Saskia performed these tasks with love and skill; she was the only one in the family who could change sheets while the patient lay in the bed. It was really convenient for us that she had been a nurse at one time. Ada had not wanted a stranger in the house, it took a vocation to take care of the dying, Saskia thought. "Yesterday the doctor wanted to give her a pill for her heart, just like that, one of those huge pink capsules down her throat. Let me do that, I said, you will choke her to death. I ground the pill to a fine powder and dissolved it in water. Ah well, they're so clumsy." I was feeling too guilty not to agree with her.

Saskia had been nursing Ada for weeks, she came every day to wash, to iron, to massage her bedsores, and every night she called me to tell me how tired she was and how much she had done for her sister. I did not tell her that Ada had complained to me, "She is nursing me into my grave. I am not dying. The bad moments are only temporary. The sinking spells are getting shorter."

And the sinking spells did get shorter, but Ada had no more ups, only downs, a straight downward slope into the grave. She no longer left the bed, her skin no longer healed, she lost weight by the pound, she became incontinent, her legs began to swell until the water settled behind her lungs. Her breasts withered, but death brought two bubbles of water to her back in return. Provisions for the journey. Saskia saw the spots of dead skin grow, we could not see them, we could not smell her death as Saskia did; but then, we had not been trained to do so.

Ada would not swallow painkillers, she did not want to pollute her body. No chemotherapy, no surgery, the quality of life was what mattered. Only nature could heal her: injections of Iscador, an elixir of mistletoe. Just as mistletoe strangles the tree, so this elixir was supposed to strangle the cancer. A symbolic medicine of anthroposophy. Alas, my sister was not a tree.

As her body weakened, her mind must have searched desperately for an anchor. It radiated from the bookcase behind her bed: *Vital Questions, Mysteries of the Soul, The way to Insight Into Higher Spheres*... one esoteric work after another. And then the drab pictures on the calendar from the organic food store: expanding universes, vague creatures with auras and chakras, lots of smudges, very few outlines. But ah well, there was something comforting about all this, our house by the sea had been full of such images. Our mother happened to believe that all manner of invisible things float between heaven and earth, she had experienced it in the East Indies, where there was a vacuum in the universe, and anyone who had lived there a long time and was receptive to it became naturally initiated. On every child's birthday she read a new horoscope for the celebrant, she planted and sowed by the full moon, and on Christmas Eve, when the cosmos was full of positive energy, she put out a loaf of wholewheat bread for the sick. With such cosmic blessings the bread would never grow moldy, and whoever had some ailment or other received a slice of bread that had been thus exposed to the beneficent rays. Ada, too, did not escape her portion.

It was a world that belonged to the dunes, and to the guna guna magic of the East Indies, of which the perfumes lingered for a long time about the cabin trunk.

Saskia refused to give her sister Iscador injections. When Ada grew too weak to inject herself, Saskia threw all the needles and vials in the garbage. The cancer was too widespread, there was no point in slowing down the process. As a trained nurse, she would devote her skills only to the living, she said. She would have no part of torture. She used big words, mentioned the Hippocratic oath and her respect for death, which would, in the end, overtake us anyway. Though she had only briefly exercised her profession, she never lowered her standards.

The last days of her life Ada was given a single paracetamol pill for sleep.

Saskia firmly controlled her sister's dying. Pulse, breathing—each faltering exhalation was observed with a lifted index finger. When Ada's breathing slowed and she was clearly letting go, Aram's protest also diminished; he could no longer steer his mother to her salvation. He left the room and began to kick a soccer ball around the hallway. Maarten, his father, who had been sitting by Ada's side since early that morning, cornered between Ada's bed and a dried-out ficus tree, looked up in distress.

And it went on and on, until Saskia stopped us from leaving the room, even Aram had to return to his post. He put the ball under the bed, looked at his father, and straightened his back. The sun threw a beam of light into the back room, somewhere far away a group of children assaulted a garden, one last death rattle, and Saskia announced solemnly, "Ada is gone." She took her sister's pulse and looked at her watch. "Ada passed away at five fifteen." She closed her sister's eyes and suppressed a sob.

Maarten laid his head on her pillow. We withdrew from the room. But Ada changed her mind. She began to shake, her husband pulled back, and the ficus tree lost some of its leaves from the shock. Her chest heaved, scraping and squeaking like an old cart, but she was breathing. She looked at us and wept.

Saskia took over at once. Firmly she closed Ada's eyelids and brushed away the tears. This time she did not let go, as if glue had to dry. Rigor mortis didn't have a chance. "These are post-mortem reflexes, don't worry," said Saskia. "It's quite normal."

"Perhaps she isn't dead yet," I said.

"I've seen hundreds of people die," she countered, offended.

Such authority could not be questioned. Ada had died. We kissed her good-bye, and again she opened her eyes . . . brown diamonds. Half an hour later she let out a final breath, a breath from no-man's-land, and her eyes became dusty coals.

We went to the front room and closed the glass sliding doors. Saskia stayed behind to make the bed, removing the blankets and smoothing the sheets. Ada was now no more than a fold in the whiteness. She yawned at the ceiling, for she simply couldn't manage a smile. And yet she had died with a smile; after the pain, peace had returned briefly, she must have seen something very beautiful until, with a sneer, death turned her rigid.

The anthroposophic doctor dropped by (socks knitted from goat's wool, sandals, and a fringe of whiskers, sometimes every cliché is true). He officially declared Ada dead, then disappeared quickly. Too quickly to suit me. Did he suspect that I would have loved to take him aside? This man had encouraged Ada's denial of her illness, and now he sat here by her dead body filling out the forms. I couldn't help calling him a murderer, rather too loudly. This made the family so nervous that before I knew it, he had been urged out the door.

We were waiting for the undertaker.

"My condolences to you all," said Mr. Korst. Ab Korst was from the Verduyn Funeral Home ("Your adviser at a time of personal loss" was written on his card.) He dropped a bulging black attaché case next to the chair and bowed slightly, causing his black trousers to ride up and reveal a stretch of hairless shin, white as a whiting. He himself looked rather like a fish—bulging eyes, a mouth gasping for air, weak; his black suit and vest shone like scaly armor.

"Forty-two years in the business, madam," he told my mother, "And we still don't understand grieving. I cannot take away your grief, but perhaps I can give a little relief."

We nodded in agreement.

"Milk and sugar?" Saskia asked.

"Yes please, Madam, but first I would like to look at the deceased." Mr. Korst went to the back room and leaned over the body.

"He's kissing her!" exclaimed Aram.

"No, he's smelling," Saskia said.

We were all grateful that she had had nurse's trained.

"Divine, Madam," said Mr. Korst as he swirled the last sip left in his cup and then gulped it down. "At home or in the funeral parlor, Sir?"

"I think Ada would rather stay home," said Maarten.

"Then let's do that," agreed Mr. Korst. "It's not the same, of course. At Verduyn there's ample parking, and our parlors are provided with appropriate music and with flowers that are always fresh."

"I'd rather keep her here until the funeral," Maarten insisted.

"Just as you wish, Sir. We'll make sure that Mother looks her best."

The coffin. Mr. Korst opened a folder with samples of seven kinds of wood, as if it were a question of a new floor. Maartin looked away, but Mother pointed without hesitation at the least expensive kind. "This one," she said. "Ada loved birches."

"Simplicity, Madam. You prefer sober and plain?" asked Mr. Korst. "We respect that."

The limousines. "Two? Perhaps one extra for the elderly mourners, who will be driven right to the hall? It is still quite a walk from the parking lot."

Big hall, smaller hall? The coffin visible or behind a partition, a red glow indicating its presence? Black or gray border on the envelopes? Coffee with or without cake? A little wine? Anything was available, there were still a lot of choices to be made after one died.

The urn. "The gentleman does not wish an urn? Present at the scattering of the ashes, yes or no? And does the gentleman wish to be advised of the date?"

Mr. Korst was making his calculations. "Fifty envelopes are included in the burial policy. A hundred more, that will be an additional hundred and five gulden. A third limousine, two hundred and fifty extra. Sure you wouldn't like the ashes scattered over the sea? No? Then shall we do it in the rose garden? That will fit nicely within the price range. Simplicity also has its charms," he stated as the total amount appeared in red on his pocket calculator.

"And what about the announcements?" he asked while taking down the quotation. I gave him three texts we had composed just before he came, while we were sitting around the kitchen table.

"Do forgive me, Sir," he said. "You wrote 'After a short illness.' We always recommend, 'After a brief illness.' After all, *short* is a measure of length."

"Another cup of coffee?" Saskia asked.

"It was divine, Madam." Mr. Korst grinned as he underlined another word. "Is 'in truth' not better than 'true'? And may I change 'with' to 'withal'?"

"I'd rather you didn't."

"I mean, considering the occasion, it is and will always remain a solemn one."

I lit a cigarette—the first one in months, snitched from Saskia's purse—and blew a cloud of smoke at the glass doors. For a moment Ada disappeared from sight.

"I have the weight of experience on my side, Sir, forty-two years in the business. Have you thought about the music yet?"

"I want to play the French horn," said Aram.

"Are you sure you want to, young man?" Mr. Korst asked. "You'll be upset, you know, often people don't know how they're going to feel on such a day, perhaps you'll play out of tune. We advise against it, we've had unfortunate experiences."

"You can play at my funeral," said my mother.

"We'll make a tape of it, Aram," his father suggested.

"With two ten-second intermissions, please, one while people are seated, and one when they leave," said Mr. Korst. Aram left the room, stomping. "It's bound to be emotional, isn't it," said Mr. Korst. "I recently buried my mother-in-law. Everyone said, 'Now that's right up your alley.' I laid her out myself, should be nothing to it you'd think, after forty-two years. Well, I tell you Madam, I was standing there bawling, with a capital B." He spread the thumb and the index finger of his right hand as far apart as possible. "I was amazed at myself."

"Yes," Saskia agreed. "I used to be a nurse, and I've seen hundreds of patients die, but family is something else again."

"That's so true, Madam. Here you have two veterans of the profession." Mr. Korst slid his chair close to Saskia's. "Tell me what you think. Shouldn't we change that to 'brief'?"

She looked at me questioningly. "Perhaps it's better."

"Certainly," said Mr. Korst.

Aram's ball was bouncing in the hall.

Saskia had been prepared for the day of Ada's death three times already. She was in touch with a great many essences these last months, including Sheila, one of the astronauts on *Challenger*, who had crashed with the crew a few years ago during the launching. Sheila now flew in a cocoon around the world and had chosen Saskia as her contact. The day of Ada's death would have something to do with the number nine, and according to my mother, that made a lot of sense, since nine stands for Mars, and is a number that governed our entire family from birth to death. Nines are fiery and passionate, their lives are noticeably difficult and full of strife, but they are not frightened; all these details fit the picture. Both her husbands had been born on the twenty-seventh day of a month, and two and seven add up to nine. The girls, too, were born on a twenty-seventh, and they had all been married on a twenty-seventh day. All the children also had the letter A in their names, because A (which equals one) stands for the sun, the spiritual bearer of light (positive and creative). At first Saskia thought Ada's death would happen on July ninth, but instead, her cleaning woman died on that day, which was also a blow but the wrong one.

On August eighth she telephoned the family to prepare them for the worst. "Will I see you again tomorrow?" she had asked her sister the night before as she stored the ironing in the closet.

"Yes, why not?" Ada answered, surprised.

The following day a man who lived in Saskia's street died. This, too, had upset her, even though she had not known the man. The month after that, she got it almost right, for her sister died on September 6. The number of the month fit, and flying upside down so far up, it is easy to misread a six for a nine.

Judith also put Saskia in touch with our deceased fathers, hers and mine, our mother's first and second husbands. Not only were they born on the same day, but both of them also happened to be called Justin. So as not to confuse them, the family referred to them as Just I and Just II.

Just I had been an Indo boy, as people born in the East Indies and with brown skin were called, and you were called a boy as long as you lived, no matter how impressive you might look in photographs in your dark dress uniform with stars and braids and ribbons, stitched collar, white-plumed helmet, and a sword dangling by your side. Justin van Capellen, first lieutenant in the Royal Colonial Army, son of a Dutch planter and a native woman.

My father was also in the Colonial Army, but he was not as high-ranking a member, his uniform was a simple battle dress. In his case, a sword would have dragged on the ground, for when he died, his trousers were already almost too short for me. Though he was undersized, he was a handsome fellow, even baldness looked good on him. His pate shone, brown as a peanut, but he wasn't half as dark as my mother's first husband. Just II said that he was tropical yellow, caused by the climate, for near the equator the sun burned right through your clothing. (Was his body as yellow in death as in life?)

His family had remained "pure blood" through six generations in the East Indies, and good Catholics besides. I'm afraid this mattered to him—not so much the faith, for already in the camp he had given that up, but the color of his skin. He preferred to see himself as a Dutch gentleman, never a boy (in fact, when I hear myself say "boy" with a colonial accent, it's as if I heard his words sizzling in hot oil like *Krupuk*). He joined the army when he was only sixteen, already a gentleman, never a boy.

He must have begotten me just before we all left for Holland, in Palembang, where hundreds of repatriates were waiting to be shipped home. Anything to kill time. That is how Just II also became the stepfather of Saskia and Ada and of Jana, the oldest of the three girls, who emigrated to Canada when she was only eighteen. Though we did not look like each other and had different last names, when we lived in the dunes, we played at being *one* family. Words that undermined this oneness were avoided at home. "Step" and "half" existed only in unpleasant fairy tales.

The astronaut also communicated visions of her father to Saskia. Apparently Just I was ready to receive his dying daughter attired in his full dress uniform. He stood waiting in the green light of dawn under a panoply of waving palm trees, at the head of a procession of bearers. Even in the car on the way to the funeral parlor Saskia saw her father gird on his sword. "He still keeps watch over us," she told her mother.

"He must have postponed his departure for her," was my mother's cool reaction, for to her the world was simply a transient abode, a coming and going of old and new souls.

My father, too, manifested himself. "Your father says to say hello to you," said Saskia when we first met at Ada's bedside. I had not seen her for a few years, and I immediately remem-

bered why. She'd always carried on about my father, no one had
been quite so warm and special a person: the rijsttafel he
cooked (it burned your tongue the minute you took the first
bite), the stories he told at the dinner table (we didn't sleep a
wink at night in terror), the kindling they used to gather
together for the open fire (she would have to carry all of it), the
books he read (books about the war), the originality of his
thoughts, his aristocratic frame of mind (pain is the best training, capital punishment for all traitors, and why not stand all
socialists up against the wall and shoot them, for they had, after
all, sold out the East Indies for a pittance).

Yes, he was willful, hard at times, Saskia agreed, but he definitely had his tender side. (Which meant that he spent my
mother's money like water, dressed like a dandy, and never
lifted a finger, the spoiled colonial brute.) But she, Saskia, had
discovered his remarkable qualities when she was young, they
had been kindred spirits. The tension between talent and duty,
how familiar she was with it. He gave her her first drawing
lessons, he taught her photography, and oh, how much pleasure
these things had given her. You'd damn well think she was the
fruit of his loins, and she made him out to be such an ideal
father that I was actually jealous.

Yet Saskia knew better. As she fussed about Ada's deathbed, I
was struck again by the size of the scar on her left thumb. It
marked a cut tendon that made it impossible for her to hold a cup
by its handle. She bore the traces of my father's love on her hand.

Mr. Korst had filled out the forms. ("Oh, the entire family was
born in Indonesia? The emerald circle, our best clients come
from there, warm-hearted people.") After the last signature had

been appended, two men appeared at the door with the coffin. Its finish was birch veneer, for solid wood was not covered by the policy. A little earlier Mr. Korst had communicated our choice by telephone to "the boys in the grief business": "And oh, please bring a slipcover as well." We had all been present.

Besides the slipcover, the undertaker's men also dragged a refrigerator table to the back room, a weekend would pass between death and cremation, and my sister would have to be preserved for five days. We turned our chairs away from the sliding doors and stared out to the front of the house. Some neighborhood kids were peering through the frosted glass windows of the double-parked hearse, disappointed that it was empty. Saskia closed the curtains. Now we stared at gauze drapes, and behind us a bed creaked, wheels squeaked, a zipper zoomed, and we heard Mr. Korst's instruction: "Careful, boys, don't force it."

I could see too much with my ears, and I went to the kitchen to find a tablecloth and some thumbtacks. As I pinned this improvised curtain to the sliding door, I saw Mr. Korst unfold a pair of my sister's clean pajamas. His fat fingers had trouble with the buttons, in spite of his forty-two years of experience. His hands were trembling.

They would make Ada look beautiful, and Mr. Korst came with a few final questions. The flower arrangements. The funeral parlor had sent along a catalogue, would we make our selection from it. "Guaranteed fresh." He showed us some color pictures of crosses, wreaths, and clusters filled with asters and carnations, "Sometimes even the flowers these fellows deliver die before they're laid on the coffin. Really terrible." We agreed,

I could not take my eyes from the illustrations. What would we say to a little ship, a musical note made of white carnations (Ada had sung in a choir), or perhaps a portrait in flowers? Exactly like a photograph, a mere thousand gulden, we would be amazed at what could be depicted with flowers. "We'll pick something from our own garden," Saskia said. She had already brought a small oasis into the house.

The eulogy. Who would deliver the eulogy? We all looked at Maarten, who sat in a corner mumbling to himself, "Without Ada, without Ada, how can that be?" For years now he had suffered from a debilitating illness that affected his nervous system and was hardly able to walk. The disease was also eating away at his brain. No, he would be unable to say anything, perhaps I'd be willing to thank everyone in the name of the family? This course was decided upon, and I was resolved to tell all.

"You will keep it short, won't you, Sir?" asked Korst.

"No, it's going to be a long story."

Mr. Korst leafed through the policy. "You are entitled to twenty-five minutes in the hall. If you want more time, we will need to charge you extra."

The undertaker's men required attention. These guys had become one with their profession, pale as corpses, their backs permanently bent from lifting. "How would you like the mouth?" asked the head undertaker. "It's a little open now, very natural, but we can close it altogether. What would you prefer?"

We couldn't decide so quickly. I searched for Saskia's cigarettes, and our hands met above her purse. We gave each other a conspiratorial pinch. When was the last time that I had touched her? I had not kissed her since my father's funeral (which I had not been allowed to attend, too sensitive). At that time she had cried harder than I liked, my father belonged to me, I would not kiss a traitor.

"When the mouth is closed, people often say, 'No . . . no . . ., that's no longer our mother,'" the undertaker explained. Being lovers of the natural, we chose the parted lips.

A few minutes later Mr. Korst invited us to come and admire the work of art: Ada, propped up high in her coffin, cushioned in some gray fabric, half under glass, her black hair dried and brushed, with a little makeup on her cheeks and lips, or perhaps it was the reflection from her pink pajamas on which blue swallows fluttered cheerfully between forget-me-nots. Her hands held a portrait of her father—Saskia's idea. A white plastic folder lay at her feet, the register of condolences. A dance card for her final party.

Maarten took his camera and flashed a picture above the glass, he hadn't seen his wife look so beautiful for months. There was a rumbling under the coffin, louder and louder, the ground shook with it. Ada trembled (so did I), and the leaded glass in the sliding doors rattled. Mr. Korst crept beneath the coffin, something was wrong with the mechanism. As the family left the men behind on their knees ("You don't suppose it has something to do with the cooling system, Ab?"), Aram's football came rolling out from under the coffin. The ball left a trail of slime on the linoleum.

Tomorrow I would come and address envelopes.

Maarten did not have a date book, his days were too empty, no address book, nothing. Ada had made all his appointments for him. What were the names of her friends? Who should be invited? Maarten had no idea; it was all too much for him. He

wanted a quiet cremation, tomorrow into the oven, and preferably with no one present. "Ada, without Ada," he kept repeating,
like a dull prayer, that's all I could get out of him.

We started with the family, the aunts and uncles-in-law.
Aram knew where they lived but not their last names. After
much telephoning we had a vague list, barely enough to fill *one*
row of chairs in the hall. Was this appropriate for my former sister, Ada, who was always writing letters, who attended camp
reunions and who year after year got together with her school-
mates? She must have kept her correspondence somewhere. "In
the drawers of the bookcase behind the coffin," said Aram.

I did not want to go into that room again. Last night I had
seen Ada die over and over, she was still gasping in my ears. First
I would try Maarten one more time. "Where do Namunia and
Aunt Nikki live?" I asked.

"Namunia . . . who is that?"

"Your Moroccan cleaning lady, Aram says."

"Namunia, Namunia . . . never saw her."

"And how am I to find this Aunt Nikki?"

Maarten shrugged. "Don't know her." The leaded panes
started shaking, the refrigerator had started up.

"The lady who saved Mama's life in the camp," explained
Aram.

"We haven't heard from her in years. She doesn't need
a card."

"Perhaps we should at least let her know."

"Yes, sure."

"And the name of her choir?"

"Something Christian, I think."

After an hour-long cross-examination I summoned up my

courage and stepped into the back room. I had to search through Ada's drawers, perhaps I would find more addresses, there was no avoiding it.

The stench and heat overwhelmed me, as if someone had left a pan of dirty dishwater on the stove. Saskia seemed to have brought flowers very early—sunflowers and long wild grasses, natural, as we had wanted. Aram had put them in front of the gas heater, but it was still lit, for Ada had been cold when she was dying, and the stems had become pulpy. The flowers were trembling. The refrigeration table fought against the heater. The sight of Ada had grown more unpleasant: she was yawning, one eye open, the other half-shut; the ficus valiantly tried to block the view with a final autumnal offensive. I blew the leaves from the glass and covered her face with my handkerchief.

To rummage through other people's drawers can be thrilling; it is improper when there is a body lying alongside. What all did I not discover: picture postcards from museums and countries visited during holidays, coupons, clippings, paper souvenirs, snapshots from the East Indies—Ada on the veranda playing with a raccoon, Ada standing proudly next to her father, who had shot a tiger—and Ada half erased on a drawing together with her sisters; three beribboned girls' heads. It was signed "Justin," in the same fine handwriting with which my father signed my report cards. The paper was almost falling apart and crumbling at the corners. I also found stacks of envelopes from which the addresses and the stamps had been cut off. I sniffed them, looked inside, read a sentence here and there: love letters from the time Ada worked as an au pair in London, with snapshots of boyfriends from the old days. My hands trembled. A violation of the grave. I did my best not to read further, I was searching for addresses and should not look at anything else.

I began at the bottom, on my knees, my head at the level of the coffin, but the higher the drawer, the better I could see Ada, peering at me from under the handkerchief. I did not want to look, but her drowsy eyes forced me, and I caught myself whispering to her, asking for advice. Did you really not keep any addresses? Never wrote anything down?

The top drawer was stuck and twisted, I banged it and shoved until it flew open and fell out of my hands, almost onto the glass lid of the coffin. A fan of green notebooks fell out onto the linoleum; they were faded and yellowed by the sun. One notebook had fallen completely apart, the binding was loose, but it had been ransacked before, pictures and pages had been torn out; the dried-out strips of adhesive tape lay on the ground.

I picked up the pages, quickly, so as not to be too sorely tempted, until I read the word Bankinang, the name of the camp in which my sisters and my mother had been imprisoned for years. This I was free to read, this was something I might use in my eulogy, and I began to read, any old where, the first sentence of a page picked at random.

"It was stiflingly hot there in the daytime and cold at night. There were five big sheds, 60 yards long, each shed for five hundred women and children, two corridors, sleeping places to the right or the left, no room to be alone, four lamps, one above each entrance, a *tampat*, an area 2 feet wide and less than 6 feet long per person. I could barely stand up there, Mama had to bend over. The four of us shared two mats. Aunt Nikki lived above us, she was a member of the committee and snored. When she peed and missed her chamber pot at night, it rained on us. For the rest, lots of busybodies you were supposed to call Auntie. They stole each other's laundry, I saw them, and accused us children. Liars who . . ." the end of this sentence was scratched out. "Women among each other worse than the Japanese!" Ada had written next to it.

Hello, Ada, this is how I recognize you, dear pest. What is this, an attempt to write a diary? And why these snatches, sentences without beginning or end?

No two pages were consecutive, whole passages had been blocked out with brown ink (India ink, it still smelled of school), supplemented with remarks written in a visibly more grown-up handwriting, as if she had later wanted to take revenge on her memory with pen, scissors and Scotch tape. "Indian = Indonesian!" was written several times in the margin, "Japs" had been crossed out and replaced with "Japanese."

"'Hunger does not taste good,' Mama says. I now know how you can eat the most disgusting things; close your windpipe, don't smell and swallow. I keep thinking of the two Japanese soldiers in Fort de Kock who slit our little pig's throat and drank its blood before our eyes. I thought it was very cruel and disgusting. Later I too ate fried blood and had to squeeze out a cow's eye. Mama didn't dare, but it contained half a liter of oil, now we could bake with it for a while. Anything tasted better than goat's bladder with glue."

I would not be able to keep a hallful of people entranced with cooking in the East Indies. I wanted them to laugh, or to cry, but the camp? No, I did not want to talk about things the whole family already knew, even though they used to tell nothing but lies about them.

I sat down on the linoleum, next to the gray drape, in the chill of the refrigerated table that was no wider than her sleeping area in the camp, her little *tampat*, and I drew the notebooks toward me. Some of them buckled with the clippings and dried flowers glued in them: evening primrose, wild violets, milkweed, dunerose, and snapdragon, the flora of my native village.

In these, the writing was a mixture of war and school. Pages of teenage purple prose, illustrated with pasted-in pictures, cut from magazines, of Rock Hudson and one of Edmundo Rossi singing in front of a red double-decker bus: London is the place for me. Already then. I never realized my sister was such a passionate diary keeper. These writings, too, she must have expurgated later on. The more grown-up her handwriting, the more rigorous her intervention. Her scissors attacked even the movie stars.

One notebook seemed to have escaped her censorship—the earliest, judging from the girlish handwriting, decorated with pictures collected from Van Nelle's coffee and tea packages. The label read, "In the Tropics," each letter written in a different color, the whole in the shaky script of the anthroposophists.

"I was born in Malang. An old native woman told us once that malang means evil. When my mother heard this, she made a tour of the house with a candle to chase away the evil spirits. It's true that there was a *kuntilanak* in the mango tree, a nasty she-devil to whom the natives sometimes made offerings of a buffalo head. We never had any problems with it."

A school composition, discarded. Impatiently I leafed through the notebook and looked at the Van Nelle pictures: women weaving, a Balinese dancer, bulls wearing pink parasols on their heads. Only the tops had been pasted down. I lifted one of these pictures and saw that the writing continued underneath. Could it be the same story? Ada's handwriting was so terribly small and so mysteriously hidden within the square frame of the pictures that I could only decipher it with half-closed eyes. I longed to stand up and look Ada in the face to ask for permission, but my curiosity won out over my sense of propriety.

"What are memories? Things you still know you have experienced. Most of them I am no longer sure of, often I cannot remember a thing. Last week I was sick and shivering with fever, and suddenly I remembered things from the past. We stayed in three different camps in Sumatra, first house arrest in Fort de Kock together with five other families, then a temporary camp, then that dreadful confinement in Padang, where a thousand men were already imprisoned, joined by two thousand three hundred women and children, and later the barracks of Bankinang in the interior. Aunt Nikki gave me the numbers. All I know is that it smelled of piss. It was impossible to get any sleep because of the roar of the sea. Some of the mothers thought that it came from Allied ships coming to liberate us with their cannons."

I had found the most secret of Ada's secret diaries. I lifted the other pictures as if I were lifting her skirt and read on.

"What I'll never forget: I see myself in a little yellow dress with glass buttons, which I got in exchange for a book. I hear the women as they return from fetching wood. I'm lying in the little hospital in the middle of the camp. A lizard is climbing the gauze of my mosquito net, looking at me with a pitiful expression. Am I dying? He looks as if I were. The room smells of pus. They bring in a girl who has fallen into the hot ashes. Her mother has wrapped her in a mosquito net, and now the gauze is stuck to her skin. I'm nauseous, my bowels are emptying. All I get is tea with salt and pepper. Every day a Jap comes to my bedside. He is kind, wants to talk with me, but I do not understand him, he speaks a few words of Malay. He takes me on his lap and massages my cramps away. The Australian woman doctor forbids this, but I let him do it anyway. He promises to take me to the men's camp, where they have received new medicines that might cure me. The doctor and my mother won't let me go with him. A little later he lifts me onto the back of a truck and lets me sit on his lap. Mother is crying at the gate.

"When I come back, the Jap has given me two coconuts and a whole cabbage. Mother beat me, I was never again to accept anything from him, but they ate it all up anyway. The Jap did the same thing to Els. She didn't tell me until we were on the boat. He always gave us something extra if we would sit on his lap.

"I don't know how much longer I was sick. If I ask about it, Mama says that the Japs were nice to children. I forgot the rest."

Here even her memory had become a pair of scissors.

How many memories had I myself cut out of my head? Was the picture I had of my sister correct? Ada, the most balanced, most intelligent of the lot, wary of emotionalism or trendy nonsense, had I ever heard her talk about the camp in the old days? "I was too young," she would say whenever someone introduced the topic. Saskia did. Each little ailment she attributed to Bankinang; whenever it rained, her right shoulder burned from fetching water. Ada made a point of sticking her fingers in her ears at such talk, but she didn't miss a word. If Saskia said, "concentration camp," Ada snapped "It was an internment camp," and if anyone ventured to compare the Japanese to the Germans, she would say, "Beating is not the same as gassing."

My mother would not stand for any complaints, either. I can still see her angrily shaking the dishmop while doing the dishes, if after singing the cheerful camp songs one of the girls dared to complain about the Japanese. "You know how to chop wood, make a fire, cook, slaughter, sew, mend, nurse, make frames with bamboo, paint coconut shells. What child your age learned to do all that? Think positive! You learned to read and write better than any Dutch child. The teacher had an advanced degree. You're way ahead, thanks to the camp."

Scratches in the notebooks.

But this Els about whom Ada wrote, her bosom friend on the ship, which friend could that be? I knew of only one Els from the old days, Els Groeneweg from the Hague, the daughter of the notary public. Our parents were acquainted, her mother had been in the camp with ours. Mr. Groeneweg advised us on our paperwork and helped Mother in her battle with the Department of Overseas Territories. Mr. Groeneweg would come to our house as soon as a single brown governmental envelope was dropped on the doormat. He brought his own typewriter, with a silver ring around each key, and his sentences were as long as the ribbon. Sonorously he read his missives aloud to us, seated at our table at home: letters to the Minister and to the Pension Fund and requests to the Queen. Requests . . . what visions that word arouses, Father and Mother under the yellow light of the lampshade, the smoke rings from the notary's cigar, the letters being typed on paper . . . we harassed Her Majesty with requests. We had been done a great injustice, this much I understood, but my parents bore this fact in silence. When we complained, it was done formally.

The Groenewegs were rich and elegant. Els wore a signet ring (and my sisters her old clothes), her father drove a shiny Land Rover. Half the village came out to stare when his car stood in front of our door, we rarely saw one as splendid. It had a walnut dashboard and a fan of dials. We were used to the vegetable man with his tricycle and, in the summers, little German cars. As soon as the notary finished, we children were given a ride along the boulevard, it was like touring in a black top hat.

Later Els would visit us in her own car, a blue MG with an open top. I, a little boy, rode in the rumble seat, inhaling her blond hair. (And I can still hear the tinkling of her charm bracelet as she shifted gears. All the old sounds come back to me. My ears have the best memory.)

Els was my first secret love. She should definitely receive a death notice.

The bell rang. Maarten called for his cane, and Aram stormed up the stairs. I hid the notebook about the tropics under my shirt, shoved the rest back into the drawer, and ran to open the door. Usually by the time Maarten did the honors, the caller had already left. This time the visitors were just about to turn away; it was the neighbor who lived in back of the house with his son, Pieter. They were coming to pay their respects. Pieter was Aram's best friend. I called him and heard a key turn in a lock upstairs.

"Would you like to see her?" Maarten asked, leaning like a drunk against the wall. Without waiting for an answer, he preceded them into the back room. I warned them that it would not be a pleasant sight, the undertaker would have to come back. But the neighbor waved my objections aside. "It's about time Pieter saw his first corpse."

I went upstairs to look for Aram. On the landing the carpeting had been torn away, the tacks still stuck out along the baseboard, you could get cold feet just from the hollow echo. I hadn't ever been upstairs before, and I opened the first door, the marital bedroom with its unread newspapers, stacks of unopened mail, and a double bed slept in on only one side. Here too the floorboards were bare, dust had gathered between the cracks. Maarten was right. No cleaning woman had been in his room for weeks.

The side of the bed that had not been slept in was covered with slips of paper torn from a scratch pad. On each a trembling hand had written a single sentence: "Aram makes too much noise! Aram a nuisance! Aram does not obey me! Call the food delivery service! Aram's insurance! Pay for the music lessons! Aram should help! Take off his shoes, no French horn practice in the afternoon! Go with Ada to Terschelling, make reservations now! Must be nicer to Aram!" Reminders to a memory full of wormholes.

A large drawing hung on the wall, it looked like an old print, yellow and shabby, but when I stood in front of it, I saw that it was the enlarged photograph of a drawing, its perspective awkward, a study in stark simplicity: a wooden floor, four rolled-up straw mats, reed walls, four tins, a pail and a broom. "Our *tampat* in Bankinang" was written underneath. So this was the cubbyhole my mother and her daughters had shared. Looking once more at the drawing I understood the simplicity of Ada's house.

Aram was not in his room. It smelled of unwashed feet and dirty sheets. The floor was strewn with books, models, and notebooks, the most recent proof of his exemplary life. Above his desk hung a picture of King Arthur and the Knights of the Round

Table and a poster of a Roman fort. He had wanted to become a
knight, any book about chivalry would do as long as there were
not too many illustrations, for those were forbidden at home.
He gave reports about all this in school, dressed in homemade
armor with a cardboard helmet. This was also why he chose to
play the French horn.

Above his bed hung the tools of his naughtier life; a ripped-
off traffic sign, posters of Guns n' Roses and other heavy-metal
groups with much nudity, tattoos, and leather. He had also been
busy with a spray gun. Obviously Ada had been unable to climb
the stairs these last few weeks. Aram, the well-read nerd, so ami-
able and thoughtful, with his pageboy haircut, his Dr. Scholl
shoes and baggy trousers, had taken control of his own life.
There were even comic books strewn across his bed. The only
evidence of his parents' waning authority was a hand-written
sign above the bed: "Be nicer to Papa and Mama!"

Where was Aram? Not in Maarten's little office (the drawers of
its child's desk full of dinky toys; now that I was snooping in
other people's affairs, I had no more scruples), not in the bathroom (towels hard as cardboard), not in the toilet (gray, recycled
toilet paper). He did not answer my calls, and then I heard
creaking overhead. I pulled on the rope handle of the trapdoor,
but it did not give. Aram had locked himself in the attic.

"Won't you come down?" I asked.

"No."

"Pieter is waiting for you."

"I don't want to see him."

"Why not?"

"Because," he sobbed.

"Are you afraid you'll cry?"

"Yes."

Who was up there? He was up there, so was I, struggling with our shame.

The day after my father's death I was the one who had to go and tell people. Because my father had not been married to my mother, announcements could not be sent—in those years people still obeyed the rules of propriety. First to the post office. Within half a day the whole village would know whatever was told there. The postmistress, a fat woman with a cardboard chest, came out from behind her counter. "Poor child," she said. "We were expecting it, what will happen to all of you now?" And she clasped my face to her breasts. I told the grocer, who always smelled of alcohol from early morning on because his daughter had died two years earlier of scarlet fever, and he squeezed me against his beer belly. Mr. Key, retired sea captain, took off his hat to me. All the people I met on the street extended condolences, and each time I had a dreadful weeping fit, not because I was sad at my father's death but because I couldn't stand their pity. They did not give me a chance to be a man, I longed to be a regular guy, a guy without tears.

"That's okay, Aram," I said. "Pieter will come back some other time."

Downstairs Pieter was sitting on the sofa, waiting. He stared straight ahead with glazed eyes, his mind fully occupied with his first corpse.

That night death invaded my dreams once more. I can hear a saddlebag rub against the spokes of a wheel. The newspaper boy? Most dreams come in the hour when darkness gives way to dawn. And I saw my mother, still young but also old, as all mothers are in childhood memories. Bent over, she's pedaling into the wind, on her bike with its frayed saddlebags that have always made me feel ashamed. I'm eleven years old and sitting up in bed, listening to the sounds of the night. I'm dreaming within a dream. My father is dying in the hospital. He is fighting for his breath, like an airplane pilot in rarified air. The hospital has called, it is all over.

Water is running, doors creak, voices whisper in the hall. Quiet, quiet, I am not to know, don't turn on the light. I hear bicycles on the garden path, the rubbing of saddlebags against the spokes, and off they went, my mother, my sisters, but not me.

A storm has come up, the wind tugs at the shutters, and there's a creaking in the hall. I hear shoes on the linoleum and recognize my father's footsteps. He's walking toward my room, he opens the door. There he stands in his motorcycle coat, his face partly hidden by rubber biking goggles, his eyes glistening by the glow of the nightlight plugged in day and night. My father sits down next to me on the bed. I move over a bit and shiver with the cold he has brought inside under his leather coat. My father has come to visit me while my mother and my sisters are leaning over his deathbed. We're outwitting death. My father pushes up his right sleeve, the leather creaks, he takes off his watch and holds it against my ear. The light-green phosphorescent hands beat like a heart. Woosh, woosh. I push away his hand, I don't want his watch. It ticks too loudly. I'm afraid of the poisonous light, the metal is chilly, and the strap cuts into my ear. I duck, but I'm unable to get away from his hand, the hand that always hits me, a hand that when it wants to caress, suddenly pinches. A heart beats inside his treacherous hand. Woosh, woosh.

The newspaper dropped into the mailbox. I could still hear the woosh, woosh. My alarm clock was ticking under my pillow. In my restless sleep I had pushed it from the nightstand into the bed. This is how dreams reflect real sounds.

During the final weeks before her death Ada could not endure the sounds of life. Aram and Maarten had to go around in stocking feet, the French horn playing had stopped. Distant children's voices, the wind, the first leaves drifting against the window panes, each sound irritated her, even a watch hurt her ears. She tapped her wrist (so brittle, so thin) and motioned for me to take mine off. "I'm not wearing a watch," I whispered. And yet she could hear the ticking. Ada knew I never wore a watch, and she also knew why.

When the returning bicycles woke me up on that night of my father's death, high heels were clicking in the hall soon thereafter, and a cold wind entered with my mother, whose face, in the light of the little lamp, was ashen. She kneeled at my bedside. "For you," she said. "Now you are the man of the family." She held a stainless-steel watch against my ear. Woosh, woosh.

I would not accept it.

Mr. Korst was amazed. "There must be a hundred people, and there's only room for sixty." He could not provide extra chairs, we should have hired the larger hall (not covered by the policy). "And what about the cake?" he asked.

I slipped him another hundred gulden. "Add another forty slices." Korst turned out to be not such a bad guy, and when I asked, he managed to find folding chairs behind the curtain. The call for mourners had had its desired effect: rows of women,

friends from the camp, had shown up. My mother complained
that her hands ached from all the telephone calls, but it was a
satisfying pain. To see all those faces from the past . . . hey, wasn't
that Nikki? And how about Els over there? Mama waved as I led
her to the front row; she was dignified, but she waved just the
same, her other hand pressed against her stomach, like a retired
diva recognized by her loyal public.

Half the choir was there also, some neighbors had managed
to find the conductor. What a gathering, now all we needed was
the music. Where was the French horn? We were all set for sobs,
but there wasn't a sound. Mr. Korst came forward and wanted
me to start my eulogy. "Music," I whispered. He leaned forward—once more I caught sight of his white shins—and said
with a nod in Maarten's direction, "The gentleman does not
wish it."

"None of his business, my sister loved music," I said. "Don't
you have something handy?"

Saskia caught on to the problem. You couldn't leave anything
up to Maarten, that was obvious. She had brought a compact
disc, just in case, something with violins, would that do? She
had nothing with a French horn. She handed Mr. Korst an envelope, and he hurried to the back. Aram kicked his father.

Nervous feet shuffled on the tiled floor, people eyed each
other curiously. "First some music," I called across the rows
of chairs. A few seconds later a sweetish moan seeped through
the hall, tremulous violins, creating the effect of syrup on a
tooth cavity.

My neck was hot with embarrassment. "First some music"—
how in heaven's name could I have brought myself to say such a
thing? I sounded even more banal than the announcer on

"Musical Favorites." Would I really be able to say later that Ada had good taste? "She brought music and literature into her home, she kept out everything that was vulgar, materialistic, and ugly." I had written these words the night before because I wanted to show Ada as I had known her, not as the ascetic looking for deliverance that she had become. It had been difficult for me to remain kind as well as honest on paper, meanness kept slipping from my pen. The eulogy I held in my hands had been cut by half, and as the music played, I kept stroking the erasures with my fingertips, tactile proof that I had held my fury in check.

Was there ever a more idiotic death than hers? If she had allowed herself to be operated at once, she would be alive today. Cancer didn't exist. Maarten's illness didn't exist. She had found him a practitioner of magnetism who came and prayed over him twice a week behind his back. And oh, how it helped! Thanks to those healing hands, Maarten did not need a chairlift or a wheelchair yet, and it took him half an hour to climb fifteen steps, after which it took him an hour of sitting on the sofa to recover.

But I controlled myself, I would dissemble in a muffled voice, as is expected of someone delivering a eulogy. I even lowered myself to free-floating metaphors. "During her studies of English literature, Ada immersed herself in the Arthurian legends, and just as the Knights of old searched for the Holy Grail, she spent her life looking for the sublime in herself and others."

How could I deal in such lies? The sublime in others . . . she had, on the contrary, distanced herself from others. During her final years she hardly ever saw her old friends, she was annoyed by their greed, their twaddle about mortgages, she became difficult to get along with, and she became especially hard on herself. In her house laughter sounded like a curse. One cookie with tea, then the lid came down on the box, economizing became a hobby, one baggy dress lasted fourteen summers, no brassiere, one bottle of wine in the entire year, mulled wine jazzed up with an orange stuck with cloves. Merry Christmas!

More and more she lived according to strict rules. Early to bed and early to rise. Mopping, scrubbing, everything done by hand, shopping for organic vegetables, reading the labels of every product with a magnifying glass to reveal poisons and preservatives. We thought it all fit in with her obsession with health, her weaving loom, and her preference for "honest" raw materials. Ada advocated a renewal of purity, and more and more she ate plain food, eating for nourishment's sake, barley with beans, pleasure was not allowed on her plate. She longed for absolute frugality, for asceticism. Her house became as bare as a *tampat.*

Ada had a horror of possessions. She did not want to be tied down to a house. Another war might start tomorrow, it was important to be ready to flee at a moment's notice. So that's how it was, everything fell into place now that I had read her diary.

She also compared her illness to having been sick in the camp. "I have been at death's door once before, and that time I also made it," she told me at my next-to-last visit. The light filtering through the gauze curtains reminded her of the mosquito netting in the camp hospital, and she placed a photograph of her father on the bedside table. The less of a future she had, the further back she went into her memories. She also talked for the first time about the camp with her younger sister, and she cried—a triumph, thought Saskia, Ada in tears. . . . To her these tears were like a gift, no greater repayment for all her nursing was possible.

During her final weeks Ada really did not want any more visitors. The present no longer existed, in her thoughts she was once more the child locked in the empty waiting of the camp, lying still and hoping for liberation.

When, after much insistence, I was allowed to visit briefly, I tried to evoke more pleasant memories. We leafed through her old art books and spoke about beautiful exhibitions seen in the past, about the good books she had given me to read. And then I couldn't help teasing her a little, for now she disapproved of the new every bit as much as she had welcomed it before. Pop music, Hollywood, nudity, all of it made her shiver. Only surrealist black-and-white movies that ran for two hours and were praised by a cranky critic were any good. Whenever she recommended such a movie to me, I would praise, by contrast, *Airport* and *Airport 1975* and *Airport '77*. I pretended to be more of a populist than I was, and I defended mass culture with the same arguments she used to defend classicism and elitism. I lied just to shock her. If only I had known that as teenager she had swooned over Rock Hudson.

Why did I resist her so strongly? Now that she lay in a coffin, I was reproaching her, something she didn't deserve. I should, on the contrary, be grateful for the formative role she had played in my life. She was the one who gave me my first poetry anthology—*Poets of Our Time*. She took me to my first ballet performance, Kurt Jooss's *Green Table*—the first time that I saw men with bulges in their tights leaping about on stage. And I saw my first play with her—*Cat on a Hot Tin Roof* by Tennessee Williams. I was twelve or fourteen. I didn't understand much except that the leading character, the cruel father, a fatally ill cotton planter, was like my father, and I imagined myself as his son Brick, a sensitive son, but with enough guts to slap his father's face.

Ada backed me in my war against my father. She dared to make fun of him, laughed at his ridiculous discipline. This was the bond between us, it had made us eternal allies. She had written about him as well in her diary from the tropics. "Mama's new boyfriend used to serve *under* our dad in Java"—she had found it necessary to underline the word *under* three times. "When he comes into my room, he always turns Daddy's photograph to the wall. I don't say anything, I just put it back the way it was. He thinks he's still living in a military barracks, everything has to run like clockwork. Home from school *one* minute late, and I'm punished. When he loses his temper, he slaps you in the face, a sergeant major from tip to toe. His favorite form of punishment is to lock us in the bathroom. Sometimes I sit in there writing for a whole half of a Sunday, but the other day he tore up my notebook. I don't show enough respect, he says. From now on I'll take my flute in there. The calmer I remain, the angrier he gets."

I copied this passage three times and each time crossed it out again. On a day like this, civility is what matters.

The violins were cut short. I went and stood at the lectern, unfolded my speech and could see the light of a videocamera coming from a brick wall. A watchful eye? Was Korst the disc jockey keeping watch over me? The actor in me praised Ada's sensitivity and her motherliness. "Maarten needed care and attention, so did Aram's education, and in spite of her own illness she was full of compassion for her sister Jana in Canada, from whom we'll soon have to part as well. Caring Ada, always present, never in the foreground."

A tremor went through the hall. Jana ill, too? Almost no one knew it yet, and we didn't want to think about it at this time, but from a telephone conversation I had with her right after Ada's death, I understood that she too had only a short time to live. Cancer. My mother refused to believe it and bombarded her oldest daughter with diets, irradiated bread, and the latest homeopathic rubbish. Jana accepted it all sweetly but was in control of her own death. She had ovarian cancer and had agreed to treatments until the birth of her first grandchild. Two more months, and a new life would be filling her arms, just a little while longer and she would finally be allowed to die.

I thought I should mention it on this day, for too much had been kept silent and hidden. "It is unfair that such a young boy should lose his mother. It is unfair that my mother should lose two daughters, whom she kept alive with much sacrifice during the war, children who are now slipping from her grasp, broken and wasted. There is no justice in nature."

Nature, not God; no reincarnation; man as chemical process —that's all there was to it.

The cake was delicious, and Mr. Korst spoke with his mouth full. He handed me the register of condolences, the ribbons and the silver frame that had held Ada's father's photograph. "We are not allowed to burn metals." I understood. In "gratitude and as a souvenir" he gave me a videotape of the ceremony. "You don't want it? But it is customary, a gift from us to you." A little later he also returned Saskia's CD, a prized recording from the series Musical Meditations, violin fantasies that, according to the accompanying text, represented the quiet restlessness of rotting waterlilies.

I was last in the reception line, shook many hands and received wet kisses from old ladies who called themselves Aunt and whom I had never seen before.

I recognized Els Groeneweg at once: blonde, long-legged, with hazel eyes, laugh wrinkles, and still a touch of the East Indies in her voice. I could not hold back my tears any longer, and immediately fell in love again. Besides, she looked exactly like my girlfriend, blonde, same laugh, same eyes, same figure; how was it possible that subconsciously I had been looking for my first love?

"How terrible about Jana," Els said. "She was really my best friend. I always hoped she would marry Joost, my oldest brother. He died last year."

"So if you'd had your wish, Jana would be a widow now," I said.

"A happy widow," she replied with a laugh, and mentally I kissed her tiny wrinkles. "Too bad nothing came of it between those two. They were very fond of each other. I still have piles of letters from her. Perhaps you should look at them. Jana fled Holland, there's no other word for it, but then she didn't have much luck over there either. What a hell of a life that girl has led!"

Fled? What was she talking about? Jana, my father's darling. She had found Holland too cramped, like so many of the young people repatriated from the Netherland's East Indies. She wanted to go to Australia, but that didn't work out either, she was too dark-skinned for that. In the end, she chose Canada. I always thought that my mother had encouraged her, a woman has to take a chance, get out of this frog pond, she herself had left home when she was young. She visited Jana every other summer and would return with a frizzy permanent wave and a pantsuit in flowered nylon. This was enough to discourage me from wanting to visit my sister.

And now, suddenly, it seems Jana had fled. Els wouldn't elaborate. We exchanged telephone numbers and promised to get together soon.

I only knew Aunt Nikki by name, she was in her nineties and had come by taxi all the way from the country. She could hardly walk and wobbled from one arm to the other until she fastened onto me and drew me to the nearest chair. "I came for Letje," she said. "I felt an urge. I had to be here."

I had never yet heard anyone call my mother by her childhood nickname, she was usually Lea to her friends. "That was sweet of you," I said.

"You know your mother and I were in the same camp?"

"Yes."

"Your mother told me once that you found it so strange that she always attended our *Kumpulan*. Reunion, don't you know. You never understood how much we enjoyed each other's company. But you know, your mother found strength in our reunions. She seems tough, Letje, but she felt discouraged at times, just like the rest of us. I always had to stir her up a bit, like an old stove, yes." She shook my wrist, and drops of spittle flew. "Without her old friends she wouldn't be able to keep going, she always goes home with new energy. You know that morale was very high in Bankinang, and this strength always returns when we have a reunion. Only once did she almost give up, she stopped taking care of herself, ate hardly anything, just lay there on her *tikar* and waited, ready to let go. Edema, yes, and water on the lungs. Jana would have to take over. Letje, I said, think of your girls, don't let go, Letje, you still have a job to do. And now, too, she mustn't give up, she's sure to live another ten years. Aram is going to need her." We both looked at Aram, who still had to deal with a line of mourners. "You don't have to worry about Ada, she's in good hands. But you must hurry to Jana, she doesn't have much time left, and she misses you, she wants to mourn too, she needs you."

"Mother and Saskia are planning to go next month."

"Now!" It sounded like a command. "I see you leaving next week. And you must go along, you've never visited her. Come on," she tugged at my wrist as if the airplane stood at the door. "Jana was your second mother, she was the one who took care of you when you were born, your mother was too weak."

She could tell from my expression that I had absolutely no intention of going to Canada. I had only seen Jana twice since she had left, briefly, and I did not have happy memories of her. Wash your body with snow in winter! Nice mother. It would be autumn by the time my mother went, and by then it would be snowing in New Brunswick.

"You will go, whether you want to or not. I foresee it all. Jana can tell you a lot about you father."

Aunt Nikki grasped both my wrists and looked me straight in the eye. "You have his eyes," she said.

I tried to disengage myself, but she wouldn't let go. I blinked, but she forced me to face her.

"Your father had good qualities, too. You think you hate him, but if hate was all you felt, you wouldn't be who you are now. You also loved him, and he loved you. He expected so much from you, you were his only son. He must have taken hundreds of pictures of you. But he was ill, too, I know. I saw how much you looked up to him when you were little, how much you admired him and longed for his affection." Aunt Nikki smiled at my surprised expression. "Yes, perhaps you've forgotten. During the first years after the war I used to come for a visit now and then, to keep up Letje's spirits, but after I moved to the east of Holland and my legs began to fail me, I saw you grow up only in the snapshots she would bring to the reunions."

I didn't remember her, and yet she must have been just as impressive in the old days, sturdy as she was, with her piercing brown eyes.

"Let yourself remember his good qualities, you've got them too. If you hate everything about him, you're hating yourself." She spoke firmly, with great conviction, and though I resisted her with all my being, I was touched by the great peace she communicated.

She signaled to Aram. At first he did not dare to leave his post, but after repeated signals he came toward us, relieved. "Well, my boy," she said. "You can consider yourself lucky with what your mother has left you." Out of the corner of my eye I saw Maarten, exhausted, sitting in a chair, shaking every hand that was offered him, looking as if he had no idea where he was. What role would he play in Aram's life from now on? No one took him seriously anymore, and even though he had moments of lucidity, he was hardly consulted whenever Aram's future was discussed.

Aunt Nikki laid her hand on Aram's hair. "During the service I also felt a hand on my head," said Aram. "Very strange, I felt that someone came and sat next to me and touched my hair. It was a man, in uniform, really creepy."

"You were absolutely right, young man," said Aunt Nikki. Proudly she took his arm and together they walked toward the cake.

Poor Aram, I thought, a perfectly intelligent high-school student, and already affected by higher powers. I lit a cigarette and went into the hall.

But my mother would not let me go. "Ah, there you are at last. Come, there are still so many relatives who want to talk to you."

"I won't see any more family," I said. "I've had it."

"There are some van Capellens you haven't ever met, come all the way from Groningen." She meant the relatives of her first husband, with whom she had lost touch after the war. Regretting their decision to stay in Indonesia, they had returned in the mid-1960s and were later readopted as new aunts and uncles by my sisters.

"Spare me," I said.

My mother faced me squarely, her purse resting against her stomach, her hands on her hips. "Do you realize that Just was present?"

"Which Just?"

"Just van Capellen, Ada's father." All I could do was heave a deep sigh. "He stood behind the coffin, in his uniform. He held Ada in his arms. He came to take her away." She couldn't have used heavier artillery. She was holding back her tears.

"How great for her," I said. I went outside, to the rose garden, for a pleasant stroll through the ashes.

At the end of the hall stood Mr. Korst, receiving the mourners for the next funeral. He saw that I was pale with emotion and shook my hand with fatherly concern. "Ah yes, death, my dear sir. We will all experience it some day, if only we live long enough."

2
ACT OF DENIAL

═══════════

THE WHOLE family could go to the devil. There was no consolation, everyone withdrew into a private sorrow. Whenever I talked to him, Maarten looked at me with glazed eyes, he could not imagine what we were all looking for in his house after the cremation. While we were making coffee, he put a frozen dinner into the oven for Ada, and he couldn't understand why he should have ordered one less meal from the catering service. He stuck to the daily schedule tacked to the kitchen door.

Aram acted awkward and tough, shying away from any well-meant approaches, and carried his dinner upstairs, where he locked himself in with heavy metal.

My mother especially took refuge in a world of shadows. It was painful to see such an intelligent woman cling to so much nonsense. Ada might be dead and reduced to ashes, but to her she was still with us. Her spirit was not yet ready to depart, she said, there was still so much to take care of: insurance, custody, the care of Maarten. Ada had avoided all plans for the future. Maarten was not up to making plans, and now it was up to her to supervise everything from the other world and to make sure that all went well.

I used to be able to laugh at my mother's attitude, it seldom caused complications, for she was too sensible in spite of her fuzziness. Every week we consulted the tarot or threw a coin to consult the I Ching, and she would explain to us what to expect. We giggled at the vague predictions and forgot whether or not they ever came true. The cosmos could vibrate as it pleased, we mustn't neglect our obligations. She, too, did not quite believe in it; she checked out horoscopes to see how her stars stood, but if she didn't like the outcome, she was ready to ignore the whole thing. The stars guide, but do not decide. We never acted cynical about any of it, but accepted it as family entertainment, no more; cynicism upset Mother, and she had suffered so much already. Anyone who had lived through such hardship had a right to play with the stars.

But lately reality and magic had become more and more intertwined, especially since she had fallen into the hands of two ladies in the retirement home where she lived who held séances. "Delightful ladies," she told us, "with remarkable contacts." One of them had been a handicapped child in a previous life, and later a bandit. "She killed tens of people at the time, she has a lot to account for, that's why she wants to help me now. She's a great support to me." The other one had met, on the bus, a Hindu whom she recognized from a previous life. "Now he has tea with her once a week. A really interesting man, a spirit who can materialize. He is a chosen one, imagine, he just appeared on the bus."

"Ada must depart in peace," said my mother. "Let's help her as much as we can, there is nothing worse than a restless soul." That afternoon, right after the cremation, she ordered me to sort all the official papers. "Ada will guide us through this mess," she said. I had to control myself to keep from asking whether her wandering husbands wouldn't be able to give a helping hand. The Royal Colonial Army, always at your service.

Grief had washed away my mother's last remnant of common sense, and without some fantasy she could no longer cope. Ever since Saskia had told her, while eating the undertaker's cake, that she had given Ada two sleeping pills the night before she died—without consulting the doctor, crushed and mixed with custard, fed to her bit by bit through clenched teeth— Mother insisted that her daughter had died of an overdose.

"It's the pills that did it, right, Saskia?" she asked at least five times in the limousine on the way home.

"It gave her the strength to die," said Saskia. "The pain had stopped her from sleeping, she was too tired to die."

"Yes but that pill, those pills is what finally got her."

"Cancer, it was the big C!" I snarled from the back seat. I aimed my words at her neck, and the purple hat acquired especially for the occasion dove forward.

Frightened, my mother turned around. "Why are you so heartless? You destroy everything with your words."

She got her wish. I would show her how heartlessly I could keep silent. Once back in my house I took the telephone off the hook and cut off all communication.

Only Aram got to me. I wanted to take him out of that house of the dead, spoil him, buy him new clothes, drop his stinking socks into the collection box for the Third World, shower him with material goods. Perhaps he should come and live with me. I tried to imagine a routine of coming home from school on time, tea at four o'clock, and listening to him recite his Latin verbs. But it would be impossible. I couldn't very well take him out of his present school and say to his father, "Your wife's dead, just hand over your son and we'll stick you into a home." I changed my will—everything would go to Aram—and measured the attic to see if it was possible to turn it into an extra room.

And as I mentally made space in my life for my nephew, I could see him walking through the barren halls in school, with sleep still in his eyes, his hair standing straight up on his head, with no one to see to it that he left home looking neat. Would he be downcast or proud? A death in the family used to be a good thing in school, classmates whispering behind your back, a smile from the girl who never noticed you before. And was there a better excuse for playing hooky or for bad grades? But how long would he last? His attitude, his loutish behavior, all reminded me of my own years of mourning as a boy.

There I stood on the playground surrounded by the other boys, telling them about my father's brave death, "Yes, he'd suffered from a very special disease, his case was written up in the papers, without mentioning his name. He was the first one in the area to undergo a commissurotomy. A what? Yes, it comes from the Latin. A surgeon drilled a hole in his heart valve and just poked in it with his finger. A knife cut straight through his heart!" And I lifted my shirt to demonstrate where the surgeon had sawed his chest open, making an almost complete circle. I pretended to be my father, who had also bared his body at appropriate and inappropriate moments to show of his scars. Finally he had a scar worth showing off, better than the scar tissue on his back. This was a wound he could be proud of, almost a mark of distinction, more important than his decorations. They snatched the newspaper clipping from my hands. Fantastic! For a heart operation you had to be frozen in ice, you were unconscious for eight hours, and all the time the thing just kept on ticking. My father was a medical miracle!

But the new valve tore, nurses watched him day and night, even adhesive tape didn't help. My father turned blue once more, and there wasn't a surgeon who could save him.

I was the hero of the playground, a heart with a hole drilled through it, not even the worst of the bad boys could top that one. My father had been sitting at home, without work, there had been no reason to be proud of him, not until he was dead could I finally brag about him.

But I was not really telling the truth, his operation had taken place a year earlier, and his heart had functioned perfectly. It was the cold that got him, just an ordinary Dutch cold. My father died of the flu.

My childhood came back to me even during my daily routine. I saw myself looking at my father as he shaved (I have his chin)— so this was waiting for me too, a dangerous knife, boiling water, lather, the shaving brush, and making faces. But by the time my beard began to grow, I couldn't remember how to hold the razor. It was the first time that I had missed my father, about six years after his death. There was no man in the house to teach me manly things. I still don't know which way to turn a light-bulb or a screw, the directions to electrical gadgets drive me crazy. From whom could Aram copy these skills? His pathetic father was no example, no one needed lessons in stumbling and forgetting.

I realized that the person I mourned was not Ada but my father. I thought I had him well under control, securely trapped under layers of cynicism, and here he was, suddenly popping up from the grave. For years my hatred of him had guided me, everything I did or did not do I could attribute to my resistance to my father: he was a profesional military man, whereas I painted my nails to escape military service; he was a punctual man, while I never wore a watch and, if anything, was always late. Strength, muscles, sweat—no matter how weak he was himself, he studied the sports pages; I could throw up at the mere sight of soccer shoes. My hatred was a source of energy.

I didn't allow myself any subtle distinctions, I refused to think about him at all. But as the years passed, I noticed that I looked like him more than I found comfortable, and even if I weren't aware of it myself, the members of my family were there to point out the resemblance to me. I, too, couldn't handle money, I too indulged in temperamental outbursts and fits of sensuality, I had his charm, his volubility, and his tendency to exaggerate. And no matter how much I disliked these traits, they took possession of me, and I was unable to ward them off. As I shaved, I noticed how I began increasingly to look like him. It dawned on me gradually that I didn't know my father at all.

Since Ada's death a vague understanding was becoming clearer to me, and this is precisely what drove me crazy. I refused to understand the man who had humiliated me for eleven years.

I stayed home and delved into the past. I sat and ruminated and wasted time. My father was lodged in my brain and began to talk about the past. I could not chase him away with liquor, and finally I drowned out his voice in bitter self-pity.

A week later I made the mistake of plugging the telephone back in. I was once more ready to face the world. Saskia found me out. "You see, I've got to tell you this, I want you to know, I must get it off my chest, but don't tell a soul, especially not Mama. . . ." She paused dramatically, her voice was hoarse with tears, and I noticed how tensely I clung to the receiver.

"Go ahead," I said coolly. "Speak up."

"I've been going to Forty-Five."

"To what?"

"To Forty-Five, Center '45. I'm in therapy, three times a week, nothing but tears, all I do is cry." She was weeping, with great big sobs, snatching for breath; I said nothing, waiting at the other end of the line, too long. Saskia slammed down the receiver.

I called her back. "Yes," she sounded as if she were dying.

"Tell me," I said. The sniffling resumed. This time she got hold of herself.

"We also talk, you know," she said with an apologetic laugh. "So much is surfacing, you have no idea—finally. If only Ada could go through this. Did you realize that most of the children who spent time in camps die earlier than the average age? Scientifically proven. We've always adjusted to the outside world, but inside, the war simply went on." She spoke slowly, she had said it before.

"Do you think it does any good?" I asked. I could hardly pay attention, too irritated by the therapeutic clichés. "Unresolved suffering brought to the surface . . . long-suppressed phantoms exorcised . . . East Indian identity refound . . . after many war years still searching for rescue."

Only two years old when she had entered the camp, she nevertheless retained the most vivid memories.

How those people must be delighted with her, I thought. The war bothering you? Let it all come out, we did the same. Now that the real victims are losing their minds, our appointment calendars are empty. There's enough unemployment in our profession as it is. We'll help you, and you're helping us. Grab that client.

"For years they wouldn't listen to us," said Saskia.

"Come on now, there are more than enough social workers."

"Do you remember when the Moluccans held up that train? I was searched at least three times at the station during that week, once I had to lie flat on the ground. We're outsiders, they'll always remind us that we're different, we don't belong anywhere."

... "Why don't you say something?" Saskia asked.

"What should I say? You're confusing two different issues."

Saskia answered with more tears. "We've kept silent much too long," she said.

"I'm glad you're being helped," I said. I heard her lighting a cigarette and lit one myself. Finally we dared relax.

"I've got to ask Mama so many questions, but whenever I mention the camp, she starts talking about her own ailments. She says I'm exaggerating."

"Yes?"

"There are still so many blind spots."

"Blind spots."

"After all, we have a right to know what happened."

"Yes."

"She refuses to talk about it. Forgotten, she says."

Just say yes, repeat the final word and they keep on jabbering, a simple psychiatric trick. In the meantime your mind can wander. ... Saskia's reproaches were familiar. Her mother would not listen to her, she lent a deaf ear, just as the Dutch had done right after repatriation. A single complaint about the camps, and people would start to speak of their own troubles. She had had to swallow so much. "Oh, you colonials didn't have it all that hard, some annoyances, a few years without a nanny, but you had permanent sunshine and bananas growing on every tree. Compare that with our starvation winter, we had to eat tulip bulbs!" My mother's suffering was second-best, she became tired of complaining.

More than a year after the war ended, she was officially advised that her husband had died. After that she had to fight for years with the ministry to collect his back pay and a pension. "A boy from the East Indies who sided with the Dutch, come on! Didn't all Indo with an education collaborate with the Japanese and the Indonesian nationalists?"

"But he held Dutch citizenship," my mother replied. "He fought for Queen and Fatherland, he joined the resistance."

"Resistance against the Japanese? But my dear lady, there was no such thing! The Dutch were all interned, they couldn't resist."

She had to wait five years for her pension. After a lot of negotiations, Notary Groeneweg managed to round up enough witnesses to testify that Mother's husband had fought on the correct side. Not only that, he was suddenly promoted to war hero, rehabilitation followed, and Justin van Capellen was posthumously awarded the highest military decoration.

"Too late," my mother wrote to the minister. "Permanently too late. First I had to spend years being told to be ashamed of my husband, and now I can buy his hero's title." For thirty-six gulden and twenty cents she could buy the decorations of the Military Order of William of Orange. "Just pin it on your own chest!"

My mother reacted with silence. The fifteenth of August, the day the Japanese capitulated, was marked with a cross on the calendar in the toilet. Our second spring in the Netherlands my father bought a Dutch flag, flown at half-mast on the fourth of May but raised to the top of the mast on the fifth. Otherwise we never hung out the flag, not even on April thirtieth, the day of our arrival in the new homeland, the new queen's birthday. We flew no flags for the Netherlands, but we did want to be part of the war.

Our mother did not complain. "Think positive," she said and rarely spoke about the camp. Whenever I asked her about it, she'd say, "My God, child, hunger, yes, always hungry, it's a strange feeling you know, but otherwise we just laughed it off. *Sudah*, let it be."

And now the daughter was appropriating her mother's suffering.

"Yes, yes," I said, and Saskia wept.

Between sobs I understood that she did not see the psychiatrist alone; she met with a group of her own generation, all of whom shared their experiences and feelings of being misunderstood. Most of them had been in a Japanese camp, but some were born after the war. "We all have parents who won't talk. This affects all children."

"Children?"

"Children at the time," said Saskia. "And you should come too."

"I have no problems."

"But at home, by the sea, with your father, was the war ever over?"

Suddenly I was alert. Don't touch, I thought, Father belongs to me. "Is it because of Ada that you're so obsessed with the camp?" I asked.

"No, I've had these weeping fits for a long time now, for the silliest reasons. When I pass by a display of baby foods or diapers in the store, it comes over me, who knows why, those grinning baby faces on the labels. We were never children, maybe that's it."

For a week or so she had been unable to control herself, the weeping fits broke out more and more frequently. Her husband attributed it to menopause. "I keep dreaming that I'm a child, there's no one around except behind barbed wire. Every night I wake up screaming, in a terrible sweat. I'm unable to concentrate, and without a sedative I can't sleep at all. Don't you ever get that way? Do you know the feeling?"

"I didn't live through the war."

She sighed, I sighed. Bad chemistry, even as children we irritated each other.

"Some months ago I went to an exhibition with Ada about the resistance in the colonies," she continued with renewed courage. "One display case was dedicated to Pa van Capellen's group. There was a picture of him in prison, so emaciated that I could not recognize him, together with three others. Next to it hung a photograph of the same group, probably taken and distributed as propaganda to frighten people about the resistance, this time on their knees, in their uniforms . . . headless. His head lay on the ground in front of his knees. I could see his eyes staring straight at the camera, upside down, two black spots swimming in the white of the eye, looking surprised. His collar was still neatly around his throat, and you could see the neck muscles, white threads in a gaping stump. Blood streamed down his jacket."

There was silence at the other end of the line, and in a flash I saw the framed picture of her father standing on the cabin trunk, wearing his dress uniform with the gold-braided collar and a plumed helmet.

"Jesus, I never knew that."

"Neither did we, Mama never told us. The executioner was standing next to them, laughing, one of those nasty, sneaky Japs. The blood dripped from his sword."

"But why do you go looking for this kind of stuff?"

"I just had to see it. I have a right to know who my father was. Shot by a firing squad, Mama said, that's how it's recorded in the Register of War Graves. We know nothing about him. At that exhibition I read that he was with the guerrillas for two years, blowing up radio stations, messing up the railroad switches, derailing trains. Fantastic. And do you know what was written in Japanese script underneath that picture? 'Traitors get their rightful punishment.' How dared they! My father was a hero."

A fool, I thought, fought for the wrong party, chose sides with the country that had appropriated his own, and resisted the nationalists. History did not prove him right. To console her I said, "A father to be proud of."

"We weren't even allowed to be proud. Mama always kept us in the dark about him."

I was too overcome to answer and could not think of another nice thing to say.

"I think it's so sad that we no longer see each other, we'll be the last ones left, you're my only brother, after all." Ada had brought us together, she thought, and in her honor we should reestablish contact. Her therapist agreed. "He says we should talk it over, work through our mourning process together. Let's make me into an autonomously functioning person."

I really felt sorry for Saskia, in spite of her weeping and her dramatics.

"Can't we plan to get together?" she asked. "I have to tell you some more about your father, a voice has surfaced from the past."

Oh God, Sheila the astronaut must have been at it again. The damp receiver stuck to my hand. "Come to my house," I said as gently as possible. "Then you'll see how I live."

"No," she said firmly. "I don't want to see your house, you've never once invited us."

"Then I'll pick you up, we'll drive to the sea, by our old house, and we'll take a walk along the beach."

"No, I don't ever want to go back there. I want to remember the village as it was, I wouldn't dare see how it has changed."

"Nothing has changed, it's still as empty and bleak as ever."

"The woods across from the house are gone, I heard. I want to go to the woods."

We decided on the forest behind the dunes. We would go the following day, to talk and eat pancakes. I like to have a destination when I go for walks.

Were Saskia's problems not much more obvious ones? Her failed career, her unhappy marriage? For years she'd been talking about getting a divorce, and each time she resolved to start painting again, the way she used to, when every summer she'd peddle her watercolors on the boardwalk. The whole village praised her talent, and the drawing teacher had nothing more to teach her. Saskia was the artist in the family, and she longed for only one thing—to leave school and go to the art academy.

My father had always been against her artistic aspirations. It was much better for a girl to take up nursing. First get into a profession that will support you, preferably with a pension, that's what life was all about. He spoke from personal experience. Saskia resisted, her schoolbooks were filled with her paintings, she wore a tight sweater, narrowed the legs of her blue jeans, and sported a towering Brigitte Bardot hairstyle. My father was already too ill to be angry, I was angry for him. She played hooky from school, and Mother secretly slipped her some money to take lessons from a genuine painter. Saskia hid her canvases at a neighbor's, and she made sure that no trace of paint remained on her fingers when she came to the dinner table. Without my father's knowledge she passed the entrance exam to the school of industrial arts. He wasn't dead yet when she took her paintbrushes and left. In a single season I was delivered of two tormentors.

She found an attic room, started to paint, and made posters protesting against the atom bomb (which our mother tore up at home, for the bombing of Hiroshima had saved her life). In her rebellion Saskia flourished and was given a show of her own. Not one picture sold. Disappointed, she switched to nursing overnight. She married, gave birth to a daughter, and moved to a bungalow in the Gooi region. Her husband, a sucker, and most important, a rich one, had preferences of his own; he liked rural antiques. Their first living-room table was a wagon wheel.

The easel and paintbrushes went into the attic. After only a few years Saskia was ready to leave her husband, but she lacked the courage; she couldn't take her child away from her father, at least that's what my mother said, for I never spoke to Saskia herself. But she was also too frightened to be on her own and too dependent on the money and luxury her husband heaped on her. So she tried living like an elegant country lady—working in the garden, playing bridge, and espousing charitable causes for all suffering creatures. Every summer she ran away to come and weep her heart out at her mother's: tea for the nerves, the I Ching, and a séance with the lady friends. A week later, her husband would come and get her, and she resigned herself to her lot once more. This situation lasted for years. All caused by the war.

The wind tore the sea mist to shreds, and from far away we could see our old house rise out of the gray world, a wide red roof against the silhouette of the dunes. Saskia did not want me to drive past, but we couldn't avoid it, there was no other way into the forest, and when I pointed at the peak of the roof— "Look at the green patina that covers the copper bell tower now"—she looked the other way, toward the barren stretch of land on the other side, where an infestation of beetles had killed all the pines years ago, though she had not wanted to see this devastation.

Sand had taken over the front yard. Without a fence, the wind had free play here. Before the war the house had served as a German children's camp, which explained the bell on the roof. After the liberation it was confiscated and allotted to four repatriated families. (Everyone was brown, except my mother and I. Every summer the sun remedied my deficiency; seven layers of pink, and then I peeled; a freckled nose among the Indos, not golden skin like theirs.)

"It seems better kept up than it was," I said. "Fresh paint." I couldn't help stopping a minute in front of our house. The more chaotic I feel inside, the more I appreciate wholeness.

Saskia turned to me cautiously, tears dribbling down her cheeks. Her eyes refused to see it clearly. "Do you come here often?"

"For me there is only one beach, and that is this one. I love this landscape, the gray-green beach grass behind the dunes, the clumps of wild oats, blue thistles, yellow evening primrose, the silver of the poplars, the black of the pines. When I can't go to sleep, I think of these colors; when I'm at the dentist, I concentrate on this landscape."

"And you always said that you were unhappy here."

"Not in the dunes. Slogging knee-deep through the sand with a stick in my hand, I found a horizon without people."

"We were still here."

"You refused to see anything, you were blind. Look, on that spot I was knocked unconscious." I had to wipe the steam off the side window, our breath condensed in the cool sea breeze.

"We loved your father. We were the ones who chose him for Mama."

"Where did you get that? Our fathers knew each other in the Colonial Army. My father was supposed to help Mother find your father, but he looked in the wrong places, and I was born. Don't make more of it than it was, he seduced the wife of his friend and got her pregnant."

Saskia plucked an imaginary bit of lint from her Hermès scarf; again the tears welled up. And I had made such resolutions to be gentle and careful. "We met him for the first time in forty-six, when we were waiting to be repatriated to Holland, in a big house somewhere in the European district of Palembang. It was jam-packed, ten families, only women and children, everything you touched was clammy. We weren't allowed to leave the grounds, cooked out in the garden, grew our own ubis, and played behind a wall made of atap."

"Atap?"

"The oldest of us secretly cut peepholes in it, so as to get a glimpse of street life. You couldn't get us away from there, spying on men, I had never seen a man dressed in civilian clothes, and each time a group of them walked by and we squealed too loudly, the adults pushed us away so as to look for themselves. Mama was in a state, she was worried about her family in Holland, she didn't have a cent, she'd sold everything, even her last ring. The Army wouldn't pay her as long as nothing was known about our father. The people at the Red Cross were of no help. We heard all kinds of conflicting stories, someone had seen him in northern Sumatra, somebody else had seen him on a boat from Borneo to Java. Anything was possible. A few soldiers from his regiment had been taken prisoners of war in East Java, but later they turned out to be Dutchmen. We understood that Pa van Capellen had probably never been interned, because if the Japanese kept to the rules, people of mixed parentage could stay out of the *kawat*. Anyone with twenty-five percent Indian blood or more was not considered Dutch."

"You're very well informed."

Saskia looked at me with hurt feelings. "I hear a lot of stories in therapy."

"And all that Malay."

"I'm taking a course, it's part of my identity, this is my calling."

She picked up her pocketbook from the back seat and took out an elegant little notebook, bound in expensive leather with a gilt ballpoint pen stuck in a loop, a trinket for the woman who has everything, and wrote out three Malay words for me: *ubi* = sweet potato, *atap* = rush matting, *kawat* = fence. Lesson number one for beginners, as if I were a dummy. Her manicured fingers caressed the paper, and the words seemed false, memories of poverty written by a wealthy hand, a hand that had not peeled a potato in years. Even her rings seemed fake, emeralds set in gold, tropical colors, green against brown. If it should ever become necessary again, they could keep her fed for months.

"When the war broke out, we were much darker than we are now," said Saskia. "But that did not keep us out of the camp. We lived among Dutch military people, and we were put under house arrest right away. I envied the natives who could go free, I did not want to belong to the *kaaskoppen*. I belonged to the brown people, and I had to be fenced in all the same. I just couldn't understand it."

Don't be ridiculous, I thought, you were barely potty-trained. But I was determined to be gentle, and I kept silent.

"Odd, now that I think of it, I realize that may have been when I first became aware of my brown skin." She patted her chest, I had never yet seen her so clearly proud of her descent. "Twenty-five percent. At Sunday school in the camp we sang 'I see a portal open wide,' and I imagined a lot of brown kids walking in a free heaven. I dreamed that I slipped out between the legs and skirts of the wood gatherers, to join the native smugglers who were rummaging around outside the gate. Only later did I learn that it wasn't much safer out there."

It was growing stuffy inside the car, and Saskia's perfume was getting on my nerves. I opened a window but had to close it again at once. Her thoughts were wandering in the East Indies, she said, and the cold sea air was distracting.

"When the war began, Pa van Capellen was on a secret mission to Borneo. Mama reassured us and said that he had gone underground somewhere. But where? And why didn't we hear from him? Searching for him was useless, the mails weren't working properly, it was the beginning of the Bersiap period, the big purge. Many Indonesian nationalists were hostile to the Dutch. Sumatra was not safe, there was fighting everywhere, women and children had to be repatriated as soon as possible. If there was any news, we'd be sure to hear it in Holland.

"A government employee told Mama that Pa van Capellen had joined the resistance with several other Indos. The rumors drove Mama crazy, some other Dutch people insisted Pa was a traitor. How could she prove otherwise? Mama knew nothing, she didn't have a single official paper.

"We had no more clothes or linen to trade. The English gave us Japanese uniforms, horrible, but we had nothing else. Mama made mud-colored dresses out of them for us. She herself went around in military pants that floated around her middle like a balloon, tied together with a white belt stained with rust around the holes. I remember it perfectly. We had no shoes, there were no children's shoes in the Red Cross package, we wore wooden clogs with wide leather straps.

"Our neighborhood was guarded by the Japanese, this time to protect us from fanatical insurrectionists, the former enemy had become our protector. Luckily we didn't have to bow to them anymore, but I was more afraid there than in the camp. At night you could hear shooting, and you could smell fires burning in the city. After a while the British took over the security. Diagonally across from us a group of men lived in some sort of old mission house. They played soccer in the front yard and made a lot of noise, especially in the evening; they played music until all hours. The mothers all said it was shocking, but when we were in bed, they would sing along softly out in the garden.

"We girls had to absolutely stay away from that house. The women who frequented it were bad. As soon as we were allowed to move about more freely, we carefully walked by it, to look at bad people. We couldn't see anything exciting, just a lot of old men, some of them wounded, lying on stretchers under the tin roof of the veranda, others walking on crutches. They were homeless, grim, dressed in rags, not the men of our mothers' dreams of whom they spoke at night and with whom they had danced the rumba so wonderfully before the war. They looked like death in the story of Pierlala, crooked, with hollow bellies.

"One of the men stood out, wearing snow-white pants with a crease and shiny new black shoes. That one's got to be a dancer, we thought, you could hear the steel taps clicking under his shoes. I had never yet seen such polish, we only knew of open-toed linen shoes, clogs, and boots. The dancer spoke to us and addressed Jana in a very friendly way, without winking or making risqué jokes like the Allied soldiers did. He often strolled around the little square at the end of the lane, where he stood bargaining with the natives. We admired his shoes, and he let me stand on top of his toes in my bare feet, then we danced. He spoiled us with candy that he'd been able to get from the natives. I couldn't remember my own father at all, but I loved being so close to a man. In those days, many of the children in our house got their father back, trucksfull of fathers were being distributed, I thought we could choose one, too. The fact that he was called Justin made it that much easier to appropriate him. Yes, all three of us fell in love with him. So that's the man who later became your father."

Saskia looked at me expectantly. What did she want? Should I throw myself into her arms and thank her, sobbing, because she had chosen my sire?

"When he heard our last name, he told us he had known our father during his military training. We went and told Mama at once, but she didn't have the energy to seek him out. Every time we saw Justin, we questioned him. He had been a boxing champion and could draw beautifully. We posed for him and gave Mama the drawing. Never saw it again, of course, thrown away like everything from the past. We thought she should come with us to thank him, but she was ashamed of her Japanese pants. Jana almost forced her, she was the go-between, she called Justin by his first name. They weren't that different. She even went to the nuns to beg them for a dress, and when she got no for an answer, she stole a sheet from their laundry line; she confessed to me later. Mama made a jumper out of it.

"They met on the little square, Jana had set it up that way. Mama on the bench, your father by the gate, and behind the barbed wire were two vendors. And we just held out our hands: condensed milk, a piece of material, a box of chocolate, all into mother's lap. He also gave her a flower and a letter, and she accepted everything but refused to go dancing with him. That, she thought, was not proper. She was waiting for her husband, she didn't know yet that she was a widow, and she thought of your father as just another young man."

"You sure have a good memory," I said. "A jumper, black shoes, rust spots on the belt. . . ."

"It's the small things that stay with you."

"You were still small yourself."

"Five years old, almost six."

"And already with political insight." I mistrusted the whole story. Roughly I put the car in first gear and drove to the lane in the forest, some hundred yards behind our house. At the end of the dead-end road there was a parking space, but I didn't stop, I tore at full speed into the lane. I made my own rules here. The sand splattered against the side windows, the motor roared. As a child I had often helped to push Germans out of the loose sand, this time I got stuck myself. We looked at each other angrily; as far as I was concerned, we had nothing more to say to each other, and yet our walk had not even begun.

"Ada told me all this," said Saskia as an excuse. "But you know how it is, when you hear about it, you relive it. It's my story too."

To escape my cold questioning she suddenly produced an envelope from her pocketbook and put it in my lap. "A voice from the past," she said. "Here, a letter for you."

My former family name was written on the envelope, my father's name. It had been my name as long as he was alive, and later, too, in school, but as soon as I went to college I adopted my mother's maiden name. I didn't want to be reminded of that man, and since he had never been married to my mother, I had a perfect right to her name. I thought that in this way I could simply erase him from my life. Besides, my mother's family was of much older stock. I was a snob as well as a bastard.

"It's been opened," I said. It had been sent to Ada's house, the return address used on the death notices. Maarten didn't understand. "Who's it from?"

"Read, just read. With an Indo accent, you're so good at that."

> Dear Sir,
> It is difficult for me to address you as sir, for I held you on my lap when you were a baby, but I expect you've grown considerably and I hope for your sake that you deserve the title of 'sir.' First of all I want to extend my sympathy on the death of your half-sister. I remember Ada much better than I do you. Ada

was a strong-willed girl. I'm sure you loved her. The bond between half-brothers and half-sisters can be strong, as I well know from personal experience.

It must also have been a shock for your mother, please convey my best wishes to her. The reason I am writing to you is the following: why did you not sign the announcement of your sister's death with your own last name? Why do you use your mother's maiden name? Even though your father was not able to marry your mother because of wartime circumstances, he acknowledged you legally. He was especially proud of you when you were born. I remember this very well, for I am your father's half-sister.

You are denying your descent. From acquaintances of your mother I hear that you frequently speak of your father with condescension. I can understand that you do not wish to stay in touch with your father's family; you also imply that we are of mixed blood.

Your father was a highly respected man and a brave soldier, of ancient lineage, related to the famous textile manufacturers of Leiden, residents of Batavia as early as 1827, and of pure Aryan blood in every line.

Your Grandmother Didier, my mother, was a Frenchwoman of noble descent. We are definitely not Indos. I had to get that off my chest.

Very truly yours,

Mrs. E. Taylor–van Bennekom

P.S. It is imperative that you get in touch with me.

"Who is this creep?" I asked.

"I think it must be your Aunt Edmée."

"Edmée? Never heard of her."

"She lived in Cyprus and was married to a British officer, Uncle Jeremy, a stiff sort of man with a mustache and a pipe. They came to see us at the seashore only once; she was a worldly woman. Don't you remember? I'll never forget her, she wore a hat with a veil over her eyes, very elegant."

"And a pure Aryan, besides."

"You were four years old, maybe five. Strange, but of course not everyone remembers things from that early an age. Perhaps you supressed it." She couldn't help laughing bitterly.

We left the car standing in the sand. My anger had disappeared, but with it went the energy to push the car out of the ruts.

As we walked, Saskia asked me to put my arm around her. I did, even though I had to force myself not to push her away. She was overdressed for the country, too much makeup, wealth clung to her hips. And then that pleated skirt over her ass, like a pumpkin in a lampshade! I soon chose the narrower side paths, where it was sandy and we had to let go of each other.

Autumn had crept into the beach grass, green and yellow alternated in the wind, a dry summer had colored the shrubs red, the gorse bushes were weighed down with orange berries, predicting a cold winter, Saskia thought, and we wondered how cold it was in Canada and whether Jana would die in winter or during Indian summer. I wished her a death in mild weather, Saskia hoped she would live to see the snow.

We had never agreed about anything. As children we were always quarreling. She'd see me mope in front of a full plate, spoiled, growing up in prosperity. I felt excluded and could not share her past in the East Indies. She was jealous of my peacetime, I was jealous of her war.

But the matter was more complex than that, I understood as we rested in a tearoom on the way back. The sea mist had crept under our coats, and we ordered hot chocolate and pancakes. (Fried in deep fat. I left half, she ate all of hers. "I just can't throw away food," said Saskia. "Well I can, I throw food away every day. It's my contribution to prosperity.")

We chose a table near the open fire—the first fire of the season—and I asked her if she and her sisters had done right to choose my father.

"What do you mean? He took good care of us," said Saskia.

"He humiliated you."

"Sometimes, when I did something wrong."

"Thirty seconds late for dinner, sixty seconds late from school."

"He was a punctual man."

"He beat on time."

"Not me."

"Right, he menaced, and you sweet-talked him to avoid his anger. You massaged his neck with tiger balm, ironed his slacks. You begged for his love."

"You were jealous."

"Yes," I said, my mouth full. "My father was mine, no matter how mean he was. You played him off against me. You took his side whenever he took his anger out on me and then I felt abandoned, or you made fun of him behind his back and then I was ashamed. If people looked down on him, they did on me too. And my father enjoyed the game, we squirmed under his hand."

"But he was also afraid of us. Whenever we touched him, he cowered. We loved him, and he couldn't bear it." Saskia looked at me in despair, her shoulders hunched anxiously, her hands stretched out, her whole attitude pleading for understanding. We were aware of having been rivals in love, this was why we begrudged each other everything. I rubbed her left thumb with mine, over the scar my father had caused. Too much gesturing with her fork, and wham, a slap with the carving knife. A little accident, a temperamental outburst, that was all; he didn't realize that the knife grinder had paid a visit. The incident happened before I joined the family at the table, I was still in my crib.

One thing we agreed on, for the first time: Perhaps we fought mostly about our mother, our constantly pacifying mother, blind and East Indian deaf. She always managed to stay out of the argument, she remained silent or shushed quarrels and agreed with everyone, not caring who was right; she found a way to excuse everything.

"She was the one most afraid of him," I said.

"She did not dare take sides," said Saskia.

"She did when it mattered, she let Jana emigrate behind his back and helped you get painting lessons."

"Yes, when he was already dying, and it wasn't even her own decision, she went to a medium for advice." Her face relaxed at the memory. "I'll never forget her coming back one night from a séance, and before I went to sleep she whispered the words that set me free: 'You must go to the art academy.' *Must*, that was literally how it had been communicated."

"And why didn't you finish that school?"

"I never dared tell anyone at home," she said. "During my second year I was given an exhibition by a friend. I wanted to show everyone what I had made. My color was sepia. My work was still abstract, monochrome paintings on a white background. It wasn't deliberate, I just had to get that color out.

"My friend had reproduced one of my pictures on the invitation. Soon thereafter she got a call from an acquaintance. He had shown the card to a Japanese friend who thought it was beautiful, he had just moved to the Netherlands and wanted some Western art to hang on his walls. My friend called me at once, what did I think, could any Japanese come to the opening? Fine, I said, just let my former enemies shell out. I thought it was really exciting. But when I saw that man leaning over, looking at my work at the opening, I had an anxiety attack. In a flash I understood what I had tried to express with my paintings: fear, imprisonment, bamboo fences, the shuttered gate. I ran away and never wanted to see those paintings again. After that I didn't dare paint for years, and much later, when I cautiously started again, I preferred to create safe little landscapes rather than the subjects I was too emotionally involved with."

"Therefore, nursing."

"Clean and white."

"And you were obeying my father."

"Yes and no. When Mama moved to the retirement home, I found an envelope at the back of her linen closet. There was nothing inside, but something was written on it: Saskia must go to the art academy. What's this? I asked. 'Ah well, I might as well tell you now,' she said, 'but how terribly frightened I was that evening of the séance. The medium received a written message, her hand and pen were guided by a superior force. This is your father's handwriting.'

"I know you don't believe in it, but I think that my father made me paint those pictures, he wanted me to express my fears in paint, but I did not continue at the time, I wanted to obey two fathers, yours and mine."

We walked back along the wider paths, my arm encircling Saskia. I pulled an orange-colored shovel from a fire pole and dug a trench under my rear tire, *Ja, jetzt geht's los*, I still knew the phrase in German, and together we pulled the car out of the sand. Four hands against the car trunk, pink beside brown, now really at one with my difficult sister.

"Any news from the hereafter?" I asked my mother when I called her from home.

"No, nothing special."

"You're not being abandoned by the spirits, are you?"

"We're out of touch."

"And that Hindu of your séance-holding friend, wasn't he a chosen one, can't he reach someone?"

"He was an impostor, he decamped with her table silver. No, Ada is too tired now."

"Tired? You think she took her mortal remains along?"

"Of course not, her spirit is tired. Don't forget that she went through a hard time, and then those sleeping pills."

"Say, who's Edmée?"

"Which Edmée?"

"I have a letter from a lady who calls herself my father's half-sister."

"Goodness, don't you know her? She's the youngest of the lot. Edmée is a child of Grandma Didier's second marriage, she remarried a lawyer, don't you remember? A van Bennekom, a crooked lawyer from Batavia; he was terribly sly. Goodness, that little Edmée, so she's surfaced again."

The letter, Edmée's reproaches, my mother wasn't surprised. "You can break away all you like, in the end relatives always find each other again," she said. "It's a mystical bond, an umbilical cord that ties you to your origin."

Dig them up and dig them in, tear yourself loose from these crazies, erase your memory with quicklime and forget your family, forget them forever . . . the words were on the tip of my tongue, but I wanted to be a good son and said, "How nice to have a new aunt."

"So long as she stays at home. I have no desire to see her again."

"What was the last time you spoke to her?"

"God, ages ago, at your father's funeral."

"Then how does she know what I think of my father?"

"Come now, you've been going on about it all your life, every chance you get you broadcast it all over the place, there isn't a single one of my friends from the camp who doesn't know; some people go to every possible reunion. And everyone knows that there was no love lost between your father's family and ours."

"Everyone except me."

"They thought the girls were too Amboinese. Nonsense, Justin van Capellen was the son of a Menadonese."

"What does that mean?"

"The Amboinese are family-minded, they stick together like burrs. The Dutch looked down on them because in Holland they kept on living together in camps, or forty people to a single house. Well, you know your father's family, conceited about the color of their skin, they feel superior. After his death they wouldn't have anything to do with us."

Where did she get this? The pot calling the kettle black. What a delicious family. And I was hearing all this only now.

"Your father's side was embarrassed by us," she said cheerfully. "You were an illegitimate child, and Catholics think that's a mortal sin. That is also why they did not consider you one of them."

I didn't know what to believe. My mother had a tendency to rewrite family history each time some suppressed fact surfaced from oblivion. As she became older and more vague, she kept contradicting her own lies. A liar who does not want to be caught has to have a good memory.

My father came from a large Catholic family, he had said so himself, so that much we can believe: six children, not counting Edmée. He was the oldest and only just ten when he lost his father. Something about suicide, but of course I was never told the details. I decided to question my mother. Another brother and two sisters repatriated to the Netherlands, the others remained with their remarried mother and stepfather in an Indonesia striving for independence. Not until the 1950s, when the atmosphere became too hostile, did they emigrate to Australia by way of New Guinea.

Since he was sent away from home at an early age, my father barely kept in touch with his family. I was not surprised therefore that his brother and sisters living in the Netherlands never got in touch with us after his death. Relatives—they came and they went, and I did not miss them; but later, about the time I became old enough to shave, I did become curious. Where were they, and what could they tell me about my father? "They all emigrated," Mother told me at the time. "They followed the rest of them, the whole clan is in Australia." The story sounded plausible, and I left it at that.

The East Indies died in our house with my father's death. My mother did not want to be reminded, not only because of the camp but mostly because of all this family business and all the touchiness. She had already experienced the difficulties of marrying into a brown family during her first marriage, she had never felt quite accepted. No matter how great an effort she made to study Malay as a young girl, and to adapt to the new culture, her husband's family still saw her as a menace and never tired of subtly making her feel excluded. Let it be, the East Indies were behind her.

So no more exotic aunts and uncles with their rolling r's and golden yellow rings and words accented on the last syllable. The kris, the piece of batik material, and the tall tales went back into the cabin trunk. From then on, rice no longer steamed on the table, only potatoes cooked until they were mush.

My father had always been the cook at home. All he had contributed to the household were a wok and a steamer; he could not repeat this often enough whenever there was a quarrel: He'd brought them himself from the East Indies. Sunday was the day for rijsttafel, and every dish sounded like an island: *bami, lombok, sajur, serundeng, atjar, ketimun.* The kitchen was his archipelago. He could not manage to work outside the home—"My valve leaks, you know"—and sometimes he was so out of breath that he spent the afternoon lying on the sofa, panting, but no matter how weak he was, he could always cook. When he wore an apron, at least, he was something of a man.

He developed a complicated network with East Indian grocers who provided him with bamboo and pisang leaves, needed as wrappers for his sticky rice. At most my mother was allowed to bake vegetable patties, made with damp bread and leftovers. After his death we could taste why: she was a terrible cook. Not until I was a student living in a rented room did I realize that a hard-boiled egg did not have to have a blue yolk.

My mother longed for simplicity. She erased my dead father,

and I became all hers and her family's: sturdy farmers, Waldensians as far back as the seventeenth century. But whenever the Dutch were horrid about my sisters' skin color, I belonged to the East Indies.

That's how matters stood, and how they continued, until my mother's world, made up of lies, threatened to collapse a year ago. A growth was troubling her, and she had to go to the hospital. Afraid that she might die, she handed me a long sealed envelope on the eve of her operation. "You have a right to this," she said in a colorless voice. "You can't open it until I'm gone. You promise?" I promised, but my nail was already prying open the seal. "No, look at me, you must solemnly promise."

I closed the door behind me and tore open the envelope. An official document fell out. It bore an orange tax seal stamped by Notary Groeneweg, now also many years deceased. Did our benefactor have some business to settle with me? I could hear charms tinkle and the clicking of dials on the dashboard. Perhaps a million-gulden legacy.

"Statement" was typed at the top of the document, the rest was written by hand. "Transcript from a legal document. Drawn up in The Hague, the tenth of August, nineteen hundred and fifty-seven." A month before my father's death. A message from the grave.

The testifying party declared "that on the thirtieth of January, nineteen hundred and forty-two, I agreed to espouse, without conditions and with the understanding that all material goods be held in common, Mrs. Sophia Munting, at that time a resident of Indonesia, currently of unknown address and no certainty as to whether she is still alive. On the second of March, nineteen hundred and forty-two, I departed on a military assignment, since which time I have not seen my aforementioned spouse again. On November twenty-seventh of that same year, during my absence, my aforementioned spouse gave birth to twins, whose paternity I deny but which said denial may be declared illegal because Mrs. Munting refused to sign an agreement. . . . It is unknown to me whether Mrs. Munting bore any additional children . . ." etcetera, etcetera.

Obscure sentences, could the "party" not have been clearer? As I deciphered the legal lingo for a second time—in the middle of the hall of the division of surgery—I noticed that the document bore an addendum. On the back was glued a handwritten note. "Act of Repudiation, August 19, 1951," someone had written in the margin, probably the notary public, for the signature next to the seal was similar in ink and handwriting to that of the other sentences.

In this statement my father also denied being the father of the twins. In spite of the services of a lawyer in Batavia he had been unable to dissuade Sophia Munting: "Some ten letters have been sent, but Mrs. Munting has not taken the trouble to reply." Different words to the same tune, except that in this document the twins were named: Ruliana and Rudiono.

The Royal Colonial Army Circus presents!

I knew, even in my father's lifetime, that he had been married in the East Indies before the war. After the war his wife seemed to be untraceable, and that was the reason he could never marry my mother. I was even aware of the rumor of children, but they had been born years after his departure. Such was the family version, and so far, nothing new.

But then what was the reason for keeping this envelope from

me for such a long time? Did my mother possibly think that those children were his after all? I studied the statement once more: March 1942 departed on a military assignment. A scant nine months later, in November, Ruliana and Rudiono were born. My mother could count. I was baffled.

I would have loved to turn back and question her, get the truth out of her. What did it matter that I had broken the promise I had only just made? She hadn't exactly choked on her last lie either. But I was more than angry, I also felt small and humiliated; she still did not take me seriously. How could my father's children possibly be dropped in my lap just as my mother was having her stomach cut open? Twins—two what? Sisters? Brother and sister? The brother I had always longed for as a child? A boy with whom I could have shared my dreams, who would give me a boost when climbing and who would save me if I walked too close to the quicksand? That night he was sent to me by surface mail.

Perhaps my father was acting in good faith and completely innocent—who knows what shameful life Sophia Munting had led during the confusion of those first days of the war? But why did my mother act so mysteriously, and why had she kept these documents hidden for so long? If I hadn't opened the envelope, I would not have known.

My mother liked to keep her distance, she put unpleasant news aside for a while, just as we left a hare caught by the village poacher to rot before we put it in the stew pot. In this case she really had left it a very long time. Hold your nose and get out of there.

In the elevator, as I put the papers back in the envelope, I noticed a penciled scribble on the envelope: "For my son, so that he may understand later." My father's handwriting. At that moment I was certain.

I ran to the hospital parking lot. I felt full of energy, determined to take off for Indonesia that very night—I was even foolish enough to ask for a road map of that country at a gas station. I wanted to go in search of Sophia Munting, I longed to hug the twins. Never before had I dared to visit Indonesia. I was afraid of false sentimentality, afraid the lashes of the palm fronds would sound like my father's slaps, afraid to eat *te pedis*, and to call my crocodile tears real ones. Just let my mother die on the table; then I'd have the money for a first-class ticket.

She didn't die. Waldensians live to be a hundred. Her tumor turned out to be benign, and a month later she was walking around again, spry as ever. My anger disappeared with her illness; I let the matter rest. There would always be time for Indonesia. On second thought, it was too much my father's country. Relatives, a new brother and sister? They were only half-related, no matter how you looked at it. The less I saw of them, the better off I was.

Not a word about the envelope, of course. Both our lips were sealed. A family trait. I know nothing. Distance. Regal distance.

I did have a lawyer look into the legality of the documents. Nothing. Notary Groeneweg had lent his name and paper to the good cause, a stamp and a lump of wax to save my father's hurt pride. The papers seemed to me destined more for my mother, letters to comfort her and to assure her once more in black and white that his legal wife, Sophia Munting, had not cooperated in any way. There was no mention of divorce. To his regret, he could not help it that his first wife remained his heir.

It was not so much because she was ashamed of living in sin that my mother would not risk putting an announcement of his death in the papers; it was also better to let sleeping dogs lie— perhaps Sophia Munting was on the lookout somewhere. She had, after all, a right to her share.

It amounted to nothing, for whatever he had left had come out of my mother's pocket: a camera, a watch, thirty coats and trousers, a bunch of ties, and twenty pairs of shoes (my father liked to show off his good taste, and she went along with him, though hand-me-downs from her anthroposophist friends were good enough for her). The coats went to the Waldensians. The first thing I grew out of were his shoes. Throughout my adolescence I went around with creased trousers.

The first few weeks after his death I hardly dared to leave the house, afraid of the evil spirit claiming my thirty pairs of pants. Jana, who was too old for ghost stories, told us that this Sophia Munting had children, she had known it even in Palembang; but my mother immediately squelched the rumor. According to her, the wife had gone off with another man. She had washed herself in the river, and in the East Indies this ritual was as good as a divorce, according to Muslim law. There were no details, we only knew that such customs were not considered valid by the Department of Overseas Territories; our country was too Christian and too respectable for such goings-on. One thing was certain: River water made you pregnant, and the resulting children were not my father's.

After the letter from my step-aunt, my indignation at Ruliana and Rudiono returned in full force. I had set their existence aside all this time as a rather comical item, but now I thought the time had come to put my cards on the table. Too many new facts had emerged. I was curious as to how my mother would handle the matter. First a telephone call; perhaps we could be more honest if we were not looking into each other's eyes.

I asked, "So tell me, this Ruliana and Rudiono—should I think of them as family members as well?"

"Who?"

"The children my father begat with his legal wife."

She thought I was too coarse, I expressed myself too bluntly, and what was I referring to? Whom was I maligning this time? She pretended not to understand me at all. Envelope, hospital, the notary . . . "Yes, yes," she said vaguely. She wasn't even angry that I had opened the envelope. Among themselves, liars don't have to stick to their promises.

"I never knew what was in that envelope," she said. "It disappeared into a drawer after it came from the notary."

I too said vaguely, "Yes, yes."

"Now look at me," I ordered my mother a few days later when I visited her in her apartment. "You did know, didn't you?"

"No, really, I never heard of this Rudie and Rulie." And she began to count the months on the knuckles of her hand. Nine. "And even born on a twenty-seventh, seven and two are nine, Mars," she said with a laugh. "The number does happen to fit in with the family."

At times I really loved my mother.

Family. You are conceived in love, lust, or boredom. You feed off your mother, you want to get out, the cake has been eaten, the knapsack bursts open. You tear yourself free, the shit comes along with it, and you make her bleed with pain. Your first camp is behind you.

And then the slap to check if you're alive. You pee. Your head under the faucet, swaddling clothes, and a warm breath blowing through your hair. Into your mother's arms, a kick, nipple in your mouth, go ahead and suck. Your mother cries. They call this happiness.

Your father is proud, he lifts you high in the air, the world is too bright, dazzlingly bright. Your sisters come and take turns pinching you. Gee, he's real, he won't go away. You don't hear them, words mean nothing to you, nor do gestures and facial expressions. But you can feel the love, the expectation, and the fear, a hot-water bottle at your feet, a rubber sheet, and pins in your diapers.

They weigh you, eight pounds two ounces, caught in a net, they buy bonds in your name, you're worth something. Again you are raised up into the air, balanced on your father's uplifted hands, this is going to be your first snapshot, it shows you crying, you're no hero.

You don't like your mother's breast, you spit, crusts form around your mouth. Your mother feels guilty, she was too weak when she carried you, such weakness causes puny children. Your father is disappointed. You keep him awake, you are afraid of the dark and of shadows that move. It is winter, and your sisters wash you with snow. This makes you strong.

An evil world streams in through your fontanel, you see your father's eyes, black, they force you to stand up and you fall, your first bump is soothed with a cool silver coin. You can do it, one hand holds on to the playpen, the other is raised on high: Mussolini greeting his fellow citizens. That will be the second snapshot of you. Mother consoles, shush shush, and the buttermilk is sour.

You're growing too fast, your shoulders grow crooked. Your father stretches your muscles, you get your first slap, you become acquainted with his cane. Your mother sews a prickly pair of short pants out of his army jacket. They put his cap on your head, you march around the table to the tapping of his ruler, your sisters clap to the beat, your mother looks at you tenderly. You're almost a man, almost like him.

Family, it'll do you in.

3

MATA GELAP: THE DARKENED EYE

═══════════

THERE WAS a call from Canada and Saskia was hearing voices once more: Jana's end was near. Sheila the astronaut again signaled the number nine, it could happen in October or November. My mother bet on October. Even though the birth of Jana's first grandchild was not to be for weeks, her bags were packed. She did not look forward to having to mourn twice, preferring two funerals in quick succession, that way she could stay in the mood.

I myself declined the honor, both dying and giving birth could take place without me. Though my oldest sister may have been my second mother and may have diapered and bathed me when I was a baby, she had become a stranger to me, and her impending death didn't affect me much, no matter how tragic I thought it was for my mother. I was nine years old when Jana married in haste and left for Canada. Since then I'd seen her only twice—on the occasions of my father's death and my mother's illness—and both times she had come back reluctantly. I never wrote to her, did not know her children, and had not been too pleased to see her husband, Errol, again. What was I supposed to do over there? Her yearly Christmas letters were full of trivial news, the accompanying photographs hurt my eyes. Fat children and a harrassed mate in a room paneled in red Canadian oak; travel trophies on the walls.

Errol had been a seaman for years, he had also come from the East Indies, a gangly toffee-colored boy from a house across the street. Our village swarmed with people set adrift by the war, the government had appropriated all the empty summer cottages for them, and when, in winter, you saw blankets hanging in the bay windows, you knew people from the East Indies lived there. The more blankets, the more exotic. In Errol's home not a window remained uncovered. "But we're pure Dutch, you know," his mother insisted at every birthday party. And the result was that in Canada, Jana bore two Chinese children— yellow, with little upturned noses and a mysterious Mongol fold around the eyes. You can never tell with these colonials.

Jana did not love Holland, so the story went at home, she and my father missed their native country the most: a fruit orchard with mango and jambu trees, earth in which you could drop a chewed-up pit that would take root and bear you a harvest, wet earth, leaves and rotting compost, the brown smell of the islands. They simply couldn't get used to the gray skies of Holland and the raw winters by the sea, the heavy clothes and dark houses, not beautifully whitewashed, *kapurd*, as my father called it. Whenever we had tea in the garden after four o'clock in summer, and the dunes glowed softly behind us, Jana would murmur about warm sunsets. The *lingsir kulon*, the most beautiful light of the Indies, the hour before the sun is slaughtered and rose-red shadows come creeping out of the bushes. *Kasian*, too bad, in our rainy weather you couldn't dance, and in the morning the trees around the house did not cause the dew to evaporate. And yes, in the East Indies the morning sky was green.

"Those two were always homesick," my mother said. "They could weep together at the sight of an old photograph. Jana is a child of the jungle, she grew up far from people and the city; we moved from one outlying post to another in those days. She never played with dolls, she took her little pig along wherever we went."

The summer after her final exams my father treated Jana to a bicycle tour of the Netherlands. They wanted to see the places whose names they had had to memorize in school in the East Indies. They would ride through the green green fields from Roodeschool to Roosendaal and to the Royal Military Academy in Breda, a castle with a moat and sauntering cadets, yes, there too they would go, and the mountains of Twente, the Holterberg, the Galgenberg, the Tankenberg, for they longed for more rarified air and distant views. All of us bent over the map, my father drew red trails like pirouettes, this was their new homeland, much smaller than Sumatra, they would explore its every nook and cranny.

They returned utterly disappointed: a week of rain and headwinds, the horizon too low and too many fences, and then those lumps in the landscape, how could people call those mountains? My father pasted snapshots of the trip in the family album. Jana was shivering in every picture.

After several wet weeks and Errol's suspiciously frequent presence, Jana made her decision: to marry and emigrate. And who didn't in those days? The milkman went to the United States with his fiancée, a Jewish family chose South Africa, classmates applied for emigration documents, the public-information bus made the rounds of the villages with a film projector. Ten million Dutch people on one little clod of earth—all those who were young and longing for wide-open spaces tried their luck overseas.

Jana received large envelopes in the mail, and the wealthiest countries sent her calendars. I hung a poster of three red mountains over my bed—The Three Sisters. Jana, together with my mother, filled in all the papers and secretly practiced English, listening to the neighbor's radio. Only Canada accepted her, they didn't discriminate as to color. My father refused to listen to any more talk about the topic at the dinner table. "Bad for his heart," said my mother.

The following summer Jana posed in a white dress in front of our communal house. Notary Groeneweg drove the pair in his black car. I found no other pictures of the wedding in the family album. No wedding feast, no aunts and uncles, both families wanted to keep it simple, my father was too ill for celebrations. The doctor came once a week to give him an injection. "He became resigned to it," explained my mother later. "The medications were a big help."

A truck delivered a crate for transatlantic transport, and Errol hammered the lid shut in our communal hallway. My mother knitted heavy sweaters, Jana raided the closets: Waldensian silverware and Sunday-best dishes with a gold border, bed linens, the pots and pans given us by the Red Cross—all our wealth disappeared into the crate. Els Groeneweg came and brought a piggy bank from Makkum, you could see the silver coins through the slot. Jana had to promise that she would break it for good luck. Our grandfather gave her two albums of old

MY FATHER'S WAR • 95

photographs, and in all of these, too, Jana appeared. The neighbors did not come empty-handed, everyone brought something. Each day I climbed the kitchen stairs to see how full Jana's treasure chest was growing.

My father lay on the sofa, bitter at being abandoned by the apple of his eye. His bluish lips trembled. Errol was not good enough for Jana—a boy from a house with blankets at the windows! What lack of toughness, and how common; we braved the Dutch winds. And what would such a boy do? What good would his training as a seaman do him in Canada? My father kept muttering his rage, and at the dinner table he invented new rules: no more hammering in the house, total silence in the hall. But the departure could not be postponed, the passage was already booked.

Errol climbed on top of the crate, tied a washcloth around the hammer head, and nailed all the boards shut. I handed him the nails, and Jana shoved the wood shavings back in. The banging of the hammer echoed through the hall. I winced at each blow and admired Errol's courage. Jana giggled nervously.

We didn't hear him, but suddenly there he stood behind us, unshaved and unsteady from his long rest on the sofa. Two fists bulged in the pockets of his bathrobe, his black eyes were burning in his skull. Without a word he went up to Errol. "Get off that crate," he ordered. Errol put down his hammer and jumped down. My father grabbed him by the collar, reached out, and slapped him on both cheeks with the flat of his hand, the way he always hit, his fingers leaving white outlines on Errol's cheekbones. I was ashamed but also relieved, even grown men let him slap them.

It became a painful farewell, Father locked himself in his bedroom and Jana wouldn't have anything to do with him anymore. For days we ate nothing but vegetable patties. Errol's parents no longer greeted us, my dad was *mataglap*, they said. This is how I learned my pidgeon Malay: *mata gelap*, the darkened eye, a blind rage that makes you see black.

And yet my father must have taken a picture of their departure. My mother still has it, hidden away at the back of her album: the young couple, with suitcases and the crate, standing in front of the truck. Errol is looking away, Jana is staring straight into the lens, tentative but beautiful. When I envision her like that, she touches me more than I am willing to admit. She was beautiful, the best-looking mother in the house, that's certain.

On the morning my mother left for Canada with Saskia, she was startled out of a strange dream. She called me quite early to tell me about it. "There was a storm, and your father was harnessing the rescue horses, you were watching him in your slicker. You had trouble climbing into the sloop, that's how small you were. Your father took the reins and the horses pulled you into the breakers. The waves foamed about you, and when the sea grew calmer and the horses swam back, I saw that you were the oldest and Aram was the child. You were rowing away together. Strange, as if the waves had washed you into an adult. Your hair had turned gray with foam."

Not bald, thank God, I thought.

"Do you suppose the dream means something?" she asked.

"It means that under no condition am I to go to Canada but should stay here to look after Aram. I'll be like a second father to him, like a rock in the breakers."

Reassured, she left for Canada.

One Sunday I went to the beach with Aram, I had neglected him since the funeral.

"You know what's strange?" asked Aram in the car. "I don't miss Ada at all." His slicker squeaked and his flashlight lay on his lap. We planned to go to the old bunkers.

"Maybe you will later on. I first missed my father when I had to learn how to shave."

"What would I be missing?" With his right hand he briefly stroked his cheek, I could see it from the corner of my eye, just as I saw the spots on his trousers, the lack of polish on his shoes, and his dirty fingernails.

"Music. Didn't you play well together?"

"I haven't touched my French horn in weeks. When I practice, it makes me think of her, and I don't want to. Is that bad?"

"What do you mean?"

"Sometimes I'm even sort of glad she's gone." Aram gave me a poke, opened the zipper of his jacket and showed me his T-shirt, a knight in armor out of whose visor crept a bloody snake. A rubber print, I had trouble keeping my eyes on the road, and I just had to touch it. The snake was sticky.

"Black Sabbath, I bought it with my allowance."

"Would Ada really have minded?"

"She was afraid the music would make me deaf. She hated heavy metal, she thought it was vulgar, fascist screaming. Dumb. She had opinions, but she wouldn't listen; I never could make her hear what they were really saying. Pieter and I smuggled the CDs upstairs, and then we played them very softly. At his house it's okay to turn the sound up. We actually are against violence, it's just that we show the world the way it really is. All that hell and devil stuff is just to scare people." Aram looked out of his window in silence. There was a strong wind, the new beach grass lay flat along the dunes, but it was a bright day and the sun gleamed on the hood of the car. "The last years weren't that much fun, my mother worried constantly."

"About you too?"

"About me and my father. She thought I was too rough. But Maarten is incapable of doing anything, and I'm not allowed to do anything. I've got to sit with him, do my homework, and stay home. I talk too loud, stamp my feet when I walk, eat too fast, can't play music at night, and he can't stand it. My father is a very old man."

"I believe we're the same age."

"But he's sick, he doesn't even dare to walk along the beach."

I parked the car in front of the gate. The stone trail led to the bunkers behind the strip of sea, forbidden territory nowadays, appropriated by the water company. We paid no attention, lifted the barbed wire, bent over. These dunes belonged to me; I knew the area, the quicksand next to the grassy marshes, the underground eddies that sometimes surfaced after a storm. The place was not entirely free of danger, but for that very reason the emptiness was etched in my brain for all time. If the dune guard were to stop us, I would insist on my territorial rights.

Aram darted ahead of me, to the left, to the right, like a dog leading the hunter. He was happy to be free of his father for the day. At Ada's deathbed he had had to promise that he would take good care of him. He took the laundry to the laundromat every week—a full bag, for Maarten peed in his pants now and then—and in the evenings he had to feed his father the last few morsels, when the spoon became too heavy for the man. We all knew that things could not go on like this, but Maarten wouldn't hear of any changes. He threw away a feather-light set of disposable tableware I had brought. Rather die than resort to plastic.

Everything remained as it had been. Saskia came to lend a hand between her therapy sessions, my mother read the cards with her women friends and saw in them that there was no better solution for the time being.

We walked over the foundations of the bunkers, they had been torn down, a scorched piece of concrete still lay half-buried in the sand. What a fire we had lit here with the summer orphans from the city, and put out the flames with gallons of piss, and measured each other's pricks! I could still smell the pee.

"I think I would have liked to be a soldier during the war," said Aram. "Bombarding bunkers."

"With people inside?"

"Well, that's not necessary, blood seems sort of creepy to me. But shooting is great—boom, everything smashed." He ran through the ruins, gathered handsful of sand, and cast them to the wind. Where the sand fell, something glistened in the sun. I leaned over and picked up an old bullet.

"From the war?" asked Aram.

"Or from a poacher."

"I think it's a German bullet. Can I have it?"

I wiped it off and showed him how you could make it into a whistle by blowing along the rim of the shell. A steely sound rang out over the dune; I hadn't lost the knack.

"A *Wunderhorn*," said Aram. He put the bullet in the pocket of his pants. "I'm sure Ada doesn't approve, she didn't like war." He looked at me seriously. "Sometimes I'm afraid she can see me and that I'm hurting her."

"Dead is dead. The dead can't see, and the older you get, the less clearly can you see their faces.

I spoke with as much assurance as I could muster, standing in my dun-colored dunes, where the sand and the wind made my eyes water. I loved the emptiness that always drew me in and where there were eddies and dangers under the surface. When I walked here I felt closest to my father.

We took the dunes by storm, Aram's sandy hand in mine. We fell and crawled to the top, where the wilderness lay behind us at the edge of the pine forest and the breakers foamed before us. A black kite dove up and down above the beach, two boys dancing at the end of the string. We sat down, shoulder to shoulder, the sand pecking at his slicker. With a wind like this I used to tie letters onto my kite, letters addressed to my dead father in heaven. I gasped and had a coughing fit—since Ada's death I was smoking heavily again. I no longer cared, I'd seen where a healthy life could take you. I almost puked with breathlessness, God, I felt old. And yet I wasn't worried, I was too glad that I was no longer a child.

After I dropped Aram off at his gloomy home, I wondered once again whether I shouldn't be taking care of him after all. I had abandoned the idea just as many times before. My girlfriend could see me coming. I had been pursuing her for eight years, but she kept running away through half the world. She was a literary agent, reading constantly, pausing for a kiss between the lines. She was not eager to have a son. Besides, she wasn't good at handling problems, and since Ada's death she had made herself scarce. Every day she faxed me a letter (her favorite word was "soon"). No, I wasn't made for ordinary domesticity with children; besides, my apartment was too small. A kindly uncle at a distance—that was all there was to it.

And yet, what a great way to revenge myself on the past—to

raise a child without ever beating him. But heavy metal in my house, and graffiti on the walls? Would I be able to leave him to his own devices? I would want to keep him safe from harm, and in so doing I would limit his freedom. I lacked the patience to let him make his own mistakes. My friendliness was just an act, I recognized the insistence in my voice, the suppressed curses, the darkness in my eyes, and my pent-up temper. I wasn't even able to take care of a dog.

How I had frightened myself a few years earlier, when I took in a puppy, a companion for my walks in the dunes, a hairy child that would bring regularity to my days. He had two tufts on his rear end, they looked like two eyes that kept constant watch over me, even though at each hill or curve he looked back sweetly to make sure I was following. I had called him Janus because he had two faces.

I meant to do better with Janus than I had with my first dog, a playful mutt that had never been given a name. We were still living at the shore, and I had found him on the wasteland by the waterworks, where the wind had covered the shifting sand with a rippling crust. No idea how he had gotten there. I heard him whine, long and high, calling for help from afar, and when I came running, he was already buried up to his belly, threatening to sink into his own pit. The stretch of land was dangerous, one false step and the ground would suck at your shoes. It was safe only along the strip where beach grass had been planted, where the sand was sufficiently tamped down. That's also where the poachers walked.

The dog slid into the shifting sand all the way up to the tops of his front legs. I held on to the dune grass with one hand and tried to come as close as possible. I hung above the rippled sand, and with my other arm I dangled a branch in front of the dog's jaws. The animal held on with a bite, but the branch kept slipping from between his teeth. He spat out the shreds and sank still further, but finally my imaginary brother gave him a shove and I pulled him toward me with a tug. His licks smelled of fish, and he followed me gratefully.

I got no further than the front hall. There was to be no smelly animal inside the communal house! The mutt would not be chased away and waited like a good dog under the kitchen window. We fed him, my mother and sisters thought the dog was cute. After two days my father filled a tub with soapy water, we washed the mutt, and he was allowed to stay. A dog, a dog, we had a dog that caught rabbits and ate washed up fish; he was a friend with whom I could run, and together we explored the secret passages of the bunkers.

But at home he did not obey the rules and regulations, my dog chewed everything. A devourer of pajama bottoms and slippers, with a preference for my father's expensive shoes, he was a real beachcomber, sinking his teeth into anything he could find. When he would not stop after being threatened and beaten, my father gave him to the coast guard, who was supposed to give him to the fishermen in the next village. The subject was discussed and understood: a dune dog could not be walled in, he would definitely have a better life with the fishermen on the northern shore.

A few days later I met the same dog in the dunes, alone and smelly. It recognized me and followed me, wagging its tail. But this time my father was adamant: no water, no bowl of rice, not even a box to sleep in at night, no *kasian*, no matter how I pleaded. That same evening Father returned the dog to the coast guard who put him in a sack and drowned him behind the barn.

My new dog was allowed to chew up shoes all he wanted and even received a pat when he rolled in some carrion on the beach. Janus was a dog's dog. He did love me, but he liked dogs even better. He always wanted to play with them, and when he lay on the floor of my study at home, he pricked up his ears at any distant bark. My home life was much too boring for the puppy, he sighed under my desk, yawned, made stinking farts, and looked at me pleadingly until I took him out to the doggy-rolling meadow, where he could have a good snuffle and dance on the trail of his buddies. Janus came from a kennel. He was used to much barking and crowding around the feed bin. The more dogs surrounded him, the happier he looked.

The silence at home depressed him, and he refused to eat. The most expensive cans of dog food, the tenderest steak—Janus would have none of these. I worried and my dog was aware of it, as soon as I went to the kitchen, he fled. He became visibly thinner.

The veterinary advised force-feeding and there I was, on my knees, a tube of chopped meat in my hand. Janus kept his teeth clenched. Caresses, sweet murmurings were no help. My hands were trembling, I shoved the tube behind his eyeteeth, first carefully but gradually more roughly. I pinched the sides of his jaws, his cheeks were puckered over his lips, and I hit him. Cursing, screaming, I slapped both sides of his head and jaws with the flat of my hand.

The kitchen was smeared with the mess, and Janus whined behind the stove. No matter how foolishly I apologized, he wouldn't budge. Hours later he crept out, terrified. I comforted him, tried to feed him again, stroked, patted, and then slapped him once more. I hated my hands, I hated my temper. I wanted to beat the puppy until he grew big and fat.

"Smother him with love," said a dog expert whom I went to for advice. "He's bound to eat, no dog starves to death." We tried again, sweet dog, good dog, but to no avail, until I discovered that Janus would eat in the company of other dogs. I took his food along to the dog meadow, and gradually his appetite returned. Weeks passed before he would also eat alone.

At home he wouldn't take a single bite when I was present, and even if I watched him through the crack of the door, he would guiltily dive behind the stove. His trust had been permanently destroyed. I loved him, at least so I thought, but two summers later I gave him to a family rich in dogs. Janus eyed me so guiltily, and if I looked back, he turned his head away. He was afraid of the black in my eyes, and because of his eyes I became afraid of myself.

Els Groeneweg's house was also near the dunes, but she lived in the built-over province of South Holland, where greed had driven developers to buy and build on every sandy hollow. Now all the rich lived there in equally ugly surroundings.

Els's house smelled of an old-fashioned Sunday afternoon, the scent of the *sajur* curry wafted through the hall, and the spice cake was on the table. "Just a cup of tea," I had told her on the phone, but once I was there, I had to stay for dinner; her husband was away on business, and she wanted to spoil me. She knew things were coming to an end in Canada and that it bothered me that I hadn't gone with the others. "In my mind, I cooked for Jana as well, " she said. "We'll be close to her."

Els went from the kitchen to the table, sat down, crossed her legs, stood up again, ran out into the hall, and as she came by, her dress outlined her hips. "I'm getting old," she said, for she had forgotten the spoons and the soup bowls.

I sighed at the sight of her dancing blond hair, her wrinkled laughter, and hazel-colored eyes. The setting sun washed in through the big window; it was as if we were seated in an old photograph, shadows creeping so lazily along the white wall and the small palm tree in the wicker basket growing taller in the twilight. Els's room was tropical.

I weighed the spoon in my hand and sat there silently falling in love. Even worse, I longed to be very small with her, to lie naked on her hips, blowing my breath between her breasts and feeling her legs about my thighs. She swerved around the table and took a framed drawing from the wall.

"Do you know this?" she asked.

"It's you, isn't it?"

"You don't notice anything special?"

The pencil lines were hard and thin, and I had to hold the drawing at a slant in the light to be able to make out the contours. I thought it was only a fair piece of work, although the mouth and eyes were a good likeness; it had to be her.

"Made by your father," she said. "His signature is under the mat."

Although his hand was supple, he had not been able to catch Els's liveliness; she sat tamed under the glass.

"He drew very well," she said.

"He could copy."

"Don't you have anything of his?"

"No, he never made it to the walls of our house." I felt as if she'd found me out; strange to hear someone admire his work while at home we looked down on it. We had managed to make even his better efforts disappear.

"Don't look so somber," she said. "I thought you'd like it."

After the *sajur* she led me to a corner of the room, to a cabinet full of photographs, her life in silver frames. We admired her father standing before his black Rover, Els in her MG, her mother next to Brother Joost in his pilot's uniform, a bent old grandmother dressed in a sarong and kabaya, dogs and cats, three shelves of happiness on display. She picked up a small snapshot: Els and Jana in summer dresses, a pig on a rope between them.

"Fort de Kock, just before the war," she said.

"I didn't realize you've known Jana that long."

"We were in the same class at school. Our mothers played tennis together. We were inseparable, saw the Japanese march in in their baggy yellow uniforms, and went through all that business together: gluing dark paper over the windows and walking to school with a wok on our heads and a piece of rubber between our teeth in case of bombs."

Els opened a drawer and pulled a yellowed piece of cotton out of a box filled with loose snapshots and papers. She sniffed it and tried to wrap it around her right wrist. "My identification," she said. "The Japanese made us wear them when we went out. Mother lengthened it so I could wear it around my arm as a pass."

Eliza Groeneweg was printed under a red circle with a white star at its center sewn onto the tape. The number and the Japanese characters had faded with time. She pushed the armband further up. "Gained some weight after all," she said then when it wouldn't go farther than her elbow. "I've kept everything from those days. Before we entered the camp, my father left a suitcase full of documents and papers with one of his clerks. After the war he got everything back, sheer luck." She pulled the drawer out of the cabinet and put it on the table. "Look, Jana's smuggled letters." She held up a handful of little pieces of paper.

Scribbles about food, as far as I could make out at first, complaints about rotten vegetables, smelly meat, not enough of anything, never *kenjang*—"enough," Els translated when my finger stopped at the word.

"You're a real *totok*, aren't you, you don't know anything. Here, there are some really funny ones among these, about the difference between lice and bedbugs, it was her job to squash them. She says somewhere that they smelled of bitter almonds."

"And later?" I asked impatiently. I wanted to know why Jana had fled the Netherlands.

"Oh, this is a very sad little note." She went on reading without looking up. "Here she says that she misses me." She brushed at the gooseflesh on her arms. I no longer existed. "Calm down, little Jana, calm down, I'm coming."

"But weren't you together in the camp?" I asked carefully.

"Not until later. She went in much earlier than we did. Most Europeans had been picked up already and were interned in a few large houses—your mother and sisters, too. Confusing times. Ah well, I don't remember exactly. Men were taken away, but some families had dug cellars in their gardens to wait for the British underground, they were going to liberate us any day, that was the rumor. We just stayed in our own house."

"But then why did you smuggle?"

"Our family did not have to be interned. We had Javanese

grandmothers on both sides, that made us Indo-Belandas, pseudo-Dutch, of mixed descent. In Sumatra the Japanese did not pay much attention to this, but my father with his authority was able to prove it. Papers, seals, stamps—the Japs loved all that stuff. Before the war everyone swept their native grandmas under the rug, but once the Japanese took over, they couldn't bring them back fast enough.

"Twice a week I was able to bring food to your mother. Look, here Jana thanks me for the ubis with grated coconut." She waved the letter, which immediately disappeared under a new pile.

"Wasn't it dangerous?"

"It wasn't allowed, of course, but I had less trouble on the street than my mother—she looked too Dutch and was always being stopped. I skipped through everything. I could get on with most of the Japanese soldiers, as long as I bowed politely to them and wore my armband. I was the *rambut djagung* of the family, with corn colored hair, and the Japanese loved young, blond people.

"I brought food to a Chinese shopkeeper who was the official provider for the house where your mother and sisters were first interned. The Chinese told me the news that I could pass on to my father, for our radio had been confiscated. I also wrote down these items for Jana—about the Allied bombardments of Germany, and things I'd seen for myself, like when the Japs burned our schoolbooks.

"It didn't last long. I was caught, and my father had to go and argue with them for hours to set me free. My brothers had less trouble, they were darker. The Japs ransacked our house, we weren't able to earn any money, and were more and more isolated. Jana had been gone quite a while. No native dared help us in the market—afraid, of course. My father once saw a group of Dutch being taken by truck from an emergency camp. They were government employees, men who had worked with him, but when they recognized him, they insulted him by calling him a traitor. That really hurt. The young Indonesians were especially rude, everyone had abandoned us, and my parents felt guilty about the people who did have to go into the camps. We no longer knew where we belonged.

"One day someone we knew was stopped in the street. He had not bowed deeply enough, and to teach him a lesson, they knocked out his teeth with the butt of a gun. That very evening my father reported us to the authorities. We literally fled into the camp. Eventually my mother and I landed in Bankinang. Now we lost all our anxiety, finally we were safe. Jana and I were delighted to see each other again.

"My brothers went with my father to a camp for men, but they were given a very different reception. Pop was considered a traitor. Latecomers like him were treated very badly by the Dutch. That's why after the war he took such pains with your mother, for if anyone knew how quick people are to judge, he did." She picked up the drawer and pushed it back into the cabinet. "There, back into the closet."

"And the Canadian letters?"

"You won't like them. Jana was right to leave, my brothers couldn't stick it out here either, they emigrated as soon as they finished their military service." She cut off a slice of cake and took a tiny bite. "A bit too sweet," she said. "If only I'd known when your mother was going to Canada, I would have given her a cake to take along. *Kasian*, poor thing, so ill, and she didn't write me about her condition."

"Did you lose contact?"

"More or less. The last few years I only got a Christmas letter. Ah well, you know how it is. We reminded each other too much of things we'd rather forget."

"The camp."

"Holland, especially Holland, I think. After the war she had a very bad time here. Don't forget, Jana and I were old for our age when we came from the East Indies, we had worked, taken care of children and the sick. In a way we were grown-ups. In the camp my mother treated me as an equal, she was my friend, she confided all her problems to me.

"In Holland we had to toe the line. Our experience didn't count in school, we were treated like half-wits, and we'd fallen way behind. I was the oldest in my class, but also the shortest. After two and a half years in camp I was the same size as when I entered, I hadn't grown an inch.

"And those Dutch kids were rude! We colonial children were used to looking up to our teachers. But actually, what had my classmates experienced? Big talk about the Krauts, that's all. I had seen how people tortured each other and how mean camp mates could be together. Lying, stealing, and cheating, and after the war, in Palembang, I saw bodies that had been stoned to death . . . rows of them along the river. Not a word about all this in school, of course, you watched your step. Some of our teachers were very leftist and were terribly down on children from the East Indies, they taunted us with tales about lazy colonials, we were oppressors, profiteers. And you could easily see that we came from the tropics, with our yellow skins and hollow eyes. On the playground they called us double-ration eaters. I could have died of shame."

Els stood up and went to the radiator in front of the window. "Cold," she said. She ran out of the room and came back with a green sweater.

"Is that why Jana wanted to leave?" I asked when she plopped herself down next to me on the sofa.

"We had the same experiences. She was also the oldest in her class and we matured earlier, I think. We wrote each other about that too. The year after the liberation we'd seen just about everything as far as that was concerned. Reams of boys were after us. My brother Joost was mad for Jana and she for him, but your father was dead set against it. When we visited at your house, those two couldn't even go to the beach together. Your father opened her letters, she had a hell of a life with him."

"But wasn't she his darling?"

"Yes, literally." She jumped up and went to the kitchen, nervous and edgy. "Sorry, sorry, let's talk about something else." She slammed the door closed and loudly began rattling pots and pans.

Pans . . . our kitchen, my father wearing an apron and Jana on the little kitchen stool, a brown crust of rice in her hand, always the pan scrapings, her favorite delicacy. Jana, the favorite, the only one with new clothes, the most pages in the family album devoted to her, the only one who went along on a vacation, his only companion in the Keukenhof gardens, at Schiphol airport, in front of the drawbridge at the Royal Military Academy.

"So what happened?" I asked when after knocking discreetly, I stepped into her white kitchen.

"What I said," she snapped. "You know how it is, they weren't that different. Jana was looking for a father figure. She may have brought it on herself. In any case, she wanted to leave home as soon as she could, so she just took that dumb Errol. I think she didn't even love him, but he wanted to get out too, and a boy from the village didn't arouse suspicion. They arranged for their escape behind your father's back." Els moved a pan on the white stove top. A glowing red circle appeared.

"Your father was a bossy man," she said. "Attractive too, and we were used to playing with fire."

"With the Japanese, for instance."

"No, for the Japs we made ourselves small and invisible, I always hid somewhere at the back of the line during roll call."

"They were nice to kids."

"Sort of," she said curtly. "But they were disciplined. If a soldier did something that was against the rules, he was severely punished. They respected us, they never came to look at us when we were washing ourselves, very correct. The Australians and the British were much worse, after the war."

"Ada had a different experience."

"It happened sometimes, yes, there was always some idiot among them."

"Was my father that kind of an idiot?"

"He could be very nice, very charming, except when he lost his self-control, then . . ."

". . . he couldn't keep his hands to himself."

"Something like that, yes."

"A bastard, in other words," I said loudly. "Just a no-good bastard who didn't know his own limits."

Els began to desperately flap her arms and then, in a fit of nerves, looked for something in a drawer.

I faced her squarely. "A dirty scoundrel, go ahead, say it, just look at me, you won't hurt my feelings." It wouldn't take much for me to slam my fist on the top of her white stove, so that I could smash the Japanese flag that glowed there into a thousand pieces. But at the same time shame began to glow inside me.

So that's what I'm like too, I thought, his character is inside me. I'm a loudmouth like him; I have the same dark eyes. I felt too filthy and obscene to remain near her. I had to get out at once, out of that whitewashed house, no curry, no kiss, only a formal handshake. My secret love must not be frightened by my lust.

4
IN THE RANKS

I AM walking with my father from our house to the station. We take the path through the woods, a winding trail between tall tree trunks. The sun is up, but daylight has not yet infiltrated all the shadows. Pine trees bow to each other, and the sea murmurs through the needles. In the distance the locomotive hisses, and Father looks at his watch. It is a weekday, his 2,448th day since leaving the East Indies. He remembers this, his head is filled with figures. My sisters have bicycled to school, five miles there and back. They don't take the train because they are tougher than the other Indo children from our village, but they do wear long stockings and thick woolen caps, for their ears are delicate. Click-click-click, week after week, Mother sits by the window with her knitting needles. Right now she is working on linings for the leather mittens attached to the girls' handlebars—there are limits to how much cold they can bear. I'm the he-man, still in short pants even though it's down to thirty degrees. If I can hold out until New Year's, I will get a chocolate bar.

We arrive at the clearing where, in summertime, the horses of the rescue brigade are put out to pasture. A misty haze hangs over the grass, and a freezing wind has dusted the bushes with hoarfrost. Father does his exercises and I join him, stretching, bending, inhaling, exhaling, blowing white plumes into the cold air. The exercises make his heart expand. He gets stiff from lying on the sofa by the window and he needs to be more active. Winter, for him, is a difficult time. We run around the meadow, my father clicking his tongue. Giddyap, I'm a rescue horse.

At the station cinders crunch under our shoes and there's a smell of steam and burned coals. The train has just left, and the platform is deserted. Father looks around for a stick. He is tired and his lips tremble with pain.

The man from the gas company comes pedaling by along the path at the foot of the dike, the barrel of his gun sticking out of his saddlebag. We wave at him, and he steps down from his bicycle to ask if anything's wrong. Father tells him what we saw along the way—a buzzard fat as a goose and a sick rabbit dragging its hind legs through the sand. The man smiles. He is the village poacher, and his bags smell of blood. At night, after supper, we hear him shooting near our house.

"Yes, there's a lot of rabbit fever about," he says. "And where exactly did you see that buzzard?"

Father points to the woods. "Back there, at the edge of the meadow." The pain on his face has vanished. He loves to chat with the men from the village, though they're taciturn and used to quiet winters without summer tourists. It has taken a long time for them to acknowledge us at all. They think of people from the East Indies as foreign, and they don't like foreigners, even though their livelihood depends on them. "I also saw two Krauts in a Volkswagen. They were looking for the bunkers," says my father.

"They always return to the scene of the crime," says the gas man. "Like murderers." He climbs back on his bike, swinging his right leg over the gun, and we walk on.

"I pointed them in the wrong direction," says Father.

"Well done!" the gas man calls over his shoulder and winks at me, which makes me proud.

We walk back the way we came, but when we reach the meadow, I ask cautiously where that buzzard might have been. "There," Father says, his finger pointing vaguely. But I can't see anything, not even a lame rabbit, nor any Krauts in a car.

"When was that?"

"Yesterday."

"We didn't meet anybody yesterday."

"Well, it must have been some other day."

My father tells me never to tell a lie, but he does, every day.

Memories gnawed at my sleep. In the middle of the night I'd wake up with a start, in a paroxysm of hatred, or weak and paralyzed with anger. And every morning my own face frightened me.

During the day I did my best to lead a calm, disciplined existence: no alcohol, a single glass of wine with dinner was enough to bring on anxiety. I also gave up smoking, for I was once more up to two packs a day, which was perhaps the cause of my disturbed sleep. I did my work, sent faxes to my girlfriend, and fulfilled my family obligations: sorting Ada's papers, telephoning to Canada regularly, and sending money to cover Jana's medical bills.

Conversations with my mother did not improve my mood. She seemed incapable of talking normally over the phone, stammered, always wanted to hang up—"What's this costing over there, I hear a click every other word." She still belonged to that generation of parents of emigrants incapable of accepting the idea that it was possible to call overseas just to say hello. She did not hesitate to contact the world of the spirits, but the idea of a long-distance call almost made her wet her pants.

In those days everything got on my nerves. I cursed at the newscaster on television, threw the newspapers across the room. War, injustice, disease—I couldn't bear it any longer. Weakness was not allowed, and to fight it I rubbed salt in the family wounds. I scornfully mocked my father's grave, but why? It did not help me to control my anger—on the contrary. Outraged at the humiliations my parents had had to suffer, I nevertheless wanted to punish them, and yes, I, too, longed for punishment. I could not understand my rage.

Whenever I couldn't put up with it any longer, I took the car and drove to the sea at breakneck speed, eighty miles an hour when possible, welcoming a traffic ticket. To clear my lungs I walked straight into the wind along the surf and paid no attention to the rising tide, the sea foam was not worth avoiding. My shoes were ruined, and the sand chafed blisters into my heels. Pain cleared my head, and wet feet brought me peace.

Continuously returning to the past, I exchanged one addiction for another and longed for new extremes—swimming naked in October, for instance. What a marvelous memory, the sting of the cold sea, followed by the sensual reward of a tingling body.

On a windy day I took off my clothes and walked into the water. My own body fat tightened about me like an armor, my scrotum shrank with the cold and became young and firm once more. I was lifted up by the waves, and my feet danced on the ocean floor; I swam. The skin of my fingers shriveled, my arms and legs went numb, but I kept swimming, and I dove into the waves, not caring whether a cramp or the undertow would drag me down.

And ahead of me my father swam, naked. There was no one to see us, our clothes lay on a towel on the beach. Later we would rub each other dry. The contrast between cold and warmth was good for his heart. I could feel his arms brush against my legs, the tiny hairs rising in the current. The waves drove us apart, then brought us together again. My father was gentle in the sea. When water surrounded us, he could not beat me.

I swam into the past and watched the memories rise.

It was winter, a high wind blowing. My father and I walked toward the big bunker. It used to stand on the dunes, like a truck made out of concrete, with a square nose facing the sea and a yard-wide lookout slit at the top, but a winter storm had worn away the sand underneath, and now it lay split in two on the beach. At high tide the nose became an island in the waves.

The tide rose, my father took off his shoes and rolled up his pants. I only had to take off my shoes, for it wasn't New Year's yet and I was in training to acquire soldier's legs. We walked toward the front end of the bunker. The water turned my knees purple, but Father's skin remained a tropical yellow. We climbed on top of the nose and waited until the highest reeds were wet. Just like hair. Suddenly Father lowered himself into the water and waded back to dry land. His pants were soaked up to his thighs. He waved me on, but I did not dare follow him. He laughed at me. If I didn't jump in, I would have to wait six hours. "Are you a sissy or a fighter?" he shouted. I chose to be a fighter and slid down into the water. The waves reached my belt, my pecker shrank in the cold, and I waded ashore with chattering teeth. My father reached for my hand and tugged at my curls. I was a fighter. Home, the wind at our back. The edges of my knee pants rubbed against each other, singing a marching song.

Regression. Whether rising stiffly from my bed or emerging frozen from the sea, my mind skipped with ease back and forth through time. After my swim I dove, still wet, back into my clothes. Purple with the cold, I cursed myself warm, satisfied. I must move, run, let the wind blow beneath my damp clothes. I tied my laces together, hung my shoes around my neck and headed north to take a look at the remnants of the big bunkers. Pestering Krauts, skimming shards of concrete across the waves, drowning my father in the rising tide—I would find out how much debris remained from the ruins of the past.

My father was more excited about other people's wars than his own. He read books about the German occupation and the first eyewitness accounts of survivors from the Nazi concentration camps. He knew the D-day beachheads by heart, just as he could rattle off the railroad stations of the Netherlands, and in each German summer visitor he recognized a sadistic camp guard. "Look, there's another one," he would say when we did our exercises on the quiet beach in summer, and he'd point to a fat man who was digging himself a hole in the early morning, or at another one on wooden crutches with one rolled-up pants leg dangling in the wind. He had plastered over the word *Kinderheim* carved in the stoop of our house. He advised our neighbors to turn away German summer visitors, no Krauts were to cross our communal threshold. And when I went from door to door selling Easter seals, he told me which houses to avoid, we would not have any dealings with collaborators.

His hatred of the Germans stemmed from his need to be understood and from shame. Finding no sympathy for his own war, all his indignation was vented on this other one. He, too, wanted to go through life as a good patriot. The first ships arriving with repatriated citizens were welcomed with flags and speeches, but by the time he arrived, there were no more dockside receptions. The Netherlands were too preoccupied with rebuilding, tired of far-away heroes and even more of the brewing unrest in the East Indies. Enough was enough, too many sons had been sacrificed. Whoever had fought over there had lost and had better keep quiet and out of sight.

During his second year in the Netherlands my father took my three sisters to the fair in the city. We were pretty short of cash, he still wore his military jacket with the orange lions on the lapels and the badge of the Colonial Army. This was the first Dutch fair of their lives, a kermis. My sisters wore orange hair ribbons, and some boys hanging out on the street called out, "Blueskins" as they passed. They laughed, considering themselves very House of Orange and thought the word was another way of saying "blue bloods." But they stopped laughing when they heard those same boys call my father a *pelopor* murderer; all four of them were only too familiar with that word: *pelopor*, a native who opposed Dutch rule.

It upset my father that he had no status, no job, no past he could be proud of. All he had were a bastard son and a wife with three brown children, tucked away by the Department of Repatriation in a former *Kinderheim* by the sea.

My father had been foolish in refusing to let himself be declared unfit for military service. Shortly after leaving the camp, he asked to be discharged from the army, because no matter how much the Fatherland needed men to suppress nationalist rebellions, he could no longer face bearing arms, and he took the honorable way out. To show its gratitude for fourteen years of faithful service in the army, the military authorities deducted from his pay the government issue of clothing lost during the war: 1 headgear, 1 short overcoat, 2 shirts, 1 pair of trousers, 1 suit, 1 pair of shoes, 2 pairs of socks, suspenders, 1 sweater, 1 kit bag, 3 handkerchiefs.

It was the bloody limit, he said, and at the mere mention of the subject my mother went crazy. My father never complained, he felt too guilty, but he did keep the list for a long time and would read it aloud as a joke during dinner parties: the bill to a sergeant major who walked out of the camp in a loincloth and who, after three and a half years of internment, no longer had the guts to go and kill *pelopors*. That, too, was vexing. The charmer who could wrap everyone around his little finger and who could strike such a great bargain had paid with his health and was given precious little in return. All right, a jacket for the voyage, a silver decoration, a few copper medals, and a measly pension.

That was where he felt unjustly treated. If he could not have a share in the honor, then at least he could hate an enemy who had done him no harm.

The shame was more deep-seated, but that I did not understand until later, after I read about people who had returned from extermination camps or who had survived great disasters. Why did the others die instead of me? That was their question. My father, too, was ashamed of his luck at being alive.

Along the beach, on the way to the bunkers, my shoes dancing on my chest and my hair white with sand, I remembered one of the little skits I had performed after the Sunday rijsttafel;

I should have understood even then. My improvised performances were often based on jokes I had heard or read somewhere. I was never shy when performing, I felt safe playing the part of someone else, and it was the only way I could get the grown-ups to pay attention to me. A dab of my mother's face cream would turn my cheeks as white as a clown's. Powder in my curls turned me into an old, gray-haired woman. A black crayon gave me a mustache and a beard. For my favorite part I wore Father's military coat. With my face painted brown with coffee grounds, his medals pinned on—"The ribbon and decoration should be displayed at all times" the accompanying directions stated—I was a fighter like the ones on the faded photographs, a brave colonial soldier.

I marched with giant steps along the railroad ties of an imaginary train track, drilled holes with an auger, and hammered bolts into the wood. This is how a prisoner of war labored on the Japanese railroad. My audience sat in rows of chairs, making up the train. I was laying rails. Then I took off my coat, stuck my legs into the sleeves, stuffed the coattails into my waistband, and marched through the compartment like a fanatical Japanese. I sold a ticket for a dime to everyone, took the first empty seat, whistled like a locomotive, then toppled over sideways, chair and all. Derailed, that was the joke, all the passengers lost their fare. My version of the war.

The first time, my father thought the skit was funny, for this is how he'd told the story at dinner himself. They'd had a lot of laughs over there, in the depths of Sumatra. The tracks had been laid in the rainy season, close to two thousand yards a day, by thousands of men crawling around in the mud, and the first time a train drove over them, the locomotive slid down the dike;

that's how badly they'd laid the foundations, and that's how dumb the Japs had been, the stupid bastards. Ha ha ha! A good reason to snort through your hot-pepper nose, have a good belch, and drum on your stomach with delight.

When this performance, because of its success, was incorporated into my permanent repertoire, he became resentful. The neighbors, too, had had enough. Father said I was ruining his coat. "Many soldiers have performed brave deeds in their uniform, don't you ever forget it." The game was over, one shouldn't make fun of a uniform, and besides, I didn't stand up straight enough—with that kind of posture I would never be able to impersonate a military man.

And the medals? Permanently locked up from then on. They did not belong on anyone's chest, not even on the Fourth of May, Memorial Day. The same with the certificates of appreciation. He hadn't really earned them, he said, for he was still alive but his friends—the real heroes, those fantastic guys, "those terrific boys"—his friends had died. Soon my mother made a pair of short, boy's pants out of the military coat.

Night fell early on that October day, and I could no longer find the bunker, no foundation, nothing, not a trace. And yet I was certain of the spot, for I remembered the wooden breakwater; the coast was weak here, and the sea often washed over it. I entered the dunes looking for remnants of the bunker, and I saw our house at a distance. This had always been the fastest way to the village, in the lee of the wind, straight through the breeding grounds where the gulls attacked your hair in the spring. A light was burning inside the house, and the broad roof was a dark beacon.

I entered our old yard, the house still lay in the loose sand, thistles and dune grass the only fence, and I couldn't resist touching the back door to see if the mailbox we never used was still there. Because the wind whistled through the oval copper slot, my mother had nailed the pocket flap of my father's military coat over it. But the mailbox was gone.

I heard voices in the kitchen, and as I sneaked past the front window, I saw a boy setting the table. I stood there for who knows how long.

The table is set. Forks on the left, tines up, spoons to the right, hollow side down, no knives, we're eating rice, but the Waldensian crystal, always water for the *pedis*, on the right with the napkins, fruit knife above the plate, everything precise and calibrated. I smell burned rice, and I'm allowed to eat the crust with sugar. My mouth waters. Dinner is ready.

That night I went, like a German hunting for his old bunker, in search of the familiar tastes, to eat Indonesian food in town, an imaginary meal with my father. I longed for spicy food, for a burning ass, for fire in the mouth and sweat pouring down my temples, and I wanted to quench the flames inside with sweet coconut. I craved a cuisine of extremes.

We ordered the most elaborate rijsttafel on the menu, twenty-two dishes for two men, only one of whom would be eating, with some extra "Mother's sambal," as the waiter called it. The sand with which the wind had dusted my hair scratched the tablecloth. Just like the old days—*senang*, cosy. I suggested that we talk about the war, his favorite dinner conversation and yet the one he brought up least often.

Here, Dad, a clove cigarette, a glass of beer—you never used to indulge yourself in the old days, but such luxuries are quite normal now. I've just given them up, but let's go all out tonight. Self-discipline never lasts very long with me; as a little boy I couldn't control my pain or my anger for as long as sixty seconds ... counting, do you remember? Your favorite pastime. Eight days without smoking or drinking, how many seconds would that be? You were always hardest on yourself, although. . . .

Quiet! Tonight I'm the one who does the counting. At this table I'll do the talking for you.

The war, then, the stage, the theater!

The landscape. This knife is Java, the fork is Sumatra—there, I'll place it at an angle—and these grains of sand are the Mentawai Islands. The bowl of *sajur* is the Indian Ocean. Now where exactly were you torpedoed? In the *sajur*, by the western coast of Sumatra, or in the south near the straight of Sunda? Ah well, let's not quibble about longitudes. We'll make this into a thrilling tale.

War was a grand gesture to you, the details weren't important. War was a paean to comradeship and heroism. Misery was something you simply brushed aside. Mistreatment, humiliation, ah well ... whatever the Japanese did was just a big joke, even in prison you treated it all as a lot of fun, and always you sang. You never mentioned that in the camp men died by the dozens every day. Hunger? Besides your daily portion of starch, rice and ketela leaves, you could always supplement your diet with your own cooking—fried bat, rat meat, python, and rolls made with flour from rubber-tree fruit. Any more and you'd explode! Do you remember when you stepped into a flooded cooking pit after a rainstorm? Up to your chin in mud; your buddies had a good laugh. Whenever it rained enough, the latrines overflowed, and you had to wade knee-deep through the shit. Then there was that fellow who, overcome by the stench, fell over backward and almost drowned in the turds.

War was about shit, and that was allowed at the dinner table. In the East Indies everyone talked about it, and at home, too, you still washed your ass with your left hand, for no matter how soft the toilet paper, you thought washing with water was more hygienic. Was that why you hit me only with your right hand? Very clever, the way you could flick the palm of your hand in front of my eyes like a butterfly. I can hardly imitate it. You had limber wrists, and after you'd slapped me, you would stretch your fingers as if you were pulling off a creaking glove.

You had stories like fairy tales up your sleeve, imitated voices, mimicked people, and always laughed loudest at your own jokes. I was too young to realize how ironic these jokes actually were, and was never allowed to ask questions. You were the sergeant at the table, and you did all the talking.

Hand me your plate; how about some *lontong* and a bit of *rendang* to start? A dead man can use some hearty food, and look, a piece of chicken, how about a drumstick? Too bad, they cut off the feet, and you can't stick the head on your finger either. But should you try that here, hide a raw chicken head in the folds of the tablecloth and then suddenly shove it in front of my face, cockadoodledoo, you can't scare me anymore.

No, hold your tongue, we don't speak with our mouths full! And wipe your mouth before you drink. Don't wave your fork like a flag. What? Rude? This is not how you brought me up? Wait until I'm finished. You'll be surprised at how well-behaved I can be.

I'm going to tell one of those stories the way you did. I'll sit, like you, at the edge of my chair, legs apart, unbuttoned, and I'll make your faces, sticking out my chin, eyes blazing, searching for your voice as on an old radio. A touch more Indonesian than the waiter, I would say, and each word enunciated clearly, especially the final n's and a double diphthong, wah wah . . . right?

Got it! Your tongue in my mouth. Listen! You're speaking through me, you're choosing my words, your voice rings loudly in the sound box of my memory.

"Did you know that you can get seasick from swimming? Yes, man, from the high waves." (Always a man, I was your man even in the cradle.) "Waves high as a houses, not like these soapsuds over here, we dove up and down, head up, head under, nothing but a board to cling to. The waves were wild horses trying to throw us off.

"And thirst! Nothing but water all around, yet so thirsty, I wanted to drink, but the water was red, clouds of red all about us, and I saw sharks' fins circling the drowning men and the water foaming up high, fountains of blood. And then I looked again and the water turned from red to blue-green to clear as glass. I drank and threw up. It was a mirage, so salty it was undrinkable.

"There were three of us hanging onto one plank, a Scotsman, a Dutchman, and I, a plank no longer than a yard, perhaps a foot wide, a few inches thick. . . . A night and a day. . . .The rough wood tore at your skin, impossible to get a good grip, the sea was lukewarm but the night wind in the tropics can be cold, man. Our arms were stiff and cramped, we clamped the wood under our armpits and treaded water like mad.

"We had to be careful that no one else would join us on our plank—one more, and we would be done for. And sleep, no question of falling asleep, no matter how exhausted. I hadn't slept a wink on the boat for three nights, too stuffy and packed too full, you couldn't lie down; we were stuck together and were maddened by the pounding of the ship's engines and the wailing of the Javanese.

"Whenever the wind dropped we were rocked to sleep, but we tried to keep awake by singing, cursing, praying aloud, and yet we kept dropping off, the only help being to pinch or hit each other. A good smack, yes, that did it. I could hardly see anymore, for in the daytime the sun reflected off the water was blinding, and the salt stung my eyes.

"Even after the second night we kept hoping to be rescued, we peered over the water and tried to catch the attention of the ships in our convoy. They picked the Japs out of the water, rafts and sloops full of Japs, and though they saw us, there were only three of us, not worth the trouble of turning back. They kept sailing by us, no matter how much we waved and called.

"On the third day, or the second, I can't remember which, a storm arose. No smoke signals from any ship at the horizon. A beam floated by and we tried to tie it to our plank to make floating easier, but our fingers were too bruised and cold to untie the straps from some backpacks that were also floating around us. It started to rain, sweet water, we opened our mouths wide and let the downpour lash us. I licked my face like a cat, the wind numbed us, the rain was freezing cold. Hours earlier, the sun had scorched and dehydrated us. Scottie almost slipped away, we hoisted him up, I bit his ear and scolded him awake, and so we bobbed on until a gunboat headed toward us.

"I still remember a hook in our plank, a hand, the hand of a Jap, and a nasty grin. I was thrown on deck and was caught on a nail or a hook, something tore my skin, that much I remember. A warm trickle dribbled down the small of my back. Someone kicked me, and at that moment I let go. I'd had it, my last ounce of strength left me, my legs slipped back into the water, and I no longer cared. Then someone hoisted me up by the shoulders, I raised my eyes and saw a white vision, shining in the sunlight. This must be an angel, I thought, and now I am dead.

"And do you know what it was? A British officer in his white dress uniform, with polished copper buttons and white polished shoes. And do you know what he said? 'Worse things happen at sea.' Something like, heads up, it's not as bad as all that. As if he were Neptune himself, stiff upper lip. And this man kept me going. During the entire crossing he'd held on to a small suitcase, and no matter how much they complained that his *barang* took up too much room, he wouldn't let go of it. In that little bag he carried his pride. From camp to camp, from Flores and Amboina to Java, for over two years, he would rather have starved than sell it. Other prisoners tried to steal it from him, some thought it held money or jewels, but all there was in it was a pair of white pants, a white jacket, and a pair of shoes—a spare uniform. He insisted on keeping it so as to be correctly dressed when he was liberated, but when he found himself standing half-naked among the Japanese, he decided to put it on for our sake, for those of us who had pulled through.

"And that man became my friend, the guardian angel who gave me strength. He lifted me to shore; and I could no longer walk, he carried me on his back and dragged me along as far as the prison. Then the Japanese pulled him out of the ranks, and that's the last I saw of him, a white speck in the twilight."

Isn't that the way it was, Dad? That's how you told the story at our dinner table, with a touch more Malay; sorry, I've lost the words. You at the head, hidden behind steaming platters, spoon in hand and dishing up, the guests were served choice morsels. Now that you're dead, I dare to look you square in the face. With the years your eyes have grown lighter and less stern, as in the faded photograph behind glass. Our sun is stronger than you thought.

Let me put another helping on your plate, I'll color the rice with *sambal*, blood, and I'll inhale the aroma with delight.

Your stories kept changing quite a bit. Sometimes it wasn't a plank on which you floated but a raft, tied together with straps from the backpacks. Sometimes you were in the water longer, or the weather was different: a full moon and a sea strangely becalmed, so that the lamentations of the *romushas*, the Javanese coolies, could be heard far over the water. But your tale was always spellbinding, you wanted us to laugh, though we felt more like trembling.

The Javanese boy, remember? Suddenly it all comes back to me. He was hoisted up by one leg, the other one was bitten off by a shark. A medic wanted to tie up the bleeding stump with a rope, but the Japanese wouldn't allow it. A horizontal body took up as much room as three vertical ones, so he was thrown back in.

It didn't stop us from eating at all. If someone threatened to burst into sobs, or hands nervously fiddled with a napkin, you would suddenly summon up a stoker from Rotterdam, that joker who jumped overboard, right under the noses of the Japanese. "Swimming home," he cried, but he got no farther than a few hundred yards, for the Japanese fished him out and after a beating, threw him into the deepest hold. Did that stoker ever lay eyes on Rotterdam again?

Even though you couldn't pull my sled in winter and you didn't manage to climb up the dune when we were flying a kite, at the dinner table you were the toughest father in the whole village.

Let's order another glass of beer. Have a drink, man, throw all that anthroposophic nonsense overboard. Vegetables also ferment into alcohol in your gut; there's no doctor here to write prescriptions. Tonight I'm writing you back to health, my pen and I are master here.

Yes, I've become a writer. You used a ruler to drill the alphabet into me, and it has stayed with me, I thank you for that. I'm still a bad speller, but my sentences are fluent. You wanted me to be able to read and write at the age of four, and you succeeded. I had to pronounce long words without faltering. It was all about rhythm. I had to read the sentences to the beat of your ruler, one tap every two lines. *Robin the Giant* was the first book I read, and we finished it. Together we celebrated by going to the movies to see *Gulliver's Travels*, another giant, an excursion topped off with orangeade and coconut macaroons (baked on a thin wafer that made you joke about the Catholics' communion wafers). I could have skipped first grade. Robin is still my hero, a giant who could let people dance in the palm of his hand. I can do it too, just close your eyes. . . .

 . . . I'll give you a pair of shoes—black, a gentleman never wears brown; I'll respect your good taste. You'll get a new suit, let the clothes from the trunk air out, and I'll set you down in Palembang, in the European quarter, in the street where my mother-to-be is living. You're holding a flower, give it to her, don't squeeze the stem, be gentle. Ask her to dance. You see what a giant I am? I can make you dance, in the street, a bit common, you didn't like that, without a jacket, the back of your shirt is damp with sweat, and don't pump your arm so much, sway, sway to the rhythm of my sentences. . . .

What? Too tired? You've had enough, your heart, even in those days? You can't rest until I let you, I'll keep you dancing, I'll let you die, but I've already done that. For the time being, you're right in the middle of your life.

I went in search of your past, Dad, and there's a lot that's different from what I expected. I asked the family, but I was told contradictory stories. Our mother wants so much to forget, and she's good at it. In the same way that our pale sun has faded your photograph, the years are wiping out her memories, and so I had to go to others for help.

About ten years ago I wrote a story about my early years by the sea, and at that time I had not heard about Pakanbaru, nor did I have any idea where and when you had been torpedoed. I wrote only about your raft, or your plank, and I can't remember how many days I let you drift—one, two or three? When I recount your life's story, I go right along with your lies.

I received a letter from a reader who recognized the story of the torpedo incident. He wrote, "The ship on which your father sailed was the *Junyo Maru* and came from Tandjung Priok, the harbor of Batavia, on its way to Sumatra. It was torpedoed on Monday, the eighteenth of September, 1944. Of the 2,300 prisoners of war who had embarked in Priok, only 680 made it to the final roll call, and of the 4,200 recruited *romushas*, only 200 survived the disaster; in all, 5,620 died, 880 survived. The following week, some thirty more would die of exhaustion. The trail of victims from Pakanbaru, where the passengers finally landed with thousands of other prisoners of war, also took its toll. The percentage of deaths among the prisoners in the military was 36.9 percent, among the *romushas* it was 83.3 percent."

A stickler for detail, that man. You all died up to the decimal point and category by category, thank God, to everyone his due. And to think that I only devoted one paragraph to your being torpedoed! The name of your ship was never mentioned at our dinner table, and I had no idea there had been that many casualties. Mother couldn't remember a thing, but at the mention of *Junyo Maru* something vaguely came back to her mind.

I didn't answer the letter until a year later, and told the writer that I'd like to look him up. Never actually did, of course. Lazy, afraid to find out the truth? No idea. I also never went to Indonesia, though I've often had the opportunity. I was perfectly content with the family myths and could interpret them as I pleased.

After Ada's death I began to dig deeper. I read books about Pakanbaru, saw your name on lists of survivors of the torpedo attack, and wrote to witnesses. I paid a visit to the few who remembered you at all—tough, elderly gentlemen who, over a cup of tea, were willing to dive right back into the Indian Ocean. But it was all too long ago, they mixed up names and facts and would rather muse about their own experiences. (And as I sat in their living rooms and saw them delving with closed eyes into their memories, you too sat there before me, an old man, and I was ashamed of never having been a soldier and of never having become enough of a "man." How did you do it?) Their hands were old and sinewy, freckled with brown spots from years spent in the tropics, and I did not dare ask them whether they beat their children. They seemed like friendly fathers, every one of them.

I finally visited a gentleman in Limburg who said he had been your bunkmate in Batavia in the infantry. His memory was pretty moth-eaten by then, he could tell me little about you. He considered you a "very decent sort." "After I was declared fit for transport, I suffered a severe bout of malaria. I could hardly walk, and things looked pretty bad for me. Then your father drew a portrait of a Japanese guard in exchange for some quinine. He could make the Japs look more heroic than they were, he was very clever at it, his drawings sold like hotcakes among the guards. I think he finagled a lot of things with that talent of his." Nice of you. As he saw me out, he added that I looked like you. "Only it seems to me that your father was a lot shorter." A whole day's driving, and that's what you get.

But all in all, when I combined the various tales, I was able to reconstruct your transport to Sumatra.

In the ranks. You stand in line on the parade ground of the former Tenth Infantry Battalion in Batavia.

Hundreds of emaciated prisoners of war have been assembled from various camps in Batavia and selected for an unknown destination. Roll call. Counting and recounting, for hours on end ... *ichi, ni, san, shi, go.* There's great confusion, for without an abacus they have a lot of trouble. The shouting drives you crazy. Civilians and soldiers together, Dutch, English, Americans, an occasional Australian, and a group of colonials in the military whose loyalty to Dutch rule is being rewarded with imprisonment, in spite of the false promises of the Japanese.

You've already spent two and a half years in camp, probably somewhere in Java where you had gone to military school and had no doubt remained—here my information fails me. Amazing that you were still in Java, most of the young men had already been dispatched. How old were you, twenty-nine? Perhaps you were overlooked.

You march through the unlit streets of Batavia early in the morning, a silent procession clattering toward the station. Hundreds of wooden-soled sandals echo from the houses, your infantry boots have long since been abandoned, the straps made out of rubber tires cut into your arches. You inhale the smells of the market, kerosene lamps smoking in the stalls, the vendors look on and say nothing.

What did it feel like to be marching like this through your own city? Didn't your father run a funeral parlor as well as a stud farm here? Plenty of cars and carriages, as a boy you didn't have to wear out your shoes, and if there was a shortage of deaths, your father changed the little curtains and drove wedding parties. These could have been prosperous times for the business, there had never been so many deaths, but now others are calling the shots. You have to bow to the Japanese—humiliating? And yet to them it's a perfectly normal greeting, just think how often you made a native squat before you when you were a child.

You remember these streets from the days of your wealthy childhood, when you rode your father's horses and the servants ran alongside. On Sundays a coach and four, giddyap, past the kampongs, how grand you felt seated way up there, giddyap, to the planters in the mountains, the sun, the view, and the scent of a thousand perfumed flowers.

Sentimental memories will do you no good now, you must keep walking, you've been approved for transport. Only a day or two ago you marched past the Japanese with your shit in your hand. Dysentery parade, with your feces on a piece of cellophane to show whether you're fit for the job. You tried to cheat, who didn't? A watery dog turd or ground peanuts did wonders. Whoever had dysentery could sell his shit at a good profit, it would let you off the hook, and if one couldn't find some diseased turds, a blob of snot from a companion with a cold would do, preferably with a trace of blood in it. But when you walked by, those damned slit-eyed Japs wouldn't look. You're in for it, giddyap, into the truck.

The locomotive points north, that means transport overseas, say the prisoners of war who came from other islands. They tell stories about bombings and torpedoed ships. Nobody believes them. You have all been given mosquito nets, and you expect to be taken to warmer regions. After a voyage in an armored train you can smell the sea, in spite of the vomit and the shit from the dysentery patients. You march toward the inland harbor and wait, and wait.

Then the *romushas* come stumbling in, gaunt Javanese in rags, some of them with stinking wounds. They have sold their lives for five gulden, most of them picked out of the dessa by the village chief and destined for transport: old men, children, it makes no difference, there is even a seven-year-old boy among them.

(Your former comrades did not talk about these things to me, I found them in archives and books. One man said, "As time goes by, you wipe a lot of things from your memory, you have your hands full with your own problems, you can't survive on pity." Did you see those children? Or did you have shit in your eyes as well?)

It is daylight, but you have no idea where you are. To you, these inland harbors are coolie territory. The *Junyo Maru* rocks along the quay, a rusty old wreck. A little longer, and the Japanese and Korean guards chase you into the holds. The ship casts off and lies at anchor for hours in the blazing sun, the men on deck are burned by the scalding sheet metal. Then, finally, the open sea, rain and sun alternating, at night a raw wind blows, and the days are unbearably hot. The ship is much too crowded, not every prisoner has found a bunk to sleep on, a whole rack collapses, dozens are wounded. The latrines are overflowing and hard to reach; the weak piss in the hold, the ones suffering from dysentery hang on ropes overboard, often too late, so that you wade up to your ankles in brown muck.

Is that where you learned all your shitty jokes? Or were you sitting between the bags of cement, a gray old man? Or in the coal bin in mourning among your friends, or did you manage to find a spot on the upper deck?

The food is good: soup, rice, vegetables, and salt pork, better than what you were getting the last few months in the camp. But the chow lines are long, the spaces cramped, you shove and fight over water and rice. Though there's enough to go around, you let others starve. When the sick start dying, they are thrown overboard without ceremony; you can count how many there are by the number of wristwatches the Korean guards wear on their arms. One of them has nine.

The *Junyo Maru* zigzags to the northwest, Sumatra's coast comes in sight, with some luck you can see the outlines of the

Bukit mountains. At 18: 10 Tokyo time the first torpedo strikes the bow. Bodies and beams fly through the air, and only seconds later the stern is hit. The ship does not list, no one on deck realizes how fast she is sinking. Sure, take your time, stand around arguing whether it was an English, Dutch, or American submarine that hit her. Or blame each other. If only the Japanese had stuck to the rules; according to the Geneva Convention, prisoners of war should be transported under the Red Cross flag.

Panic reigns in the holds, men kick each other down the stairs, the wounded and the sick are trapped and trampled underfoot. When the stern goes under, panic breaks out on deck as well, you fight to reach the railing. No life jackets are being distributed, the Japs claim the lifeboats for themselves and fight off *romushas* and prisoners with their swords. One group somehow manages to get hold of a dinghy, but when they lower the ropes too quickly, the boat flies apart on the high waves. Planks from the bunkers and life rafts are thrown overboard, men jump into the water from all sides, and some drown as they are hit by a piece of falling wood. The sharks feast on the corpses that drift in the wake.

One more explosion, and the *Junyo Maru* sinks into the deep. The sea boils over and turns bright red. Not blood, as you knew damn well: a cargo of red deck paint has burst open in the hold.

Never mind exactly how many days and nights you floated, you were sighted and hauled aboard one of the ships in the convoy. That's when you must have torn your back on a ragged iron scrap, which would explain the strange scars between your shoulder blades—a vertical strip on the left, a vertical strip on the right—that used to swell in cold water, as though you had sprouted tiny pink wings. Touched by an angel, worse things happen at sea.

After days of plugging along, you, like everyone else on board, end up in prison in Padang. No cots, no bedding, dry rice and a soggy green leaf, unboiled water, piles of shit, and thousands of maggots in the open sewers. You look to each other for comfort, but the following morning the corpses of the men who had been kept from the boats with axes and sabers lie in your midst. No time to rest, after a few days the first group leaves by train. Chugging up a mountain as cold creeps into the armored cars, then hurtling down into the valleys, no one knows your destination. Where the rails end, open military trucks stand waiting. You drive through dense forests along waterfalls and ravines. Just beyond the highest peak you cross the equator. Did you see the monument, the stone globe with the thick red line around the middle?

The trucks sway down into the lowlands, the heat of the marshes clings to your torn back. Your first camp, the bridge builders' camp. Here is where I lose sight of you. Nearly a hundred and fifty miles of mud, ravine, and jungle lie ahead of you. Rails and ties have been trucked in. You can go to work.

Not until now do I realize that you lost everything. You could no longer bargain, you had nothing left to barter, nor could you ingratiate yourself with your drawings, for your pencil is floating somewhere in the ocean. No mess kit: the first few days the survivors from the *Junyo Maru* had to eat with their fingers. You had no mosquito net, no clothes, no shoes; you were handed a rag to cover your private parts. It took a while before you could bring yourself to wear the pants and shirts of the dead.

I won't suggest that those things you had to do without became unusually important to you after the war, but honestly, was anyone ever as preoccupied with cutlery as you? The way we had to hold our knives and forks, as if we were dining with the queen, my fingers still cramp when I remember. You claimed you could tell people's background by the way they held their knives and forks. You, who shoved food into your mouth with a stick. And how tidy you were with your clothes, you, wearer of a loincloth, always pressing your pants and brushing your coat.

And your mania for counting, did you get that from the Japanese as well? Every morning on your way to the latrine you did your own roll call of the dead, counting the bare feet that stuck out of the charnel house: ten, twelve, thirteen pairs. How many dead, how many hammer blows still rang in your head after eleven months of work on the railway? Were you still working at counting them as you lay at home on the sofa after one of your fits of temper?

Thirty times thirteen is three hundred and ninety, times eleven is four thousand two hundred and ninety. Four thousand two hundred and ninety plus five thousand six hundred and twenty is . . . you could lie there for hours doing your sums aloud. Those were the hours in stocking feet. Shhhh . . . no bicycling in the hallway, no rattling in the kitchen, don't flush the toilet. No recorder right now, Ada. Shhh . . . Saskia, your pencil case. Mother brings in the door mat. A rag muffles the doorbell, the curtains are closed. Come on, no giggles in the bedrooms, no sighing while you're reading. Hush, hush, on tiptoe, sh. Daddy is counting.

Come, Dad, my plate is empty, I'll pay and we won't double-check the bill.

Shortly after my swimming session one of the survivors of the *Junyo Maru* to whom I had written sent me a copy of an account that might shed a different light on my father's mania for counting. It concerned the eyewitness report of a certain Mr. De J., who in the colonial period had worked for a drilling company in the East Indies. This Mr. De J. tried to take legal action against a fellow prisoner, Mr. X., after the war, "A traitor who sent at least one of my comrades to his death." The account looked to me as if it had been endlessly recopied, for not only was the typing blurred and barely legible, but lots of notes and names were scribbled in the margins in different handwritings. With great pains I managed to make out that Mr. X. had acted as interpreter in various camps along the railway. In the 1930s he had worked for several months in Japan as a ship's agent, and he prided himself on speaking fluent Japanese. Actually he knew no more than a few polite phrases, but whenever he got the chance, he used his knowledge to ingratiate himself with the Japanese. Mr. X's unsolicited services had already caused problems, and his fellow inmates avoided him as much as possible.

Mr. De J.'s report gave no indication as to the guilt, or eventual punishment or settlement, of the phony interpreter. These are not really relevant. Save your own skin. The only thing that mattered to me was a single line in the account that concerned my father.

Mr. De J. described how, after working all day with a crew of six men, he walked into the paddies, supposedly to look for a consignment of railroad ties that had been washed away during a downpour. In reality the men were going after an escaped water buffalo. Without considering the consequences, they grabbed the beast by the horns and led it back to camp, all under the supervision of a Korean guard and a Japanese soldier. In exchange for half the booty, these men were willing to look the other way. Unfortunately they were unable to perform the slaughter in silence, there was too much excitement among their companions in the barracks, and no one had a decent enough machete to chop the buffalo in pieces. The crew of railroad workers was caught with blood on their hands. It turned out that the interpreter had reported them to the commander. He was afraid of reprisals. "Better punish only six than the whole barrack," he argued.

The men were tortured for two days. Their names were listed in a footnote, and my father's was one of them. One man died of his wounds the following day. Four others, including Mr. De J., were sentenced to a week of solitary confinement. My father managed to so impress the Japanese that after being tortured, he was the only one allowed to recuperate in the infirmary. Apparently during those two days he behaved like a "fakir." "Thanks to a kind of self-hypnosis, he was unaffected by the pain." One sentence, no more. I wanted to speak to this Mr. De J.

Pension funds do wonders. Mr. De J. was still alive and lived elegantly in Wassenaar. We decided to meet on neutral ground, in a tearoom on a square that was brown with autumn leaves. De J. had been too busy all his life to think much about the past, constantly traveling and drilling, in Brunei, Latin America, Nigeria, all over the world, fascinating, but now that he, "an Indo boy," was getting on, he'd opted for his native country. And here, where everyone was constantly babbling about the war, all these damned memories came surfacing. "What is it you want to know?" he snapped. No, not his life's story, nor did we have to drill into the camp experience. My father, what did he think of my father?

"A man who could move about, a mind traveler, I'd say. He could endure pain as if he were somewhere else. When they pulled out one of his fingernails, a real live nail, he didn't make a sound. Justin could hold a pail full of water over his head with outstretched arms, not just five minutes, the way we did, but a quarter of an hour, fifteen whole minutes, without spilling a drop."

Mr. De J. took his time, and he made sure that I wrote everything down accurately. "Please note, fifteen minutes . . . that was most unusual, and I remember it exactly, for your father was counting every second and minute. That was his secret." And as I wrote, he slurped his coffee and gazed dreamily at a dog playing outside among the leaves.

"If you dropped the pail, you were whipped. We all got it, even your father, but he could take it. The Japs didn't know what to make of him. A strong fellow, that father of yours. Heart trouble? That surprises me. . . . He was also quite a mimic, could croak like a toad or roar like a tiger, he was so good at it that you thought there actually was an animal in your cell. The guards were scared to death! Justin pretended that he felt no pain, yes, yes, that's what it must have been, concentrating so intensely that he stepped out of his own body. But if it served his purposes, he could be a terrible sissy. He talked himself into the sick bay with all kinds of ailments, that's what saved him in the end.

"For two whole days the Japanese amused themselves with us, every six hours they dragged us into those cells, one at a time, so I never saw your father, but I never heard him, either. We groaned until there was no life left in us. Not long afterward we were finally separated, I was sent to the coalfields as punishment.

"I ran into your father again after the liberation, in the convalescence camp. I asked him how in heaven's name he had managed it then. By doing complicated sums, he said, taught him by another fakir. Interesting fellow, interesting fellow," said Mr. De J., and his eyes wandered back to the dog playing on the square.

My father taught me too how to count, without a whip, without pain. I learned from hearsay.

I didn't know what to think of my father's fellow prisoners. Mr. De J. seemed so distracted that I didn't dare ask him how he had endured his own pain. Packed it away and taken it along on some business trip? Bellowed it out later, down a drill hole? He added drily, "Haven't shed a tear since that fingernail, except once, actually, when . . . oh, never mind." I left it at that. And the others?

They had suffered, that was evident, and they were proud of it, too. Three and a half years as prisoners of war, three and a half years of torment. They had been in the pit of hell, and yet they were jubilant at having survived the ordeals. Their expressions were triumphant when they thought of the tricks they had played on the Japs, they were naughty children. They rejected weakness, and I showed them mine.

I said, "He beat me."

"Does that still bother you?" asked one of them.

"Yes."

"A beating never hurt anyone."

"The war still troubled him," I said carefully.

"What nonsense!"

They reacted uneasily, I reminded them too much of the difficulties of surviving. Who hadn't taken the bowl of food from a comrade who had given up, or accepted clothes from the charnel house? War is war, we had to survive.

So the camp had gotten to my father after all? Yes, yes, and they stared dully into space. But that wouldn't happen to them. They had no problems, and yet, if I looked deep into their eyes, I could see that the food of a dying man had not agreed too well with them, and a stolen shirt could be awfully tight in the dead of night. To look back made no sense, the past must be kept in its place, and I was not to disturb the peace.

I too, had the same reaction: How was I to imagine a tortured father? I saw grimaces without pain, a father without feeling. Would understanding be able to drive out hate? I hadn't the courage to make room for these new facts yet.

After meeting these men, I'd had enough of war and bravery, I longed to hear gentler voices and reminiscences of the green mornings of my father's youth in Java, hoofbeats and creaking carriages in Batavia—with wedding curtains—I'd had my fill of corpses. I decided to look up his half-sister Edmée. I'd have to endure shaking the hand of a self-proclaimed Aryan, but I didn't want to miss the chance of getting closer to my father.

My most recent aunt staggered into my arms, I almost choked on the makeup and rouge that covered her cheeks. In spite of her wrinkles she still looked surprisingly young. But what a tart! She wore something pink and fluttering; heavy black lashes like an owl's flapped at me.

I had announced the hour of my arrival by letter—teatime—very proper, a bunch of flowers in hand, but I didn't even have to ring the bell, she was lying in wait. "Finally," she said. "how deliciously tall you are, finally I can clasp a family member to my bosom again." She crushed my bouquet and pushed me into the living room. The candles were lit, glasses and dishes of nuts stood ready, and she swore she hadn't planned anything, the appointment had gone clear out of her mind.

A slight smell of kerosene hung about her, sherry, as far as I could make out from the label on the empty bottle on the coffee table. Her rouge could not disguise the fact that she was a boozer. While she let go of me to pour me a glass, I noticed that the entire room was pink: lampshades, pillows, antimacassars, a carnival kind of pink, three balls for a quarter, and above the door hung a tasteless Christ on the Cross.

I had barely finished drinking a toast to the new relationship when I was made to get up and stand by a photograph of my father, a retouched portrait that she had put on the television set for the occasion, on top of a lace doily, a candle burning beside it. How little I looked like him, Justin was barely twenty in the picture, the darling. Edmée took me by both hands and drew me a few feet away, the better for us both to look at the photograph. She made a sign of the cross, and as I disentangled myself from her embrace, she wanted to hug me again. Gestures, but I did not fall for them. First she had snubbed me, and now she wouldn't let me go. The annoyance I had felt at our first contact now turned to nausea, as if my face had been shoved into a bowl of candy. Everything about her appearance was false—her eyelashes, her jewels, the plastic pearls in her cleavage, and possibly the long nails painted with a wobbly hand.

She was incapable of conversation without holding on to me; I felt sure that she hadn't seen a soul in weeks. And she went on and on! She made no bones about it, her husband, the British officer, had traded her for a young mutt. Some gratitude! She'd followed him all through his service career, Aden, Cyprus—"He did the killing, I did the cooking"—to end up emigrating to Rhodesia where, after thirty-four years, she'd been dropped like a hot potato. Their only son, Ken, her darling boy, had died in the war in Rhodesia. She only got some token alimony, the pound had gone down in value, her lawyer had cheated her, and her ex did not answer his mail, and wouldn't I be able to do something about it? She couldn't expect much help from the rest of the family, her last half-sister had died the previous year. Who? Aunt Pop, Aunt Régine? Both of them, yes, *kasian*, very sad, all dead, her brother too. Pop was the last, yes, her heart (a congenital defect, I began to worry immediately). Only one brother and one sister were still alive, in Australia, very bad correspondents, and the nieces and nephews I had never heard of before were scattered over the globe. And hadn't she heard that I was now a writer, and weren't relatives supposed to help each other? My father was her darling brother, "I miss him desperately."

Drop dead, I thought, how come I never met you in the old days? Tell me something about my father; did you know his first wife and Ruliana and Rudiono?

No, first she must finish her list of complaints, one endless lamentation, as if I were leafing through an old issue of a women's magazine. Dizziness, hyperventilation, agoraphobia, lumps in her breast, and now she had just read about new vertigo symptoms, she had those too, she was spared nothing. She could no longer afford a car, and just look at how old her refrigerator was, and those worn places in the carpet. . . .

She rattled on until her pancake makeup ran. Excuses to leave came to my mind, but in the end you just chatter along, give advice, and point to Jesus, he never gave up either. And I looked at her again: did she look like my father or not? Same dark eyes, the nose flattened against the window pane a bit too long, and a touch of the tar brush, her too, you can't quite cover it with paint.

Ah well, what can you do. You just accept it, have another sherry to wash away that cheap taste of kerosene, the two of you together kill a whole bottle, you take her out for dinner, and you can be sure that she'll order the most expensive dish on the menu. Drink lifts her spirits, she dabs on some more paint, hoists up her old bosom, and her lipstick leaves smears on the wineglass. You look at her sweetly and ask about the East Indies. She doesn't listen, she ignores almost all your questions, she stumbles, she becomes obsessed with a minor incident, you help her on and mention an island, Java, a city, Batavia, a quiet suburb, and with great difficulty you make sense out of her drivel.

Finally you are seated together on the veranda and the toucan screams and the lizard clings to the screen with its toes and two native boys sell you a parakeet for a gobang—a two-and-a-half-cent coin, they still had those then—and the chameleon changes color, pink; the whole atmosphere turns dark pink, for night is falling and the house servant trots about and you can hear the cicadas in the clicking of her pearls.

"Our garden at sunset . . . all the greens flowing together into a single color, a reddish black, and all the plants mingled into one perfume, the gardenias, jasmine, yellowish-white frangipani, lemongrass, a perfume that made you faint. And there we sat on a Saturday night, outside, in the wicker chairs, milk punch in the pitcher, my hair still wet from my bath, and Justin in his new white uniform, his chin tight against the stiff collar. Justin was on leave and full of tales about his military service. I sat at his feet and listened with my eyes closed, the better to picture his adventures. Even my half-sisters stopped squabbling, the servants stood with heads bowed behind the screens, and our bored mother was filing her nails, exasperatingly slowly, in contrast to Justin's excited tone, as if she were playing the violin, wanting to fill the darkness with her own sound.

"We had a beautiful mother, a mother you could admire in silence, a mother who did not need words, one look at her and you were hushed. She had black irises and long, heavy eyelashes. The daytime bored her, the heat made her lazy and tired, but toward evening her strength returned. On Saturday nights she went out, her dresses lay ready for her, and I was allowed to help her choose."

Edmée bit her pearls and let them click against her teeth, which were also false, judging from the dull sound. "Oh dear, is this necessary?" she sighed. My, how she'd let herself go. The East Indies were a closed chapter, completely ruined since Sukarno came to power. Gone back? Don't be silly, she knew better. The embers of old loves should not be stirred. She actually preferred the nights in Africa. "The drummers telling each other tales across the open land, the dry heat and the smell of burning wood, you know how it is. . . ."

"Then let's talk only about Justin."

"In spite of her indolence, my mother had a passionate nature, adulterous, there is no other word for it. She enjoyed secret rendezvous, small lies, surreptitious escapades. Her evening was a failure if, after a concert, she didn't come home with a handful of notes from admirers. She'd been like that even as a girl, all the men knew her, at parties you heard people whisper about her behind her back. The Rose of Surabaya, there goes the Rose of Surabaya, that's where her family came from, French aristocracy, fled before the Revolution. You didn't ask me, but I'll tell you anyway, it's not easy for a daughter to compete with such a name. She was a star who dazzled everyone, she meant to remain a seductive enigma to all men, she denied being the mother of her own children. According to my half-sisters, no one ever saw her pregnant—she favored loose gowns. She literally gave birth to her babies in the outbuildings. None of the children was allowed to call her Mom or Mother in the presence of strangers. We had to call her Odile or Madame. Sometimes she went away for days on end, she did come home but remained out of sight, for she found it so sad for us to have to keep saying good-bye."

Edmée took a sip of sherry and sighed deeply, and whether because of the wine or the taste of her memories, she made a sour face.

"All week she was busy with her wardrobe, the dressmaker came daily. I still have a black beaded pocketbook of hers. . . ."

"My father was a lot older than you. . . ."

"Men, sons, it made no difference, she danced with anything in pants. The boys were much more spoiled, the dressmaker made them the most handsome suits, they were absolute dandies. When there was a party, I, the youngest, was sent away with the *babu*, the nanny. Every Saturday there was a party, for no special occasion, just to have the house full of people. We did not celebrate birthdays, she hated the calendar, telling her age was a sin. Oh, she was such a colonial, she whined until she, too, could send her laundry to Paris, like the rich planters. Daddy went deeply into debt for her. And you know, I was at least half brought up by those native nannies, you can't imagine what I had to unlearn! I ate better with my fingers than with a spoon, preferred a pisang leaf to a dish, and then those disgusting diseases, roundworms, lice and—"

"Did my father have to dance with his mother?"

Edmée laughed at my horrified expression.

"His sisters were the ones who had the real problem," she said. "You know how beautiful they were, and Odile was terribly jealous. Either she hid her daughters, flatly denying that she had any children, or she showed them off dressed in her own clothes. She tied their hair in a bun, covered them with makeup and jewels, made them look as old as possible. When she went out riding, she pretended that her daughters were her girlfriends."

"In the funeral carriage?"

"Oh no, later! The carriage business had been sold by then and the family reunited, this all happened after the drama."

She tapped the empty bottle with her ring, and I ordered a new one. "You know about the drama?"

"My mother told me."

"What does she know about it?"

"I guess my father told her."

"It was too awful."

"You weren't born yet."

"It did decide my fate."

The waiter began to pour, but when he saw the marks of her red lips on the glass, he stopped and brought a clean one.

"Nice of you to take me here, I haven't been spoiled like this in years."

"Was it her fault?" I asked.

"Fault, fault, Odile's first husband was a complete fool. Sorry, but you asked, and I'm telling you. He was guilty as well, that man was completely blind."

"I only know that none of the children was his."

"All six of them looked like her, yes, so to the outside world the truth wasn't apparent. As far as that goes, all the make-believe was quite unnecessary. No one knows whether she ever told the truth. Odile always shrouded herself in mystery, she kept her secrets even on her deathbed, my own daddy did not know about her mystery lover. And if he did know, he took the man's name with him to the grave. Daddy was much older than Odile, he was content to show her off."

"You look like my father."

"And what are you implying?"

"Nothing. That you both look like your mother."

"Thank you, yes, I was very fond of Justin, he was the oldest and the only one at home with whom I got on well. There was a twelve-year age difference between us, but he always confided in me, age made no difference to him."

"Yes, we noticed that, he. . . ."

"Now listen, I know this first hand, your father was the principal witness. One Sunday morning after Mass all the children were assembled. Odile was away again, and their father, your so-called grandfather, was waiting for them in the front hall, dressed in his riding habit, tapping his boots impatiently with his whip. All in a row, and listen! This is how those poor kids heard about the unknown lover their mother had had for years.

Yes, he too could hardly believe it, he said, always deaf to rumors and whispers, but Odile had confessed the whole thing the night before during a furious outburst. So he wasn't their real father at all. He was sorry, from now on they'd better pray hard for their mother. Those children didn't understand, only Justin suspected that something terrible was happening. Their father climbed the stairs, a broken man. Halfway up he pulled a pistol out of his boot and put a bullet through his head. He fell down backward and landed on the wooden floor, right at Justin's feet, wham." Edmée slammed her hand down on the table and gave me a pathetic look.

"I'm sure that's not how he told it to my mother."

"After the shot the horses whinnied in the stables, your father could never forget that. Justin was a sensitive young man."

"That I never noticed."

"Don't be such a smart aleck, my dear nephew. That darling mother of his sent all her children to the orphanage even before the funeral, she had a nervous breakdown and couldn't take care of them. You should have heard your Aunt Pop talk about it later: All their fine clothes were taken away, their hair shorn because of the lice, and while they said grace, their food was stolen from their plates. Being totally unused to discipline, it was especially hard for them.

"Two whole years Madame left her children there. Oh, she did visit them once in a while, but then she played the bereaved widow and came to provide them with new mourning bands to pin to their sleeves, for though she never cared for her children at all, they did have to show their grief, not so much in their hearts but on their orphans' uniforms. Odile managed to push the inheritance through in no time at all and took a trip to Paris—to forget—and apparently she returned with trunks full of black evening dresses. On the boat she met my father. They married at once, in black, in Batavia. The Rose of Surabaya in mourning! The priest would bless their union only if Daddy would take in all the children from the first marriage. Shortly after my birth he bought a large house and was responsible for feeding six more strangers. Daddy was much too good for this world, poor man. He kept to his study and rarely went out, but he loved being surrounded by women who were having a good time."

Edmée dramatically folded her arms over her bosom, and a damp vapor emanated from her.

"Yes, our Odile was a great actress. She managed to pull the wool over God knows how many men's eyes, including the priest. Don't forget that to the outside world she led an exemplary life, attending two Masses every Sunday and, if at all possible, early Mass on weekdays. People thought of her love of dancing and parties as innocent distractions. We who lived backstage knew how unfeeling she could be.

"Of course the suicide remained a big secret, it was never talked about, not even with the children. I was already grown up when Justin first mentioned it. Strange, there was such a bond between us, and yet he didn't dare to tell me until we were in Holland. Your father always talked a blue streak, mostly to give the impression that he had nothing to hide. It was from him that I learned that Odile gave some of her inheritance to the church in order to have her first husband buried in hallowed ground. All for appearances' sake, that's what she cared about.

"Regret was a word our mother did not know. As far as feelings went, she was a tough old bird."

Edmée too had grown tough, she said. Feelings? She no longer cared about those, she had little faith in human nature, and she was right.

We emptied another bottle, and a glass of Armagnac, two, three . . . the bored kitchen help was playing cards behind the bar. Edmée began to snivel, I gave her my handkerchief, which was pink when she returned it. Ah well, so that was Batavia: other times, other customs, there wasn't a Dutch person who could understand.

I stood up, but she pushed me back into my chair. She had to talk, we were family, after all. She had been living in the Netherlands for fifteen years and still had trouble getting used to it. Everything was so doll-like and so stuffy, and so quiet indoors, no servants. She survived on tranquilizers. She didn't really know what she was doing here at all. The social security was good, yes, although she'd had to wait forever to find a house. For some strange reason she had always kept her Dutch nationality. "In the end, you do look for your roots, your relatives, don't you agree?" Yes, that's what it was, she was looking for her uprooted family.

She turned over my left hand, and with her index finger she began to trace the lines in my palm. "You're beginning a second life," she said. "After a break, everything will turn out all right." Her nail crept under the wrist of my sleeve and her shoe rubbed against my ankles. "You're not wearing a ring."

I had to control myself to keep from kicking her. Goddammit, and this person wanted to be my dear old aunt. I pulled back my hand and wiped it on my napkin, you never knew what you could catch at the dinner table, before you know it, you might grow too attached to the disease called family.

Intimately, looking straight into her watery black eyes, I asked her how white her mother was.

"Odile Didier?" she asked in a high-pitched voice. "Pure-blooded lily-white, I can assure you, her parents spoke French at home." It came out sounding colonial, her English intonation had suddenly disappeared.

And Odile's lover?

She shrugged.

"Come now, could anyone keep a secret in the East Indies?"

"Well, he was a foreigner, I think."

"A foreigner? Everyone would be a foreigner to a French-woman, even a Javanese."

"Come on, don't be silly. She was far above the kampong."

After much urging and coaxing, the full story came out: Odile had kept an Italian lover. She made love for ten years with her Neapolitan hairdresser—some hairdressing! But it wasn't at all certain that he was also the father of her children. No one was quite sure, "I swear!" After the drama the hair-dresser took the boat back to Europe. "You know those Ital-ians, scaredy-cats, the guy was terrified, of course." Edmée looked at me triumphantly. There now, it was all out in the open, goodness me, talking had made her warm. "So now you know our big family secret."

As if I hadn't heard such stories before! Italian blood, half of all Dutch colonials were supposed to have Italian blood, there must have been half a regiment of hairdressers involved.

"You mustn't put down your father anymore," she said sharply. "Maybe Justin and his brothers and sisters were a little dark, but they were definitely white. Goodness, all French peo-ple have dark complexions."

I kept quiet, she would talk herself hoarse.

"Don't give me that look, Daddy van Bennekom was also pure-blooded, absolutely." Or was that no longer correct? Perhaps brown was more interesting? Edmée sniffed, she was proud of her European blood.

"Aryan," I said, and to show me that she had understood perfectly, she threw the rest of her Armagnac in my face.

Matters were getting out of hand. I said that I did not believe in Neapolitan hairdressers, and we had an all-out fight. She didn't even want me to take her home, she insisted on a taxi, paid by me, of course. I never got the addresses of my distant nieces and nephews. I couldn't think of meeting any of my father's family ever again.

And yet, I was not quite finished with this aunt. I regretted our quarrel, we had hardly spoken about my father. Had she ever known Sophia Munting and Ruliana and Rudiono? Who but Edmée could tell me about his first marriage? And shouldn't I be helping her? She was teetering on a precipice, and with a bit more attention and money she would be able to make it. I could probably invent a camp trauma for her, an hour's weeping with the psychologist provided by some social service or other, and she'd get an increase in her monthly allotment. I would ask Saskia for the necessary forms. With this excuse I called Edmée.

Things went better the second time. We decided to meet in the morning, Edmée without alcohol on her breath and steadier on her feet, although she still held on to me when she walked. Trouble with her balance, definitely. I decided to find a good specialist for her.

Though I was forced to eat my way through a pink pastry and

had difficulty keeping her from having "just a small glass of sherry," she was finally willing to speak about my father. She too seemed to have been dissatisfied with our earlier meeting; my resemblance to Justin had confused her. If I really insisted on finding out more about him, I should begin by looking through the letters he sent home soon after the liberation. ("For politeness' sake they're addressed to my mother," she said. "But they were meant for me.")

She unlocked the door of a small room where her past was stored in a cabinet with peeling paint. We went down on our knees and began to dig into a fragrance of tropical lands. "I've never reread those letters," said Edmée. "I believe most of them were sent from the camp."

"Where were you then?"

"In Java." She pulled a reed box from the jumble and took out a pile of brittle letters. "Here, take your time, I'm not sure they're in chronological order." She closed the door behind me, leaving me alone in the unheated storeroom.

First I sniffed. . . . In my memory the few things of my father's I still owned smelled of tiger balm, the ointment he rubbed into himself daily to stimulate his circulation, a scent that clung forever. But this time my nose did not recognize anything, these papers reeked of before my time.

Letters . . . scraps seems a more appropriate word, torn strips of wartime paper, no more, scribbled in pencil, numbered but undated, folded in sharp creases, probably sent without an envelope, the return address written on the paper itself: Convalescence Camp Pakanbaru, Sumatra.

The first was also the longest, I could hardly read the penciled words.

Madame,

First of all, I survived this hell in perfect health, and I hope that you and the rest of the family are all well. Have you heard anything from Sophie? I never have, not even through the Red Cross. We hear mixed reports from Java. Ah well. I've always belonged to the fittest and am now working as a cook in the convalescence camp. When you work in a kitchen, there are always leftovers. We're very well looked after and are showered with canned food, cigarettes, and so on. At first the planes dropped these things by parachute, then later they actually landed. All the English among the sick have already been sent home. There were hundreds of Dutch boys here who didn't make it, many of whom you knew. Paul, the son of Mrs. 't Hin, died a week before the liberation. The last months were especially rough, every day more people disappeared. I could send you a list, but I've forgotten many of their names. We're all suffering a bit from amnesia. They say it's from vitamin deficiency. I'm sure it will pass. Complaints don't get you anywhere. My teeth are feeling firm again. All of them were loose from lack of vitamins. I swallow twenty-five pills a day. Once we're reunited, I want to sleep for three years and wake up like Rip Van Winkle in peacetime. All of us here are exhausted.

This week the Australians and the English are being shipped to Singapore, and I hope I too will soon be sent to Batavia. The Dutch do nothing for us. Did anyone expect anything different?

And how are things with my darling little sister? Edmée must be eighteen by now, will I recognize her when you all stand on the dock in Priok? I have no more money, but that doesn't matter, I don't need any here. Are there any dances yet in Batavia? I just heard the last call for the mail, so I can't make this too long. See you soon, J.

If the family should have an occasion to go to Australia, do take it. Safety comes first. I'll be sure to follow. Kiss Edmée for me."

How different this handwriting was from the well-formed letters I remembered. Some of the words were thickly printed, others so pale they were hardly legible, the lines wobbled, the periods were the heaviest. His script was so awkward, you could tell that his hand hadn't done any writing in years. I wondered whether I had ever laid eyes on a letter by my father before. Signatures on my report cards, captions under photographs, lists of house rules and regulations, anything to do with order and discipline, that's all I knew of his handwriting, but these lines were closer to his heart, no matter how hasty and insignificant they were. In this letter my father stepped outside his handwriting, he stood next to me, it told me more than any photograph or old tie I had kept for sentimental reasons. Here his mood flooded the paper, hope and despair, hard and gentle alternating in the lines.

Reading, writing and arithmetic—three liberal arts I had to master before I went to school. My father took all the time he had to teach them to me, and he had his own methods. Even before I could walk properly, a pencil was shoved into my hand. At the age when a child learns to color, I was tracing my first letters. The cheeks of the *d* and the *b* fitted neatly between the lines, the stroke of the *e* lay flat like a good dog, the downward stroke of the *i* was a tamed flag. I still have the letters I had to write sitting next to him at the table, carefully preserved by a proud family. What fear is visible in that handwriting, overcome, I thought, but with this letter from the camp under my gaze, I felt the sting of each slap again. Even here, in this alcove, my father sat next to me once more.

With my father's letter in hand and the bitter flavor of graphite in my mouth I could taste how, on the first day of school, I bit my pencil in two, in a rage because there were no letters I could learn from the teacher. I knew them already, I was a giant who could write fluently. She gave me a new pencil, and that one I also bit in two. Two, three shiny yellow pencils she laid in front of me, to see if I would keep on biting, and the fool kept it up, his mouth full of woodchips. All the children stared. Amazing what handwriting can reveal!

I leafed through the other letters, scribbles about more cigarettes, canned goods, and the family. Now and then something about politics: "Notice little about the Sukarno movement, everything rather peaceful, but a lot of red and white flags." "Hear Holland is ruined. In Australia life has gone on normally these four years." "We hear the news every day. Not so good at the moment. Sukarno and his ilk pretty annoying. I'm really worried about you all. KLM will resume flights on October 15, you must leave as soon as possible. See to the tickets. Edmée especially is in danger, a target for hungry soldiers. We must look to Australia for our future and return when everything has really settled down. I'm organizing a flight out of here."

Without a cent for even a fourth-class boat passage, and fantasizing about flying; already full of grandiose ideas. Not a word about the period just past, let alone a thought for his first wife Sophie, her health or possible children. I never saw the names of Ruliana and Rudiono mentioned. But how could he have known of their existence?

Twenty letters later, our Justin actually does fly, it improves his handwriting. "Today by plane from Pakanbaru to Palembang. I must write quickly, the mail leaves in 5 minutes. Beds, sheets, electric light, fantastic! It was my first flight and it really wasn't bad, in a DC 3. My address is Camp Halfway House, Palembang."

And still later: "There's also a club here. It all looks pretty good again. I'm here with the same people, very congenial company. Music and dancing at the club in the old mayor's house."

"I have appropriated a beautiful pair of American shoes, also pajamas and underwear. Have to get used to them, those clothes."

"The Dutch are at the helm once more. Quite a few people from outside the camp are being taken into custody because they collaborated with the Japanese and the Germans."

"He says nothing about meeting my mother," I remarked when Edmée brought me a cup of tea to warm me.

"But he does about me. Did you read how crazy he was about me?" She gathered up the letters and sat on the edge of a small table. With less makeup she looked better. From the letters I understood that she must now be sixty-six or sixty-seven. The tropics had been kind to her.

I was getting cold and took the tea and the letters with me into the pink room. The candles were lit, and bread and cold cuts lay ready.

Edmée took a photo album from the table and held it out to me. "For you," she said. "You knew your father only when he was ill. Here you can see him in all his glory." She took a snapshot with a serrated edge from the album: a handsome woman and a puffy, pale man in a wrinkled linen suit, in front of them a boy with a baby on his shoulders. "Justin," said Edmée, "just out of the orphanage. Look at his hollow eyes, I am the baby, and those are Odile and Daddy van Bennekom."

It was the first picture I had ever seen of my grandmother. Little Justin did indeed look like her: fiery eyes, sensual lips, as if I saw myself standing there. I recognized the gentleness in that boy, the weakness that my father had tried to train out of me.

In another picture Justin sat with a sketchbook under a tree, dapper, his head leaning slightly backward, aware of his good looks. He grew from snapshot to snapshot, from short pants to double-breasted suit, from young civilian to soldier.

Edmée spread the photographs before me like a game of solitaire: from left to right pictures showing him in uniform, with or without a cap, with pockets on his knee or with a high, tight collar, in puttees and boots, and underneath a row of images of Justin the heroic sportsman, in jodhpurs, in tennis shorts, or as a boxer raising a leather fist to the camera, and in each snapshot his shoulders grew broader. The last one, the trump card, she placed on top: Justin wearing a dress and hat, legs apart, standing on an outside staircase.

My father in drag. The one who had tried to beat me into becoming a man wore a dress. And it suited him—chin up, a sly glance at the camera, and a fan dramatically pressed against his bosom. I laughed as I held up the photo: "This one I'll frame, I never saw him so seductive."

"It was a dress of Odile's, for a costume ball." Edmée pulled the picture out of my hand and stuck it back in the album. "If that's how you're going to look at it, I won't give it to you. Clothes are just the outside. Here, have a good look at all these different faces: child, youth, man, each one more serious."

"And harsher."

"The first few months, he would come home on leave, so proud of himself. He always brought me little gifts—a wooden bird or a black, oil-colored stone. At first he also brought home drawings, landscapes of Surabaya for Odile, I think that's where he did his military training. But he stopped after a while, he became quieter, he stayed away longer; the infantry, you know, doing dirty little jobs and always on patrol. He had problems with his superior, a nasty fanatic. Odile wrote me about it after the war, probably one of her frustrated admirers. That man had it in for him all through his military service. You can tell on the photographs, his smile disappears."

"And his hair," I said, pointing to a picture of Justin in uniform on which his dark curls were reduced to two pencil stripes.

"Oh, *kepala botak*, that's a sad story."

"I know it, I know it," I exclaimed enthusiastically. "He told us about *kepala botak* God knows how many times. When there was company, our guests always asked for the story." Mentally I leafed through my father's tales and saw us sitting around a great Sunday rijsttafel, Aunt Pop and Aunt Régine flanking him, clicking their purplish nails against the crystal and clanking their gold bracelets, just let the vowels roll. My father on the edge of his chair holding forth, of course. "And where was it again, Djambi?" I asked.

"No, Djogjakarta," said Edmée, she too sat down and expectantly made herself a sandwich.

"Yes, yes, Djogjakarta, country of steep fields, forests, and man-high blooming *sepatu*." I imitated his accent, and Edmée looked hurt.

"Stop that," she said. "Don't make fun of him."

But I was not to be deterred. "Close your eyes, Auntie, I'll take you along to the foot of the Merbabu, Justin's first post after military school, where he worked as a *dardanel*, a beautiful word, but the job didn't mean much, caretaker or orderly to an officer. Not a great stepping stone for a young infantryman."

Edmée looked angrily at me. I could not go on like this. "Anything wrong?" I asked.

"You're not being fair," she said, her mouth full. "Justin had to leave home when he was only sixteen, he had a choice between the monastery and the army. Daddy couldn't see any way to send him to Holland, he was in debt up to his ears, and Odile insisted that all the children be independent as soon as possible."

"Not fair? But what exactly did he achieve? Fourteen years in the army and never advanced beyond sergeant major."

"Justin was an officer in the reserve, and if he'd stayed in the service after the war, I'm sure he would have had a good career, but your mother must have persuaded him to resign."

"In any case, he found Djogjakarta a bad beginning, he said so over and over, that's how he always started the story. There never was a headhunt, a revolt, nobody ran amok, all they did was hang around waiting for high-muck-a-mucks from Batavia to come to pay their respects to the sultan of Djogjakarta, and after a visit to his palace to climb to the top of Merbabu under military guidance."

"Kraton."

"Who?"

"The palace of the sultan of Djogjakarta is called the kraton, and it wasn't really a palace but a walled-in section of Jogja. I went there once on an audience with Daddy, several thousand people lived there. Most of the visitors got no farther than the open-air ballroom, the only structure that is still really Javanese, gorgeous, with golden pillars and a marble floor. At the entrance waited the *pangerans* who led the guests by the arm to the sultan, even the men. I had to walk on tiptoe for my hand to reach their elbow. God, how long ago could that have been?"

"So your dear Justin was bored to death there. Lugging guests up the mountain time and again, zigzagging along slippery paths, through forests and sleepy hamlets, and then, at the top, catching their breath in the tall grass and pointing to the landscape down below. And those Dutch oohing and aahing, look, the irrigation works, the terraces, the roads, all built by us. And the coolies in the rice paddies waving at them."

"Just go there once, you'll think differently. You'll see how the Javanese aristocracy—"

"He longed for promotion and dreamed of a stripe on his pants and embroidery on his sleeves, a cocked hat with feathers on his head, just like all those princes and ministers and top military officials he saw at the court of the sultan. He thought, If I just keep my little finger along the seam of my pants, never complain, and follow orders like a paladin, I'll be marching toward Breda, to the Royal Military Academy. An officer, that was his ideal! A cadet's uniform would have suited him better than battle dress with pockets on the knees.

"As long as he obeyed his superior, everything was all right, and even the superior's wife could order him about. How many times he'd had to fetch her horse from the stable for her and tighten her stirrups once she was in the saddle! After a ride she loved to let her bag fall so that, when they both leaned over to pick it up, he felt her loose blond hair brushing his temples. He didn't aim for that kind of feather, he was careful and he avoided her whenever possible. This was not a simple matter, a *dardanel* has to be available when called, unfold topographical maps, underline mountain passes, indicate routes, guide, and interpret.

"The superior spoke very little Malay, our Justin did, and he could also communicate in both high and low Javanese. His instinct for rank and class distinctions always told him how to use the right word at the right moment. All just gibberish, those languages, was the superior's opinion, and even in Dutch he could only snarl and give orders. He looked down on the natives and probably also on his *dardanel*, for let's be truthful, wasn't Justin just a bit too yellow for a pure-blooded Dutchman?"

There were sparks in Edmée's eyes, but I refused to be hoodwinked any longer. Go ahead, let's add another scene, curtains up! My father directed me from a distance. Hush!

"For the sake of Breda, he accepted everything, you know your brother, willing to bow in order to prevail. When the wife of the superior again dropped her bag, he closed his eyes when he was bending over.

"But the superior was a difficult man. He couldn't bear night sounds, and when he was awake, he felt lonely and lay perspiring under the fan. His wife was too frigid to comfort him, and so he drank and found solace in the company of his men. It happened almost every night: drinking gin and playing cards on the veranda. Plenty of bottles, he had them delivered from Batavia, they came on the daily packet. Whenever Justin went into hiding, the superior would hang on the field telephone until he found his *dardanel*.

"At first the stakes were low. The superior played for the glory of it. Sometimes the loser had to run to the barracks and back again with his shoelaces tied together, or he was dunked twice in the alligator-infested river. The superior would eat the feathers of his dress helmet. The men he had gathered cheered, what a good guy this superior was, and so friendly with everyone, the high and the low. Too bad he never lost, he was the best rummy player in Jogja.

"One evening he thought up a new penalty for the loser: the

one with the lowest score would have to pay with his hair. Every man reached for his head, terrified. Poor Justin, it was unthinkable, our Adonis, what he lacked in braid and embroidery grew in curls on his head. And what did the perpetual winner have to lose? Nothing but a few dull tufts.

"Again the superior held the best cards. The servant had already been sent to the village to fetch a barber, the liquor flowed freely, the men cheered, and things looked bad for Justin. The wife of the superior tried winks and sign language to let him know what cards the other men held, but he would not risk looking at her. How brazen she was that night, the way she danced around the table, her hair pinned up, her bare shoulders draped in an ostrich feather boa, and her long earrings glowing by the light of the oil lamp. She kept dropping her boa so as to get a better look at the cards when she picked it up. But not even cheating could save him—Justin lost.

"The barber, who had arrived in the meantime, was given a glass of gin, even though, as a Muslim, he did not drink, but they convinced him that it was spring water. He liked the taste, and soon he was babbling, "*Kepala botak, kepala botak*"—bald head, bald head. He honed his razor on a dirty strop.

"'Bald,' ordered the superior. 'Take it all off.' 'Bald!' exclaimed the men. '*Botak, botak*,' cried the servants, and the bushes rustled with soldiers who had come running. The superior's wife, too befuddled to hide her enamored state, laid her hands on the curls that she so longed to caress. 'No,' she said, and bending over, kissed Justin's pate. The superior stood up, threw his cards on the table, and pushed his wife into a chair. He undid her chignon and raised a blond lock. 'Cut,' he commanded. 'Cut this woman's hair.'

"The men objected, and the barber drew back. They took hold of Justin and forced the barber to attack him with his razor. His curls bounced on the floor, his hair was so springy, and the barber stamped his feet with pleasure. The wife of the superior ran into the house, and her husband was able to laugh again. Another bottle. The men, too, breathed easier."

"That's not how I heard the story," said Edmée.

"Special performance, family matinee, I could have told it in four sentences if I'd wanted to." And I thought, my father's stories swell inside my head, if I don't watch myself, I'll make a whole book out of what he did not tell. When I think of his stories, he speaks through me; when I lie, I lie in committee.

"You not only sound like him," said Edmée, "you have his way of mimicking, his laughter, his way of raising his eyes, the way you flap your hands about. The way you look like him is uncanny."

"But I still have my curls, and I'm already four years older than he ever was. I still remember that whenever he got going about the barber, he always took his fruit knife and waved it in the air, and your sisters would shriek."

"*Kasian*, so sad," said Edmée. She drew up her knees, nestled cozily on the sofa, and closed her eyes. "Come on, finish the story, be like him just a little while longer, let him tell one more lie."

"The barber rinsed his razor in the gin and drew white paths across Justin's skull. The men picked up the curls and held them under their noses to make mustaches. They roared with laughter and slapped the barber on the back. The razor slipped and blood trickled down Justin's temple.

"The *dardanel* was bald, the superior was satisfied. The next day my father was bent over the topographical maps with a red cut on his head. Nobody saw it, he wore his cap as a bandage, and he did not complain. It had been a great evening and the loser was a good sport. Together with his hair Justin lost his name; in the colonial army he would be *Kepala Botak* from then on.

"The following day he had a fever, the dirty razor had left a trail of pus. A week later, not hair but mold grew on his head. The doctor disinfected the wound and prescribed bed rest, the superior's wife brought him tea and changed his bandages. For weeks Justin went around with an infected head. A year later a thin stubble of hair finally grew in, but that fell out too, only a sparse black fringe remained at the nape of his neck. Small lifeless curls, as soft as those of an astrakhan lamb."

We ate our sandwiches and stared in silence at the ceiling, the only spot in Edmée's house where your thoughts could wander freely. Briefly I caught sight of my father in a corner, not as a stern director, but friendly, wistful. I had tamed him with his own stories.

"I could never get used to that bald head," said Edmée. She picked up the photos one by one from the table. "And yet he could laugh about the incident later, he thought it had given him strength. What doesn't kill you, makes you stronger, that was his philosophy then, and it reminded him never to trust people too much. Be tough, be tough, otherwise you'll just be disappointed . . . and he should know, the darling."

"Were his brothers also like that?"

"Well, they weren't exactly sentimental."

"Why didn't we hear from any of you after he died?"

"Your mother wouldn't let us."

"But how about me, his full-blooded son?"

She was scornful. "Oh, you know how it was in those years, the whole world was on the move, we were in the midst of the Greek-Cypriot war."

"Don't you have a picture of the twins?"

"So you know about those, too?"

"Did you know his first wife?"

"No. I personally never met Sophia. Justin married her in Surabaya, far away, you know how it goes."

"One day's train ride from Batavia."

"The whole family knew that the marriage with Sophia was no good, she shacked up with a Muslim even during the war. But Odile thought divorce was shameful, and she was dead set against Justin's relationship with your mother—a Protestant and those Indo daughters, and the uncertainty about your mother's first husband, a native of all things. She wanted to save Justin from ruining his prospects."

"Long live mother love."

"So long as Daddy could prevent the divorce, Justin would not be able to marry your mother, otherwise he'd be a bigamist."

I broke out in a sweat—what a bunch of criminals. Had the name van Bennekom occurred in my father's act of repudiation? I was no longer able to decipher the puzzle of my own family. Was my mother aware of all the scheming?

"Now that we're confessing anyway," said Edmée, "there's one more thing, Sophia Munting had already died."

"No! When?"

"A few years after the liberation."

"Impossible. Our family notary corresponded with her until a few years before my father's death."

"Daddy answered the letters; being a lawyer, he was in

charge, he acted as her executor." Edmée shrugged her shoulders apologetically. "Daddy was easy to win over, and God knows what a grudge he held against Justin, maybe he was jealous because his wife flirted with her own sons."

"So my father could have married my mother perfectly legally!"

"I suppose so, yes. Justin was a widower without knowing it."

"Revenge."

"Yes, I guess so."

"But why?"

"Well listen, those were different times, I was the youngest, it was a problem for my step-family, I had other things on my mind. I was in love with a British officer. I wanted to get married and leave the country as soon as possible. The Bersiap period had begun, terribly dangerous."

"And his brothers and sisters cheerfully went along with this lie?"

"It was a lie that had gotten out of hand, nobody dared back out. All of us were opposed to Justin's relationship with your mother at first, we would have preferred him to stay in the colonial army. What would he do without an education? How would he manage in Holland with a wife and three children?"

"Goodness, what concern for three little Indos!"

"We didn't talk about it, we were used to living with secrets. The few times we visited your father later on, he hardly gave us a chance to open our mouths. He kept on talking and talking, we spoke only about food."

"What a relief it must have been when he died."

"We could bury the lie with him."

"That's why you severed relations with us."

"We didn't want to be reminded."

I'd gone through life a bastard all for nothing, for nothing my mother's false shame, the juggling of family names to keep up appearances in the village, the childish bullshit on report cards and swimming tests: Well, what is his actual name? It must be legal, otherwise we can't accept it.

"Thanks a lot," I said, and I pushed my plate away with such force that it nicked the edge of the china platter.

"I understand," said Edmée, looking dazed.

Putting the snapshot back, she shoved the album over to me in silence. "And Ruliana and Rudiono?" I asked when, out of nervousness, Edmée tried to pick up the glazed splinters with a wet finger. "Whatever happened to the twins?"

"No idea."

"How, in heaven's name, do you all get along with each other? Children aren't dogs that you can just abandon."

Edmée was in a huff. "I didn't know Sophia, I didn't know those twins. I never even saw them."

"And how about your mother, Grandma Odile, she must have cared about them just a little?"

"My mother and children! She thought babies smelled bad, she could hardly bring herself to touch them." She stood up and paced, snorting with indignation, took a bottle of sherry from the cabinet, and poured out two glasses. Drink, a last resort. "Daddy must have found some solution or other, he was the cleverest lawyer in Java, he even managed to keep us all out of the camps."

Oops, a slip; frightened, she clapped her hand over her mouth. A quick gulp.

"Odile didn't have to," she said hurriedly. "She was a

Française, how should I know what the politics were in those days, the Vichy government was pro-Japanese I think, and Daddy managed to cheat a little about the children."

"How did he do that?"

"A trick."

"How? Murder, betrayal, blackmail—you people will stop at nothing."

Like a child, Edmée began to circle around the question. My hands itched. It turned out that the Italian lover had been supplied with the necessary papers to turn him into a native and the father of all the children, Edmée included. This sort of thing was more easily accomplished in Java than elsewhere. Odile safely gathered her brood about her, from young to old, even including her admirers. She remained in her own house all through the war. Daddy van Bennekom tried to find a native ancestor for himself as well, but it didn't work, he couldn't escape being put behind barbed wire, the dope. Pure blood exacted its price.

My father was unaware of this family intrigue. He was the son allowed to serve the Fatherland he had never seen, and as the oldest, he was the one who was sacrificed, following time-honored Catholic tradition.

"Freedom is worth a lie," said Edmée. Suddenly she looked crestfallen, since her confession made her ineligible for a pension as a victim of the war.

How many lies? Was there any point in delving deeper into the roots of her family tree? Where did the papers of the native lover come from? I didn't bother speculating how honorably the family had survived the Japanese occupation. Edmée was looking for purity and consoled herself with a lily-white shield. I was looking for proof of how brown we were because I'm so pink-skinned. I had to be careful not to succumb to the same folly.

That ridiculous longing for purity, my father, too, was infected with it, always preoccupied with rank and class, with elegant and vulgar, good and bad, more and less, higher and lower, left and right, strong and weak, spicy and sweet, even in the kitchen. Was that why, after the war, he embraced anthroposophy? A faith that espouses brotherhood among all men, without differentiation of race, religious belief, sex, caste, or color, the search for truth being the highest good. High-minded theories to wipe out the lies of his youth. In the same way he must have believed in the anthroposophic theory of education: the harmonious development of feeling and willpower, the learning of facts secondary to creativity, music, singing, eurhythmics. Understanding came from beauty.

He did not understand much of it. Feeling was pain, willpower the denial of pain, rhythm the tapping of the ruler, beauty and creativity meant drilled letters and lines. We had to strive for a higher self, for a pure soul and purity of spirit, the sublime must win out over the subconscious. My father could speak about it beautifully, he clung to his own words, afraid of his own darker nature and of the hell in his heart. In anthroposophy he found something gentle to cover up his harshness.

"So now you won't let me be your aunt anymore?" asked Edmée when I picked up my coat to leave.

"Sure, but not too much and not too often."

She gave me a sherry kiss, bitter and sweet, and shoved a photograph into my hand—my father wearing a dress.

5
QUICKSAND

═══════════

WE WERE rocking in the nave of the church. The pulpit was a light machine, and thunder crashed over our heads. I was caught in a vessel full of seaweed, arms waved around and under me, it was impossible to stand still, we were being borne upward. The ground under my feet disappeared, white smoke billowed around our legs. I was dancing on the waves.

My eyes looked for something I could grasp, something solid and steady that I could lean on. But lightning flashed between the pillars, and the roof rose on and off and up and down, light and dark were flashing around us.

Aram was not dancing. He wobbled and pulled himself up onto my shoulders to get a glimpse of the band, five young men with bare torsos, rings piercing their nipples, noses, and ears, their heads shorn or hair growing in waves down to their shoulders. The singer wore cut-off jogging pants, the drummer was a leather Christmas tree, the metal decorations on his cross flashing in the light. The guitar players were fucking their instruments, looking mean and spitting down at us. A raw voice moaned into the microphone, "When there is no peace, there is no sanity." The earth was a cancerous growth, God and money were a lot of faggotry, fuck the world, something like that. I had trouble understanding the words. Aram did too, but that's not what it was about, he said. It was all about sensation.

Four new musicians stepped onto the stage, bums from the Bronx. They pulled down their pants and mooned us with tattooed asses. The audience cheered. They were rough, large, strong, and they insulted us. We were motherfuckers, stupid headbangers. During their last tour they had been called fascists. Wrong interpretation, screamed the singer, they were nonpolitical, they had a positive message: "Fuck fascism, fuck ignorance. You know who is to blame, the motherfucking media is to blame." They invoked Satan and all the other toy store monsters: dragons, vampires, piranhas, and black-widow spiders.

"Gothic," Aram yelled into my ear. "This is gothic." I nodded coolly, concerned to give the impression that I was not an outsider. Once more the music kicked the crowd into the air, boys and girls climbed up on the stage, did a ragged little dance between extension wires and amplifiers, and dove back into the waving arms.

A girl in front of us fainted, a boy had a bloody nose, an elbow punched me in the lower lip. I ducked out of there, grabbed Aram by the waist, and cleared a way backward through the crowd. Plastic tumblers cracked under our feet until I felt a wooden railing at my back—the bar. Beer cans flew around our ears.

I had wanted to take Aram to a headbangers' ball. I saw boys his age in town distributing flyers—"Church Metal"—and I seized the opportunity to let him initiate me into his world. I called him, and after a preposterous conversation with his father ("Concert? But he hasn't practiced in weeks") I was given permission to take him for the weekend. As he climbed into my car, Aram did not look back. His father stood at the window, holding the French horn. No, I shook my head, we will not be needing it. Then he closed the curtain.

We would first play some records at my house and read the liner notes, and that night we would pogo and mosh—the current words for dancing up and down, in heavy shoes.

"Do we have to?" I asked.

"Yes, it doesn't sound right in these," he pointed disapprovingly at his crepe soles. So that afternoon we bought him some army-surplus boots in the Army-Navy store and some blue jeans torn above the knees. And because I wanted to look tough—a little like Robin the Giant—I chose a pair of combat boots. Aram's T-shirt with the knight came in handy that night, but when I saw him in the church, I wondered if I had done the right thing. He seemed to me too young, and all the wild behavior around him made him seem more vulnerable than he was. But Aram saw right through the madness, he found it cool, fierce, crazy, super; yes, I was a popular uncle.

The nearly naked bodies, the smell of leather, sweat, and marijuana, I inhaled it and stared at the tattoos. One boy had given his back to Jesus. The crucified Savior became the bow in the devil's hand, an arrow quivered above the crown of thorns. Others had had the name of their favorite band shaved in the back of their hair, and two snakes slithered from a girl's shoulders to her boobs. I looked with envy at all these young bodies, their washboard stomachs and their backs covered with a thick network of muscles. The mirrors behind the bar made me look browner in the dim light, but they also showed the bald spot on my head.

From the moment I brought home the tickets to the head-bangers' ball, I became preoccupied with my figure. Wouldn't they make fun of me? Wasn't my hair too gray, my ass too fat for blue jeans? I spent an hour in front of the mirror, modeling jeans, my shirttail out, collar up, unbuttoned, my belly pulled in. Boots under or over the pants legs? As I tried out different variations, I grew years older—James Dean with a pot belly.

The bar in the side aisle seemed to me a safer place, we had a good view of the stage, hundreds of clodhoppers stomped on the wooden floor, arms flashed in the light, electric shivers. One of the Bronx boys smashed his guitar to smithereens.

"Is that an expensive guitar?" I asked Aram.

"Plngt," he said.

"What?"

"Plngt." I shoved my ear up to his lips. "A-plain-gui-tar." he screamed.

I'd had just about enough of it, but Aram had not moshed yet. He took a deep breath and, raising his arms, flew into the crowd of dancers. The barmaid was dancing behind the beer tap and paid no attention to her customers. I leaned against the bar. The droning grew louder, the bottles jiggled at my back, but I also felt something gentler, a different rhythm, a hand along my shoulders and down my side.

I turned around and came eye to eye with the silver nose ring worn by a tall, pale girl. She shimmered in the light—white clothes, white lips. She swayed along with the music, her face expressionless; her spiky hair shook stiffly along, it looked like glass, a frozen white. She said something, I could not hear her, and she didn't bother to repeat it. She pulled at my sleeve and nodded toward the dancers.

"I'd rather watch," I screamed and stared straight ahead. Aram dove into sight and jumped into the outer circle of dancers, glowing with delight. His haircut was probably the tamest in the church, but the way he jumped around in the breaking light, his hair looked as if an eagle were flapping its wings above him, the hair bouncing so gently and in slow motion, up and down, up and down. He waved to me, the pale girl next to me swayed back, caught me by the arm, and pulled me by my wrists into the moshing crowd. The music sucked us to the middle of the dance floor and we jumped up and down, the eagle, the pot, and the nose ring, who could jump the highest. My lower lip trembled, my boots pinched my toes.

Fireworks went off in the pulpit. Bengal lights sprouted over our heads, smoke clouded the projectors. The Bronx boys sang about death and body snatchers . . . "A shame that you found out too late, reality is when you die." The girl danced with her eyes closed and sniffed at a Boy Scout whistle that hung around her neck by a leather thong, her fallow cheekbones turned pink. She sniffed and sniffed, until her hands pushed the whistle under my nose. A smell of sweaty feet rose from it. It was an inhaler, my heart jumped into my throat. I began to feel a tingle, and I swayed into the soap-bubble light. Pain disappeared, as did my stiffness and self-consciousness.

The music stopped, the lights went out, we heard a dull crunch and danced briefly in a sound vacuum, a last gasp, and we came to a stop.

"Short-circuit," a boy called from the pulpit. After a chorus of "fucks" and "shits," he set off another string of flares. We couldn't see a thing because of the smoke, and the explosions confused all sense of direction, so that we had no idea where the exit was.

Aram took my hand, and we let ourselves drift along with the crowd until an arm stopped me. The pale girl. She led us toward the bar, asked for a candle, and pushed a stool toward Aram.

"Just a jinx in the lightbox," she said. "It'll be fixed in no time."

"I thought it was pretty weird," said Aram. "I thought it was a raid."

She held the burning candle up to his face. "Your first concert, right?"

"No," said Aram. "I play music, too."

She did not introduce herself, accepted a glass without a thank-you, and asked what instrument he played.

"The French horn," said Aram.

"What?"

"The French horn."

"What's that?"

To help out, I said that he was a member of his school band.

"Metal?" she asked.

"No, brass," Aram yelled over a final string of firecrackers. He made a megaphone with his hands and shouted something into her ear. She laughed and did the same to him. The wise guy didn't need me at all; the girl threw her arms around him.

The three of us decided to go for pizza at the place across the street from the church. In the neon light I saw that the girl had neglected her skin, the insides of her arms were blue. She looked restlessly about her, stuttered now that she no longer had to scream, and didn't really want p . . . pizza. She'd prefer ice cream or a soft drink. "Nggrr," she sniffed disdainfully, rolled herself a ragged cigarette, and twice asked the waiter for the time.

"Are you in a hurry?" I asked.

"Nah," she said. "I've got to go to a party at the other end of town, and I don't have money for a taxi."

"But it's almost midnight," said Aram.

"I'm not tired."

"I always have to go to bed at nine fifteen."

"I sleep during the day."

"Always?"

"Al . . . always." Oh she knew perfectly well that staying up all night aged you, it wasn't healthy, but she loved dancing and music. She sniffed gently on her inhaler. Aram stared at her, full of admiration. He was allowed to touch her nose ring and her sprayed white hair.

"Like angel hair," he said.

"You're a sweet little turd," she said when he cut off a snippet of his pizza for her. Aram blushed and asked her how often she went to concerts. She lied about the bands she followed to strange cities, and he bragged about his "at least a hundred CDs." When he finished school, he would work with lights, he said, or even neater, he'd be the driver for a band.

"Does your father approve?" she asked with a nasty look at me.

"Oh, by then he'll be dead," said Aram.

"Boy, you're really cool."

Aram shrugged manfully. "Reality is when you die."

We had a good laugh. "I think you're really fun," said Aram, and she stroked his hand lightly. "You're not a bit old."

"Thank you," she said softly. She put out her cigarette in the nibbled pizza slice and swept the tobacco from her lap.

"I could have had a boy like you," she said as she kissed his forehead on her way out. She poked my stomach and said, "Say, Dad, do you suppose I could borrow a fiver for the taxi?"

Aram doubled up with laughter. I gave her the money, and he too held out his hand.

"You can't take it with you anyway," she said.

"I'm not his father, he's my nephew."

"Oh, sorry."

Outside she tapped on the window. Aram looked at me pleadingly and still held his hand out.

"You've had enough," I said.

"No, I just want to hold you," he said. I put my hand in his. "Wasn't it cozy? We were just like a little family."

I was startled. Aram needed me.

But then, there was his father. Two days without his son, and the piss grew crusty on his fly. His food was still in the oven, for he couldn't open the door and didn't understand, didn't understand, wasn't Aram supposed to be away only one night? He wanted to stroke the top of Aram's head, but his son had grown too tall, and midway his hand drew back.

"It *was* only one night," I said.

Aram opened the curtains. Maarten had been sitting in the dark the whole weekend.

I heated up his food, made some coffee, and copied out the telephone number of the visiting nurse. Something had to be done, things couldn't go on like this. Aram clumped up to his room in his boots, put a CD on the player, and stamped his feet along with the bass. Maarten sat on the sofa with his legs outstretched and laughed at the racket overhead. "Better this than silence," he said. "I've missed him."

His father needed him.

•   •   •

What should I do? I called the home-health-care office; the visiting nurse would start coming every day. I made an appointment with the counselor at the secondary school. He had been thinking about Aram, the boy was doing only fairly in school, he had three Cs and two Ds, but his D in Greek was balanced by an A. We should wait and see, he said, and if the boy did not improve, "would you be willing to look after him?" I did not say either yes or no. Was he serious or did I detect a touch of irony in his voice?

The idea of taking my nephew into my home left me no peace. I should act like a fully grown adult, either deciding that I could not handle it or changing my life style and accepting the responsibilities that the education of a fourteen-year-old boy entailed. And if I didn't have the courage or was too selfish, I should admit as much.

Once more I drove to the dunes, without asking myself whether the trip was wise. No question of getting any work done anyway, I wanted to mull the situation over in peace and quiet. As usual, my girlfriend had no time to come along, and yet I would have to include her in my considerations. Aram would be a burden on our relationship. She had never wanted to have children, and now I would be forcing one on her. If I chose Aram, there was a good chance that she would drop me. A lot of things would become clear, even though I could not foresee all the consequences.

The village lay bleak and abandoned. I took a room in the small hotel with a view over the sea and the coastal plain. The field across from our former house was more barren than ever, the rosebushes were dropping their leaves, and the area around the stable of the rescue horses looked like a dump for beach chairs and dismantled beach cabanas. My eyes wandered along the trampled paths, the pine trees returned once more, and I saw myself as a child, standing in the meadow near the nags from Zeeland. After only a few hours I was sorry I had come. I should, on the contrary, tear myself away from what lay behind me and prove to myself that I could find my own direction, away from the sea that kept rolling in and out with desperate fatalism. It should be possible, after all, to break away from my fate, to take my life into my own hands, to make decisions contrary to the expected direction. A breakwater is what I longed to be.

I did my best to stop seeing the past in this landscape. After all, nothing looked the way it used to, even the old dunes had been trampled down. Storms had erased the familiar horizon. See how the moss had grown over the roof tiles! You could walk here in city shoes. And how narrow the beach seemed, and how pitiful the dike built up by the side of the road! The smell of french fries won out over the sea wind, and half the village was *zu vermieten*—for rent.

Pools and marshes were drying up, the groundwater had sunk. Bushes lay uprooted in the dunes, concrete water pipes were being installed. No more drift sand and treacherous surfaces. Arrows and signposts gave directions, and every few miles colored maps behind glass told the visitor the birds and plants at that location. I bought a map and stuck to the rules. Before me lay a reclaimed landscape, and everything I saw was new.

But the crows still danced behind the high dune. Almost two hundred years ago ten thousand English and Russian troops were defeated here by the Batavian army, a failed attempt of the Dutch king in exile to win back his country. In his honor, the evening painted the dunes orange. Hundreds of crows pecked at the earth. Blood and iron kept it black. There was also a new paved path through the valley, complete with maps. And I stamped my feet on the stones: fly away, carrion eaters, stop feeding on the dead.

At night I felt a hand along my hand. He was caressing my arms, the blond fuzz on my skin shivered, and I was lifted as if I were leaving my own body. I was light, and felt no pain. I fell into a deep vortex, and when I woke, my eyes and cheeks were damp with tears. And once more I was awake the whole night, restless with the memories I could no longer control. I listened to the sand whipping against my window—the wind scraping its hind legs on the beach—and reluctantly walked through the seasons of my youth.

My village in autumn, a hollow of houses forgotten in the mist. Our house lay outside the center, facing the forest and the stable of the rescue horses. The roof was a buoy in the dunes, red and wide. The tower on its crest had lost its bell, melted down by the Germans to make bullets. Climbing up in it, you could see the ocean and the water tank of the steam tram.

The last summer visitor had gone, the summer houses were empty, phosphorescence lit the water for one last time. My sisters were going to high school in the city and no longer played outside. The other children from our communal house were also too old. My father and mother shivered near the stove.

In autumn the dunes belonged to me again, when storms raised clouds of sand—sand that bit into your cheeks and that made your eyes tear so that you saw everything double: two lighthouses, two beach pavilions, two horse stables, and two sets of your own footsteps. A double landscape, not to be shared with anyone.

Not long after the big flood of 1953 the local authorities installed a telephone in our communal hallway. The dune next to the big bunker had been weakened so much that the water had risen twice already and had come close to our house. From then on we had to call the coast guard in time of danger. There were three telephones in the village, and although we could use ours only for weather emergencies, we were nevertheless proud of the black contraption on the wall. Sometimes the lighthouse keepers from the villages to the north and south called with a warning to get the horses and the lifeboat ready. My father had, in fact, offered to keep an eye on the stables in the evenings and on Sundays. He mostly lounged by the window anyhow, and the coast guard lived too far away. Besides, was anyone more familiar with horses? In his youth he had spent hours on his father's stud farm, he could master any horse, the wildest Arab (with a dividing line in their foreheads and mouths so sensitive that they drank water out of a coconut shell), there was no better man in the village to look after six nags from Zeeland.

In an emergency the rescue volunteers met in our large hall. It held a chest full of flares, slickers, and waders, the stable was too damp to serve as a storage shed. The key to the stable hung on a hook painted red, and when the wind factor rose to nine, my mother had prepared a thermos of coffee.

So my father became the master of the rescue horses, I liked to convince myself of this fact. And should strangers walk near the stable, I would warn them: Those nags are ours, and my father rescues ships in distress. We have a telephone that connects us with lighthouses, a chest full of fireworks, and lamps with brass reflectors, a container of kerosene, and medals from the Queen.

But no ship was ever stranded on our shore, we did not have cliffs or sand banks, our horses stuffed themselves on ensiled grass, and the kerosene lamps tarnished in the closet. The autumn was a clammy time of year, nothing but sea mists and driftwood along the coast, flotsam and jetsam which the older boys used to build huts in summer. When it froze, the sea threw ice floes on the beach, a distant world washed ashore, slabs of ice pushed their way as far up as the dunes. I was an Eskimo and stomped through the brittle ice that came up to my knees.

Life returned with the spring, when the beach grass grew green again and drew circles in the sand. The beach chairs came out and the sound of carpet beaters echoed from the houses. Painters climbed their ladders, and a bulldozer scraped the sand off the road.

And in the summer came the orphans. Buses groaned over the road: the High House was invaded. Blankets and mattresses were hung out the windows, and the flag flapped on the porch. The boys wore blue overalls and the girls blue skirts and zippered jackets. They were pale and poor, the sun was supposed to bring color to their cheeks.

The first few days the orphans remained behind the fences and spat through the screen if I came too close. Each year I stood there again at a safe distance, looking at those strange faces. They came from the big city, spoke slang, and wore shiny black rubber boots. Their arrival was a sign of summer, even though the sun did not appear and the rain pelted holes into the sand.

Now began the time of forbidden things: skirts hoisted up, black underpants, and breasts that rubbed against jackets. The girls clung together, they hummed, they danced, they colored their lips red and laughed at me through stained teeth. The boys played with their combs, shaped their hair into a duck's ass style with their spit and trained a lock to dangle down their foreheads. I wanted hair like that too, blond and sleek. I hated my curls, nests filled with sand, and stringy in the rain. Not even a handful of spit could keep my hair under control.

If my father had been lying for days on end in the dark on the sofa, and I had to read aloud to him—my back turned, so that the reading lamp wouldn't hurt his eyes—he would weave my curls into tight little braids, just as he did with the manes of the rescue horses. (Tick, tick went the ruler as it crept along my neck to measure the length of a drawn-out curl.) I had to be a man in all things, but that did not apply to my hair. My father loved my curls.

The orphan boys roughhoused and fought in play, showed off their muscles and swore. When the retired major who wore his medals on his coat let his dog off the leash, they bombarded the animal with pine cones, and when the man from the high dune walked to the beach in his bathrobe, they sang, "*Wir fahren gegen England* . . . splash, splash." But that was allowed, for the man had been a collaborator. They said everything I didn't dare to say, without lowering their eyes. Not one of them had a father who forbade them anything.

Within a week the orphans knew the secrets of the dune. They swaggered through my marshes and broke the crust on the dangerous sands. They knew where the gullies were and where the key to the stable hung, they picked my blackberries and pinched my shells.

On Saturday afternoons the orphans had to take a bath to get rid of the week's dirt. The windows of their house misted over, and you could hear them singing, songs for the beach. I knew the tunes, but every winter I would forget the words all over again. They sang about the city and about a tower to which they had lost their heart. When they emerged, their hair still damp and the toughest with a cigarette hidden in the palm of their hand, they smelled of tar. That smell, too, was part of summer.

After their bath they walked to the beach to see the sun fall into the sea, one behind the other, noses into the wind, at a firm pace. In the evening glow the blue of their uniforms turned almost black. They sang, "Glory, glory, hallelujah, pitch black are the girls from Batavia." But when they came to our house, they nudged each other, shushed, and marched by in silence, the rubber boots slapping against each other.

I stood on the front step, my back as straight as that of a general surveying his troops on parade. My sisters closed the curtains. I sniffed the tarry smell and looked as angry as I could.

My father hated the orphans. Every summer he asked the camp counselors whether they couldn't tell the children to sing a different song. The counselors promised to do better, they too thought it a nasty song, and they had forbidden the orphans to sing it many times. Yet each new group sang it again, in the dunes, or in the woods across from our house, but never—and that really was a proof of their goodwill—never in front of our door. There they swallowed their words and stamped their feet. The orphans must have realized that my father minded that behavior even more. They passed it on among themselves, and each new group knew from the very first day what they were supposed to do: Glory, hallelujah . . . shsh shsh . . . are the girls from Batavia, quiet in front of our communal house. The orphans knew our secret.

My father controlled himself, but whenever he heard their boots, he clenched his fists. They were jetsam, trash from the city. The filth would pass, be washed away as soon as the autumn winds came. The Japanese hadn't gotten the better of him, the orphans wouldn't come anywhere near. The day would come when he'd be teaching them manners. I, too, thought that what they did was ugly and dirty, but the smell of tar was also the smell of freedom, even though they wore prison uniforms and lived behind a gate. Orphans made their own rules. I dreamed of being an orphan, a Little Lord Fauntleroy. After endless whining, I was given a pair of blue overalls. I was not given any boots. In the morning I washed myself with Lifebuoy soap so that I, too, smelled of tar. The smell gave me courage.

One morning I took the scissors to my curls. Whatever sprang up had to go. I brushed my hair forward and cut it straight across my forehead. Caesar. If I couldn't have a curl on my forehead, then I would sport the head of an emperor. I had seen boys looking like this on the beach, and a singer on a bubblegum card. My three top curls I tamed with Vaseline from the horse stables. Wearing my overalls, my collar turned up, I grew into my role. I twirled in front of the mirror the way my sisters did. This is how I wanted to be, cool, this was the boy I loved, now I was no longer alone. I spat at the mirror and cursed. This was no tear dribbling down my cheek, this was sperm. My overalls were a harness. Rebellion was hidden in hair, from now on I would never be afraid. I washed my face with Lifebuoy and stepped into the living room.

My father sat behind his newspaper. I walked through the room, tried to draw his attention by turning a few times. A gentle breeze set his newspaper aflutter. He looked up, his eyes threw flames, not a word, only the anger in his fists. He shook his newspaper and went on reading. His knuckles became as white as the paper. My mother left the room.

"Did you know," said my father during dinner, after a long afternoon of silence, "did you know that in the Middle Ages thieves combed their hair forward? To hide the brand on their foreheads. Robberhead!"

The following day my mother put my curls in an airmail envelope and glued it into the family album.

The storms came from the west, suddenly, on a summer afternoon, earlier than expected; my sisters were away visiting someone or other, and the day before, the blue bus had delivered the last group of orphans. The tiles rattled on the roof, the telephone rang, and we knew what was expected of us: getting the lamps ready. We filled them with kerosene, polished the brass reflectors, trimmed the wicks, and tested the flame. Every lamp had to burn with equal intensity. And when my father wasn't looking, I caressed the boots.

We sat in suspense by the radio, the heavens creaked on the loudspeaker. High water, a wind factor of sixty-five miles an hour, the coastal population must stay on the alert. I was allowed to stay up, and I wrote down the names of all the ships in danger. The *Despina*, a steamship flying the Corsican flag, was listing in the vicinity of the lightship, the wind was veering north-northwest, and all rescue boats and Coast Guard vessels were on the alert.

All piloting was suspended. The *Mecklenburg*, a ferry, was listing forty degrees, the furniture was smashed to smithereens, and over ten passengers had been injured. Hundreds of campers watched as their tents were destroyed before their very eyes. The dike builders were at their post, some of the outer polders were flooded. On the islands a boy was blown out to sea with his kite. The radio announcer talked about "shifting winds."

The telephone. The *Despina* had lost her rudder and was in danger of being washed ashore. The horses neighed in the stable. My mother poured coffee for the volunteer rescue brigade. They had set their hearts on the *Despina*, any wreck was a good deal, along with the bonuses it would bring. They boasted, telling tall tales, they would do this, they could do that; their slickers creaked with longing. My father, breathing heavily, sat by the phone, the radio shouted through the big hall. He muttered under his breath, for he knew that he was too weak to be a hero in this storm. I might as well go along in the rescue boat, he said. With my robber's head I'd cut a pretty good figure as a sailor's apprentice. In jest he threw me a slicker. The men of the rescue team made fun of me. I could swim only with a life preserver.

The storms kept coming, raging storms, the radio updated its reports every half-hour. The *Despina* had smashed a wooden levee but had been blown back out to sea, beams lay like battering rams along the shore. The telephone told us that no wooden life boats were allowed to set out to sea. Disappointed, the rescue brigade straggled off. There was sand in my bed, and I thanked Dear Jesus under the covers.

The next morning we heard that the *Despina* had been towed ashore by the tugboat *Holland*. Once again our village failed to make the news, and we plodded along in obscurity.

• • •

But I would never forget that storm. One of the rescue horses had suffered a bite in its upper leg—Sjors, the nag with the braided mane. He lay in his stall badly wounded, two tendons broken; he was foaming at the mouth. According to the coast guard, a rabid fox must have sneaked in after the horses had trampled down the partitions, a sign of panic. All their shins were bleeding. He didn't discover it until late in the morning. The stable door was wide open. No one from the communal house had noticed anything, for we were too busy with a ship that didn't sink. Some delinquent had tampered with the lock, the key was no longer hanging on its hook. Sjors had to be put down with a bullet, a limping draw horse was no use. The man from the gas company came and shot him that same day.

We looked for tracks, we didn't believe in hungry foxes in autumn. But the wind had erased all traces, the dune and path through the forest were pristine.

The collaborator had seen someone walking near the stable on the night of the storm, but since my father would not speak to him, he did not report it to the coast guard until the following day; the suspect had worn overalls.

My father took me aside. "Come on, confess," he said, gasping. He had hardly slept that night and had woken up with blue lips. "No no, I didn't do it." The orphans were singing in the distance. He straightened, twisted the material of my overalls about his fist, and dragged me to the road. The procession of orphans began to hiss and stamp. My father raised his hand and ran his eyes along the column. The boots came to a standstill. His glance could be so menacing that people fell silent. He called it talking with his eyes. Assuming his sergeant's voice, he ordered all the boys to step out of line. The counselors protested, but my father's eyes said, "Enough," and they took the embarrassed girls aside.

"Who left the stable door open?" he asked. The boys did not speak, the boldest laughed cautiously. I stood there, small behind my father. He barked at each one in his face.

"*You? You?*"

Not a sound.

"Answer!" bellowed my father.

"No."

"What do you mean, no? No who?"

"No, sir," said the same boy. "No . . . sir," said another. The toughest spat on the ground and tossed their forelocks. They did not avoid his eyes but neither did they look at him, they looked beyond him, at me, and nudged each other. They pointed at the imprint on my overalls where my father's fist had held me. I didn't know which was more frightening, the blue horde out there or my father's blue lips. I was ashamed, and they could smell my shame. I felt no support in the smell of tar.

My father walked by the boys with a hand raised in a frozen salute, as if to decide with which cheek to start. The tallest, a boy with a blond forelock, straightened his back and took a step forward.

The girls screamed, clutching their counselors. The blond boy held up his fists in front of his face and danced toward us like a boxer. My father jumped backward and began to flail his arms about wildly. The boys cheered and made a circle, I was given a push, stumbled, and fell against my father. They took another step forward and pushed us toward the berm. My father lost his balance, his whole body was trembling. I thought he was about to faint, and held on to him. But he recovered, caught me by the shoulders, and pushed me against a tree.

"It's you," he yelled. "You left the stable door open."

His voice rang out like a shot, hard, and from so far away, from the East Indies. The stress was on the wrong vowels. The orphans burst out laughing. They shouted after him, "Peanut, peanut." They called him a peanut man, like the Chinese peanut vendors. I tried to hold my head up. Everything turned blue in my tears.

"No," I said. "No."

"No what?"

"No, Dad," I whispered. And I felt his hand burn. He didn't stop, his fingers fluttered before my eyes. I didn't dodge, I fell, and was pulled up by my hair, and as I hung from one hand, he slapped me with the other, left and right, on my cheeks, blood spurted from my nose. The orphans screamed, the counselors tried to pull him off, but he pushed them away. I was his own blood, he shouted, his robber's head, he had the right to beat his own child. I was his punching bag, and again he pulled me up by the hair.

I really wanted to confess, but no longer had the strength to tell a lie. I fell and slumped against the tree. I have no idea how long I lay there, and only remember his hand on my neck, a hand that pushed me into the house, a weak hand from which the beating had drawn all anger.

And my mother combed my hair forward, as behooved a Caesar. Gently, gently, she caressed me, and clumps of hair fell on her lap. She cried, but I had no more tears. I was afraid only of growing bald.

My father locked himself in his bedroom and began to count

aloud, numbers in time with the ticking clock. "He is counting his friends," she said, "his friends from the war."

I'd never be able to be one of those.

After the storms the sky tore into bright blue, then a leaden sky came from the east, and heavy lethargy fell over our roof. I was so tired that I could not push my bicycle out of the hall, my eyes fell closed, and I stumbled over my own legs. I was allowed to return to bed, and my mother gave me a rusk with wild strawberries from the dunes. But neither words nor sweets could console me, a heavy hand was dragging me down. The following morning I could not move my arms, getting up was impossible. I was paralyzed. A few hours later, I lay in a hospital bed.

A mysterious virus, said the doctor, related to polio. I could only move my neck. The illness had broken out along the coast, four of the orphans had it too. So it wasn't that bad. Except that my poop was infectious, and my blood was being tapped, and I couldn't see any other children. I was put in quarantine in a glass room. No pain, for I had no feeling; I was nothing but a brain.

During the first days I learned to look slowly, endlessly at the white ceiling, at the traces left by the paintbrush, and I greedily drank in all sounds: soles on freshly waxed floors and the creaking of starched aprons. The nurses wore masks over their mouths, after their visit the doctors threw their rubber gloves in the bucket outside my glass door. I was dangerous, and everyone loved me. My sisters sent candy. My father stood at the window every afternoon and gestured to keep up my courage; when he left, he imprinted a kiss on the glass pane. Never before had I felt so happy and so safe, I breathed in the outside world and invented stories to go with the sounds and the smells. Even though I was paralyzed, in my head I went for walks all day long.

My father brought me a homemade reading board, a piece of driftwood that fitted across my bed. And although he didn't approve of pictures, at the end of each visit I was given a Classic Comics. I turned the pages with a little bamboo stick clamped between my teeth. At the end of the stick was a rubber finger, normally used for peeling potatoes: my father's idea, seen on a photograph of basket cases.

Basket cases—I'd had no idea that there was such a thing. They were soldiers who had lost their arms and legs, men condemned to spend the rest of their lives hidden from the world, hanging in baskets. The war had made them into perpetual innocents. I could already see myself dangling, fed, rocked, and always getting what I wanted. On the other hand, never again to be an Eskimo on the beach, and forever the prisoner of my father's eyes.

The heroes of the classics began to talk to me, and my mattress was as wide as the world. The horizon was never distant enough for me, I traveled to the center of the earth, rode a rocket to the moon, or dove twenty thousand leagues under the sea. I shared Uncle Tom's cabin with him, became the man who was always laughing, a Pip with great expectations, and a Nobody who misled the cyclops. I galloped with the Three Musketeers through the fields of France and helped the aristocrats find a hiding place. I chased the money changers from the Temple and was afraid of the Man with the Iron Mask. Benjamin Franklin held my kite for me, I stayed awake for a thousand and one nights. Black tulips bloomed on the ceiling.

After a week a tingling sensation returned to my arms and legs. I could be kissed again, and my mother shed tears. Now began a time of exercising, in the mornings with a nurse, in the afternoons with the doctor and with my father, so that when I returned home, someone would be able to work with me there.

Ten taps with the little finger of my right hand. The doctor counted aloud, my father counted along. One, two, three, my little finger could move again. The doctor lifted my left arm, I felt nothing. A stranger's arm fell beside me. The right leg. The doctor pushed my ankle, I should exert some strength. I clamped my teeth and pulled my leg out of a thick syrup. He lifted my left leg, pricked my thigh with a pin, and let go. A foreign leg fell into my bed. The right side obeyed, the left side was still lazy. My back was next. My father turned me on my side, the doctor bent my back and counted the vertebrae in my spine. My father counted along out loud. They stopped at six, the doctor rummaged in his bag, I heard steel being screwed into steel, the creaking of cellophane, a nail against glass. They were tapping my spine, extracting fluid, but I felt nothing.

The doctor and my father laid me down flat, they pulled the sheet tight and tucked me in up to my armpits. They pushed a big pillow under my head, slid the reading board over my stomach, bamboo stick in my mouth, and I could resume my reading.

I learned hundreds of pictures by heart, ten times the same adventure, and because I could pay such close attention, I learned more every day. That's how I knew how to survive on an uninhabited island, and how to chase bees out of their hive. The Swiss Family Robinson demonstrated how to build a hut in a tree and how to make your own clothes in the jungle. I knew the names of exotic plants and fruits: cassava, sisal, sago, copra. Another East India.

And I planned how I would make great journeys and tell of my adventures. My father had already made me a present of a Swiss Army knife, with a built-in magnifying glass and a serrated mini-saw, so that we could practice together when I got better and build huts, set grass afire, cut bamboo and weave a basket. And at each visit he repeated the old soldier's motto, "Persevere, and you shall win."

After three weeks in the hospital I could move both my arms and legs again. My nerves and muscles had suffered no permanent damage from the paralysis, I was given two crutches, I learned to walk, and after a few days I could manage without. Only my feet and my back still refused to obey at times.

Then home to practice, with my father in an ambulance in the rain, never yet had he been so gentle and kind. He stroked my tingling arms, and we listened to the song of the brick-paved road under thick rubber tires.

> Through the meadows where there are no fences
> and the cows go shitting in the road
> where the steam tram rides along the water
> we are going faster, faster
> straight into the rain
> and I shall win.
>
> By the swimming hole where men go to bob for eels
> and the child molester with his fishing rod peers
> at little swimmers in the wading pool
> we are going faster, faster,
> not passed by anyone
> and I shall win
>
> Hello, you endless lane with crooked trees
> where live the children of the well-to-do
> and weather changes right beyond the curve

we are going faster faster
catch up with the rain
and I shall win

My father devoted himself to my exercise program, a couple
of hours every day. In the hospital the doctor had given him a
book on calisthenics.

The stick was used for everything. To roll up the oilcloth on the
table, to straighten my back when it bent over, to let me gallop
like a horse, to tie to my back while I ate, to balance with, and to
beat me with when I lost courage. It was a handsome straight
stick, smoothly sanded, with elongated brown knots in the
wood and rounded at the ends.

Rolling: Me flat on my belly, my father on his knees, and the
stick rolling along my back from neck to buttocks, up and down,
up and down, like a baker rolling out dough.

Stretching: My father on a chair, me kneeling on the ground,
the stick passed through my elbows and across my shoulders.
Then pulling it up, I could feel my bones sinking. Hold your
breath, chest out and hands flat on the nipples. We were weaving a tough coat of muscles, later I would be able to lift railroad
ties.

Running: First a mug of a calcium-rich liquid to feed the
bones. My mother had been too weak when she bore me. Then
the stick in the hollow of my elbows, and I ran. I was a nag with a
shaft on my back. My muscles had not kept pace with my growth,
and a hump was sprouting between my shoulder blades.

Tied down: Sitting at the table, stomach against the edge.
Stick in the back inside my pants to strengthen the spine, and a
strap around my chest. Sit up straight! Pull in your stomach and

straighten those shoulders! Lift the spoon higher—and no spilling. I learned to eat like a gentleman.

Balancing: Before my afternoon nap, a cup of relaxing herb tea, to loosen my muscles, for cramps were pulling me askew. Lying down with the stick across my chest, making it dance up and down with my breath, in unstable equilibrium. I was not allowed to turn over or to move. If the stick fell, I was in for it. My spine must be in perfect balance, that's what it said in the book. Plenty of room for nerves and muscles. Lying crooked could be fatal.

We improved on the exercises: jumping while the stick swung low above the ground, ducking when it was swung over my head. All this activity while rattling off our lost islands: Sumatra, Bangka, Billiton, Borneo, Celebes, Java, Bali, Lombok, Sumba, Sumbawa, Flores, Timor, half-Portuguese. The skipping-rope song of my sisters. For my pain I was given an hourglass containing sixty kernels of sand. Pain must never last more than sixty seconds. Everything was carefully counted out.

So long as my muscles were still too weak, I didn't have to go to school. I already knew how to read and write. Lessons in living, that's what it was about, for danger threatened in the newspapers, worrisome times lay ahead; the Russians, the Russians were riding westward, and this time not as liberators. The crows exulted behind the dune. I must be fit and strong for the flight and be able to walk for days, but my feet were misshapen and weak, something had to be done.

A large marble in the arch of my foot. My father fastened it on with the same yellow bandages used to strap the ankles of the rescue horses when the coast guard took them to shows. The bandages served as socks, otherwise my feet would not fit into my shoes. Twenty times around the table. My father beat time, tick tick tock.

If I cried "ouch," he increased the speed. His ruler whistled in the air. By pulling up my instep I could lessen the pressure on the marble, but if he saw me, I was given a tick. Walking on the outer edge of my feet was also forbidden, the instep had to be exercised. I hid the pain in my legs, my face musn't show anything. I won.

After the circles around the table came the baths. Every day my feet were soaked for ten minutes in the washtub. Cold water strengthened the muscles. In the meantime my father rubbed the marbles until they glowed, held them over my head and made my hair stand on end. My curls came back. This is how I learned about electricity, and this sport remained a game.

(They say that pain has no memory. And yet, walking through the streets of my former village, I could feel the marbles stabbing me. It was not memory but actual sensation. Hysterical imagination. For hours on end, no hourglass could help the feeling.

I was imprisoned in a childish spirit. I had to consult old diaries to remember events from more recent years, but the slightest detail from my childhood was absolutely clear. I felt distress at the way I could recall each detail: the yellow-ocher boards in the ceiling of our communal house, the round copper screws on the little steps to the kitchen, the yard-high geraniums in front of the window—oh, our geraniums were champions, their flowers big as fists, planted by the full of the moon and encouraged to grow with violin music—the grout between the tiles in the communal hallway, especially where a small pebble glittered among the concrete, the dents in the linoleum—left by the legs of the beds in the *Kinderheim*—the lines in the wood of the wardrobes, and the faces I could read in them. All these images from the past went round and round in my head. It was a disease, a swelling that demanded more room every day.

As a child, I must have drunk it all in and stored it up as a desert plant stores up the rain. It's just an illusion, I thought for a long time, a web of dreams and imagination, memory as a magic lantern. But I returned to the old house, boldly rang the bell while the boy was setting the table, and everything still clicked. The people who lived there now were poor tenants just like us, nothing had been altered, the house had merely been painted and maintained. I could have found the pebble caught in the grout blindfolded, the screws, the indentations in the doorpost next to the kitchen, where my father measured my height with Swiss Army knife and ruler. Everything was in place, although I found myself to have been smaller than I had thought.)

The threat of war grew more serious. The village council ordered a siren installed near the railroad station, and the National Guard practiced carrying stretchers in the dunes. Communists were everywhere, even in the free West. They infiltrated factories and stirred up the workers. Soldiers' leaves were canceled, and in Siberia people froze to death in prison camps. I knew all about the gulags. Biggles, the hero of my favorite books, had flown over them. The Russians stood at the ready behind the Iron Curtain.

No arguments. I had to obey the exercise book. Train, train, and strengthen those legs. It was urgent.

The doctor came more and more often, my father was so nervous, and his heart was getting worse. His eyes sank deeper in their sockets, his lips remained blue all the time. My sisters whispered about an operation, perhaps he could be given a new heart. A letter came from a surgeon: my father was at the top of the list.

My mother hardly existed for me during those weeks, although she kept encouraging me: "Keep at it, do it for him." She cast a horoscope, fed him the bread of the sick, and twice a week bicycled to the health-food store in the city. But no pill or powder could calm my father, the doctors' injections no longer helped. The sofa became the center of the house, and he drowned us in orders. Whoever didn't want to be scolded had better run. My mother did the rounds of her family and borrowed money from the Waldensians. The housekeeping became too much for her, we got some household help, and once a week a lady came to cook anthroposophic food: my father had become too tired to make the rijsttafel. We ate raw endive with oatmeal flakes. My mother wrote two long letters to the surgeon at the medical-school hospital to ask if he could not do the operation sooner.

We had to be nice to Father. If I would just keep on with my exercises, I would be able to take over a lot of the work later on.

And God knows there was a lot to do before the Russians came! The cellar had to be cleaned out. I carried up all the old newspapers and swept away the coal dust. These chores would give me a miner's arms, and I snotted black stars into my handkerchief. We borrowed two kerosene lamps from the rescue chest and hid them under the stairs for the present. My father also screwed twenty bicycle lamps onto a board, the batteries lay ready. We would have enough light. My mother made sacks out of old sheets, I filled them with sand and carried them downstairs. Sand would protect us against atomic radiation. And we would have enough to eat until Judgment Day, twenty pounds of green beans to be canned. I wore a red rubber ring around my upper arm and walked about like a Civil Defense warden. Red was a dangerous color. We also had to can pears and pickle onions. The vegetable man brought two dozen cans of beans. We would be doing a lot of farting, but no one would be able to smell us. My father put a cloth over the hatch. Nobody knew that we lived in a cellar.

And in the evening we read the newspapers. He showed me the photographs. I could read the headlines easily. Letters were becoming more fascinating than pictures. Popular uprising in Hungary. Attack on Budapest. The inhabitants spread green soap on the bridges and streets, and Russian tanks spun around in circles. Barbed wire was unrolled, and tens of thousands of Hungarians fled to the West. A singer sang a song about Budapest. War was imminent. My father cried listening to the radio.

Back to the days in stocking feet. Shush. It is forbidden to bounce balls in the hall, watch out, don't bump into the bicycles. Not too much light. Turn off the radio. Turn off the record player. Don't ring the doorbell. Straw on the road in front of the house. No visitors. Don't flush the toilet. Don't let the water run. Butter musn't hiss in the frying pan. The clock has to shut up. My father counted the days, the hours, the minutes aloud.

A suitcase stood ready in the hall, the call from the medical - school hospital could come any day.

•   •   •

The cellar wasn't deep enough, I should find a better hiding place, our red roof would draw the bombers' attention. A hiding place somewhere behind our house seemed to me safer. I went alone into the dunes and looked for a spot in the loose sand, no tank would be able to get a grip. My exercise book also recommended digging holes. Without a shovel, I had to knead the sand to toughen my fingers. I would dig a hole as deep as I was tall. The sand crusted under my nails; the deeper I dug, the colder and wetter it was. I counted my sixty seconds. My nails were bloody, but that was no problem: clean sand was a disinfectant.

After an hour I gave up, I was still too weak and had to rest. But the next day I returned, although my father implied that there would be no place to hide from the Russians, even if I were to cut beach grass with my Swiss Army knife and weave a camouflage roof for us. For the day would come when we would have to flee together, the day on which they would make all men into slaves, and no one would be allowed to think as he pleased. And this is why I had to be in training, I must be swifter than danger. Yes, my father would teach me foreign languages, we would buy a globe and plan a safe escape route. After that we would go on a long voyage, leaving behind all we possessed, my sisters, perhaps even my mother. That's how it always was in wartime, you had to be tough and take leave of what you loved the most.

After the digging came the rest, an afternoon nap was still required. Relaxing tea, stick on my chest, and balancing. My father also rested, in the mornings and in the afternoons, and when he wasn't lying on the sofa, he shuffled through the house.

He was weak but not too tired to supervise my training. We no longer ran with the stick in my back but walked together at the pace of a carriage.

To pamper my muscles between rest and exertion, he rubbed me with tiger balm. We now smelled the same. And if he had any strength left, he would give me a massage, letting my muscles roll between his fingers, separating them from the flesh, up and down from groin to heel, digging until tears welled up in my eyes. I screamed with pain, the tiger was biting my legs. "Concentrate on something else," he whispered and continued to knead me. "You're allowed to cry, but never to scream, you must bear pain in silence. Think about your hourglass." And if I lay whimpering as I recovered, he would console me with a beautiful story, a classic he invented himself, and that, like Scheherezade, he spun into a fairy tale, a thousand and one seconds long.

My father at my bedside . . . his stories go on being told in my memory, each time with different words, although they always kept the sound of his voice.

"When I see your tears, young man, something suddenly comes back to me. Did you know that in the East there is an old belief that says tears can bring the dead back to life?"

He gave me his handkerchief, and I dampened it with my final tears.

"A strange story, I heard it from an old peddler in Port Said. You were still in your mother's womb, on the boat back to Holland. He had experienced it himself, believe it or not.

"It was hot, unexpectedly hot for that time of year. Port Said, yes, at the edge of the desert, even the soles of a camel's feet would burn. The peddler lay in his little boat, in the shadow of a landing stage, tired but satisfied. He had sold out, the money stored against his chest. Now he had to find some wares to peddle, but where? The peddler didn't know the city very well, he came from the south and had sailed with his wares from Suez to the entrance of the canal over the Bitter lakes.

"There was much more money to be made in Port Said than in Suez, where everyone was a trader, it was a fueling port, created especially for the building of the canal. Our ship had lain there two whole days to take on water and oil and to scrub the desert sand from the deck. The water around the ship was rarely still, all day long money-divers swam around us, calling and begging for coins, and at night vendors and performers stormed the railings.

"After a journey of playing shuffleboard and quoits and attending musical revues, we took leave of the tropics in Port Said. Once we sailed to the place where the mud of the Nile colored the Mediterranean yellow, we tried on our new winter clothes and paced up and down the deck. They handed out life jackets with a little red light attached, for the sea was full of mines. But in Port Said we were still dancing without a care, the whole city was one big dance party, there was music everywhere. Yes, young man, you danced inside your mother's womb under a roof of stars.

"It was a hundred and twenty-five degrees in the shade, and the peddler was looking for a rag to wipe the sweat from his forehead."

My father took out his handkerchief, shook it out in the air to get rid of my tears—"Listen, a pair of geese is flying from the delta to Europe"—and wiped his bald head. No matter how sick he was, a story could not be left unaccompanied by gestures and sound effects.

"The peddler searched through the pockets of his burnoose, and do you know what he found? A damp hand in the act of stealing his Swiss Army knife. And attached to that hand was a money diver, his legs in the water. He was as slippery as an eel, and quite naked except for a loincloth, and he had a nose like a bedouin's tent. The peddler hoisted him aboard. The little diver bowed and introduced himself as Mustapha.

"They came to an agreement right away: the peddler would not report the boy to the police if in exchange Mustapha would show the peddler the way to the Arab quarter and help him acquire a supply of goods. Mustapha did not have to think long, for in Port Said the custom is to chop off the hands of thieves. They made the boat fast and climbed ashore. But halfway to the landing stage, the peddler remembered something—his paddle, the oar as thick as a wrist with which he maneuvered so skillfully between the large mail packets. Mustapha would carry his paddle, that way no one would be able to steal his boat, for without the oar, you couldn't get very far.

"Though the little thief couldn't read, he could name every ship and knew all their dates of arrival and departure. One look at the smokestacks, and he knew all there was to know. He was clever, and could easily talk strangers into parting with some change, and when he ran out of words, he would do a little dance around the paddle. The peddler enjoyed watching him.

"The sun dried Mustapha's loincloth and lent a red sheen to his hair. He smelled of sweetish mud, and his nails were red with henna. Yes, henna, an Arab root, also good against diarrhea. The peddler was amazed at the insistence of the merchants who carried day-old chicks in the inside pockets of their coats and held out dirty pictures. He was not looking for that kind of merchandise.

"Mustapha was a good guide, he took the quickest way through the European quarter and chased away the donkeys that roamed around loose. Shoo, shoo. Briefly they stared at the display windows of the big warehouse of Simon Arzt."

(I knew the name because the man wearing the fez was on the cover of a box of Egyptian cigarettes.)

"What gorgeous materials! Hand-sewn men's shirts, hats with silk headbands . . . alas, such wares were too expensive for the peddler. Quick, to the bazaar. The Place De Lesseps was somnolent in the sun, they avoided the gambling houses where planters gambled away their capital in a single night.

In the street of the pigeon butchers the Arab activity began to blare in their ears, thousands of plucked birds hung on strings between the houses. Red drops spattered on their heads. This, too, was not the peddler's fare. Mustapha pulled him away from the begging children and led him past a tangle of shouting men with pushcarts. This is where the maze of small covered streets began, each house a store, and the sun shining through roofs made of rags. Mustapha brought the peddler to the tanners, tailors, and coppersmiths, but he was looking for smaller wares, knickknacks and jewels, manageable merchandise that he could easily display in his box and pull up by a rope. Not for nothing did the people on board our ship call peddlers boxmen. To find small goods, you had to go to the heart of the bazaar, a covered area with hidden mosques and bathhouses. Steam, yes, to chase away heat with heat.

Mustapha stopped in front of a shabby wooden door. "Behind this door is gathered all the gold of the city," he said and led the way through a maze of hallways and staircases. The paddle was too long for the sharp corners, but after much measuring and maneuvering, they managed to reach a wooden attic. Brrr . . . the spiders fled before their feet."

My father left the room to wash the tiger balm from his hands. Whether it was this story or another, he liked to maintain suspense. So there I lay, the stick wobbling on my chest, my cheeks glowing with excitement. A hundred and twenty-five degrees in the shade!

"Ten brass beds stood in a row," my father said when he returned. "On the mattresses covered with cloths sat boys and men sat polishing silver pitchers, picking precious stones out of brooches, counting change, or snoring. Not one of them looked up. The peddler was too tired to ask where he was. He shoved the paddle under a bed and fell fast asleep.

"A few hours later he woke up, his head on Mustapha's chest. It had grown dark in the meantime, and a spider was creeping along his forehead. Mustapha told him that the spider had spun a web between their shoulders and that he had not wanted to move so as not to disturb him or the spider.

"'What a good eye you have,' said the peddler.

"'We money divers have to,' Mustapha replied.

"They laughed and tore the web. It had been a long time since the peddler had allowed himself to have a friend. His entire life had been spent peddling for money, and sometimes he feared that calluses had grown as thick about his heart as on his hands. But now that he could hear Mustapha's heart beating against his cheek, he realized what a terrible emptiness it was to have no son. He wanted to be a father to the boy, to teach him to read and write, and to prepare him for an honest life.

"Mustapha laughed at him cheerfully. Look, during the first hours the peddler slept, the boy had stolen a flatbread and onions and some oily olives. The peddler objected, but the smell made him greedy, and he gobbled down every last crumb of the bread. The old man wiped a tear from his eyes, he didn't know whether it was brought on by the onions or the sentiment, for he was not used to having a diver take care of a man who was well off. Mustapha consoled him by saying that tears were the blood of friendship, and he told him the old saying that the dead could be revived with tears.

"The attic was now quite deserted, all the boys and men had disappeared.

"'Where are they?' asked the peddler.

"'They're working,' said Mustapha.

"'At night?'

"The boy laughed at such innocence. This was his home, didn't the peddler understand? This is where he lived with his friends, the best thieves in all of Port Said, money changers, storytellers, divers; there were no better people to be found in the entire harbor.

"The following morning the peddler discovered the truth of what his new friend had told him. Every mattress was occupied once again, young and old were sound asleep, and at their feet the booty of the night was displayed: coins of all sizes and kinds, rings, wallets, and silver-handled walking sticks.

The peddler himself proved to be the victim of their industry. He found that the money he kept under his shirt was missing, yes, even his paddle had been stolen, all he had left was his Swiss Army knife. He was furious and accused Mustapha and his gang of thieves. Against his will, the boy examined the booty of his friends. According to him, a thief from the outside must have come in, in this house people didn't steal from each other. The anger of the peddler lasted more than sixty seconds.

"After that night they were poor together. They shared one bed, ate out of one bowl, and whatever they still owned was also shared: the cracks in the ceiling, the tears in the sheet, and a sea of time. Mustapha wanted to teach the peddler the art of stealing, and the peddler offered to teach him to read and write. Neither of them was happy with the newly acquired knowledge, and when the fleas had eaten their fill of the peddler, he began to long for his boat. But where would he be likely to find a new paddle? The city was still too young for large trees, and the desert too dry. Yes, wood was a precious commodity.

"It so happened that one tree grew in the Arab quarter, near the spring of an old oasis, which had been a resting place for caravans. The builders of the city had used the trunk as a pillar for the bathhouse. It was an enormous plane tree, so big that you could see how its branches and leaves spread above the dome only if you were up in the sky. If you looked carefully, you could make out a ray of sunlight between the trunk and the roof, no wider than two hands, only a child could pass through that crack. Mustapha would climb up and find out if one of the branches up there would suffice to make a paddle. He stuck the Swiss Army knife between his teeth, set his nails in the bark of the trunk and with difficulty wormed his way through the crack. The peddler did not dare to look up, he was afraid that sawdust would fall into his eyes. He did not hear the sound of sawing, and yet a little later a stick as wide as his wrist fell down. His paddle! His hands recognized the worn grip in the wood. He looked up, and suddenly it was raining paper money, his money—and more, for his thumbs did not recognize the dog-eared corners of some of the bills.

Mustapha had discovered a thieves' nest in the top of the tree, and honest as he was, he stole everything back. The peddler was rich once more, he could lay in a store of merchandise and sail away. In gratitude he offered Mustapha half the money, on condition that he be willing to become his shipmate.

It was hard for Mustapha to abandon his friends from the attic from one day to the next. First he needed to catch the unknown thief, only then would he be able to go. They could not tolerate amateurs, the honor of his guild was at stake. And after the muezzin had sounded his fifth prayer from the minaret, Mustapha left for the plane tree. No matter how strongly the peddler warned him of the dangers, there was no holding him back. Mustapha reassured him and before leaving, he said, 'If someone should get in bed with you from the right side, it's me; but should they get in from the left, it's somebody else.' The peddler paid no attention to his words and fell asleep. Outside, the tunes of the ship's musicians sang out until deep into the night. 'Red Sails in the sunset.'"

I saw memories creep over my father's skin. "Oh boy! Goose-flesh!"

"The peddler heard nothing, but it was not yet daybreak when he felt a cool breeze on his neck. The bed creaked to his left side, and a strange body slid under the sheet. He understood. This was not Mustapha's smell, not the well-known sweet, muddy scent, this body smelled of blood. The peddler jumped out of bed, lit a candle, and directed the flame straight at the stranger's face. And do you know what he saw? A man with a white turban and a shawl covering his nose and mouth. But actually he saw not even that, for two bloodthirsty eyes gleamed above the shawl, even brighter than the light of the flame.

"'Where is Mushapha?' shouted the peddler.

The man in the shawl did not answer but lifted a bloody hand. Its fingers uncurled one by one, like a sea anemone in the heaving waves. A sickly smell spread over the sheets. The hand held a beating heart. The peddler took the gourd which served as chamber pot from under the bed and caught the heart in it.

In the Arab quarter the muezzins were climbing to the top of the minarets, preparing to call the faithful to their prayers, the sun colored the horizon, and they proclaimed Allah's greatness: *Al-lahou akbarou.* The murderer covered his ears with his hands and fled outside.

The peddler was inconsolable. He remembered the old belief that you could bring a friend back to life with tears, and he tried to cry, but no matter how he sighed and moaned, his tears would not flow. When the thieves returned to the attic from their night's work, he had barely accumulated a thimbleful. And the few tears that he did shed only expressed his sadness that he could not weep for Mustapha. The thieves took in the scene and understood what was expected of them. One after another they began to weep copiously. By the end of the day, shortly after the last prayer, the gourd was full of tears. They poured out all the tears a human body contains. *Al-lahou akbarou.* None of the thieves had another tear left, they all fell asleep at once. That night there was no stealing in Port Said, nor was a single story told."

"And Mustapha?" I asked.

My father smiled mysteriously. "A good story has an ending that you may dream up for yourself."

• • •

And I dreamed and heard my bed creak on the right side. A back nestled against mine—a back I knew better than my own, tropical yellow, muscular. Between the shoulder blades was a scar, one cut to the left, one to the right, two wings of proud flesh.

And I woke with a start and looked at my father's face bathed in tears. He had come to say good-bye. The letter from the medical-school hospital had been in the house for several days—no, he had not let on, he didn't want to upset me too soon, "You've got to keep your worries to yourself, you know that, young man"—but now the time had come. Notary Groeneweg was standing by in his car, he would drive my father.

The Rover billowed out white smoke. There was snow in the air. The notary opened the door, my mother led my father out. They kissed each other, a final wave, and off they drove.

We stood by the window, Ada, Saskia, and I. I didn't cry. My father wouldn't die, the surgeon would give him a new heart. My mother walked back to the house, her head lowered.

The world grew smaller, the newspapers disappeared unread in the newspaper bin. Now there was only one preoccupation—my father's heart. Would the valve hold, had the surgeon's hand not trembled too much? My mother was away for half the day, changing six times on her round trip to the medical school, her nails in mourning from the dirty buses and trains. Every day I had to write my father a note, and I used his ruler to keep the lines straight. Saskia sent drawings.

It was strangely quiet in the house, as if these were always stocking-feet days: no more stories during meals, even the radio was never turned on. Only Ada paid no attention to the oppressive atmosphere. She played her recorder in the living room, she was practicing a *valse russe*.

Frost flowers bloomed on the window panes and the pears froze in their jars, so we went ahead and ate them. The Russians remained behind the Iron Curtain. My father would not come home for a while, it was too raw at the seashore, he went first to gather his strength at the Waldensians'.

My knee pants disappeared into the closet, and I forgot what pain and bruises were. The exercises were abandoned, the road to school no longer traveled by bicycle but on the winter bus. My muscles grew mushy and once more I dragged my left leg.

The coast guard came daily by bicycle with news, back and forth from the Village Council, until we were given permission to use the telephone in the hall for ourselves. When my mother made a call, I was told to watch the clock and give the signal to hang up after one minute. For the first time I heard my father's voice over the telephone. "Hello, man, I didn't die, my motor's running fine."

He would be able to do everything again—cook and dance, ride his Solex bike, yes, he even promised Mother that he would look for work, his first civilian job; there would be plenty of money. My mother painted her fingernails the color of pearls and went to stay with him for a week. We all took heart. A new heart, a new father.

The mailman delivered a big package, a globe lit from the inside, a present from my grandfather, and a note from my father was attached: "Dear man. As soon as I am better, we will start training for a long journey. Start oiling the straps of your backpack now."

• • •

It was almost spring when my father returned to us, my mother picked the first winter monkshood blossoms in the garden and polished the wok. The Rover came to the door and my father stepped out, scrawny and shriveled, his hat sank down over his ears, and the pleat of his trousers no longer fell straight. I stood by the window, afraid that if I walked over to him, he would notice that I dragged my leg. I drank in his eyes, but he first embraced my mother, kissed my sisters, and did not glance at the window. Look at me, look at me, I whispered to myself, but he walked into the garden, turned the mulch around the rose-bushes. I tapped on the window pane, he did not respond, he crouched and poked the earth with his finger, I begged an angel to give his chin a nudge . . . Look up, look up . . . but my father did not see me. And I walked outside and held on to the door, "Daddy, Daddy," I cried. He turned around and said, "So, slow-poke, it took you all this time to show up." He laughed, he opened his arms, and we ran toward each other, and when I kissed his cheeks, he pulled my ear.

"Walk ahead of me," he said. I walked, as limberly as I could. "You're dragging your leg. Tonight we do the exercises."

Indoors, we admired his scar, and I put my ear to his heart . . . thump, thump, it ticked like new. My father was healthy and strong, he could give orders without gasping: Don't wave your spoon! Twenty times around the table on your toes! The tiger balm came out of the medicine chest, and the massage made his eyes grow angry: My left leg was thinner than my right. The ruler had a place of honor next to his plate, I got my first tap, the rice made the kitchen windows steam over, and Ada played the recorder in the bathroom. Everything was as it had been before.

The stick remained rolled up in the oilcloth for the table, my father had read a new book, the anthroposophists would be able to cure me. Dancing the letters, that was the remedy, body and soul should grow together. Eurhythmics—to feel space and walk the N, two triangles with arms wide, and humming . . . the N that stood for no, *nyet, nein* and *non,* a letter that won't allow itself to be touched. Jump upward from the linoleum and spread and tighten your muscles in the air and avoid making contact with the floor. The ruler gleefully whipped up and down. I must make my body be the vehicle of my will. And we danced the A, the T, the H, the A, the N. Ouch, that last N was untidy, do it again. My father wrote my name in the air, and more, poems: Goethe, Morgenstern, Nietzsche; and shapes— five-pointed stars, circles, lemniscates. I danced the unspeakable visible until I collapsed. And what I couldn't draw in the air I had to feel. Flip, flap, a tap on both cheeks.

My father's strength returned, and I had given up. The harmony between head and body did not occur, I threatened to become mushy, just look: effeminate flesh. He put me in front of the mirror and pulled up my shirt, yes, little breasts were even bobbing on my chest. He pinched them and made them wobble. Perhaps climbing trees would help. T R E E, what did the eurhythmics book say about that? The T was a kicking sound and symbolized growth, the tunneling of roots through earth; R was a soft purr, ceaseless growth, and EE was an exclamation of delight, an embrace. We crossed the street and looked for a tree my father's arms could surround. We chose the fattest tree in the forest. "Climb," he said. The trunk was too thick and the first branch too high, I couldn't manage it, I was no Mustapha.

He went up ahead, without panting, but his face was contorted with pain. His ribs were still too stiff, the surgeon had had to pull them apart, the better to reach his heart. He hoisted me onto the first branch and pushed me up toward the second one.

"Higher," he ordered. "Pull yourself up."

My arms were not strong enough, my knees scraped against the bark. I could not go up or down. My father lowered himself to the ground and looked up at me, furious, his eyes eating me alive. "Show that you're a man." He turned away and walked off.

I sat with legs wide apart on the branch and waited. Squirrels jumped from tree to tree, crept closer, scratched themselves, and jumped to the next tree. After an hour—or was it longer? I was too frightened to count the seconds—he returned.

"Are you a man?"

"I don't know."

He caught me by my ankles and pulled himself up. My testicles were crushed against the bark, and the pain almost made me vomit. He pushed my legs forward and back and dragged my crotch over the branch.

"Do you know yet?"

I screamed.

"Those are your balls, a man has balls. Now do you know?"

And I knew: If my mother rubs my belly with salve when I get home, I will have had a bad fall.

I loved my father, especially then. I wanted to gain his respect, to count away my pain like a friend from the war. But no matter what I did, he saw only my faults. What should I do to make him love me? I understood that he wanted to make me into a knight and that I had to complete many more tasks before he would accept me as his equal. But why couldn't he praise me just once? It did seem as if the operation had made him meaner; did the surgeon give him a worse heart instead of a better one?

At night, in bed, bent over with the pain between my legs, I gave my globe a turn and stared at the snow burning on the Himalayas and the yellow-green continents . . . I would travel, get away from my humiliation. How dared he make me out to be a woman when I was training daily to become a man? To call my haircut a robber's head when his stories always glorified thieves?

That evening for the first time I felt deep hatred—a hate that rose from my blackened testicles. The bloody limit had been reached, my bloody limit. But it was not hatred of my father and not hatred of my mother, who called a welt a scratch and every ache my own mistake, nor was it hatred of my sisters, to whom I meant no more than air; no, I felt too weak for that, too inferior, too small a man with testicles. It was myself I hated. I would be better off dead and erased from the face of the earth. The light inside the globe hurt my eyes, my hope had been torpedoed somewhere in a blue ocean, I would never return home as a great and wealthy man to take my parents in my arms. The role of proud son was too heavy for me, I had failed, even the heroes in my Classic Comics looked down on me.

I pulled the sheet over my head, bit my pillow, and counted . . . I heard a dog howl in the distance, drawn out howls, going on for seconds at a time . . . and I thought of the quicksand, of the dog I had saved. To be swallowed up by the earth, and to sink into a cool slush! I got up, looked out the window: darkness, nothing moving, only the murmur of the sea. In my pajamas I crept to the kitchen and took the key of the rescue chest from the red hook. It was dark in the hall, my parents were listening to the radio in the living room. I didn't dare turn on the light, and it took some time before I found the padlock to the chest. The kerosene lamps felt empty, the wading boots were sticky. I filled a lamp, and some kerosene dripped on my bare feet. After much rummaging, I found a box of matches at the bottom of the chest. By the light of a small flame I picked out a slicker and a pair of boots, slipped outside, and dressed behind the house. The boots were too wide and flopped about my thighs, I had to tie a knot in the suspenders, the salve stuck to my slicker. I turned up the wick and took the path to the field with the waterworks stood. My larger self strode beside me, I was not afraid, my shadow grew in the night. I was a giant.

The dog was still baying, but the pauses between howls grew longer. I couldn't make out where the sound came from. Were those voices? Or was there an echo singing in the dunes? The quicksand lay to the north, that's where I had to go, past the grassy marshes, no one could keep me from that place. Everything seemed much bigger in the dark, bushes turned into trees and the smallest bend in the path challenged my sense of direction. I turned down the wick, the howling came from two sides, when I turned around I saw a lamp flicker. Had the alarm been sounded, had someone noticed my flight?

I must try to confuse them, zigzagging through the sand, and hurry to the paved road, there I would not leave a trail. The light was coming closer, and now I clearly heard voices, two deep voices, it could not be my imagination. They were after me. The dog was quiet.

The wading boots prevented me from walking faster, they drooped down and the rubber flaps between my legs made me trip. The lamp knocked against my stomach, the flame flickered and threatened to go out. I should raise the wick, dangerous, but without light I could see little, the moon and stars were hidden behind the clouds. I wanted to walk toward the strip of sea, the source of the murmuring, that's where I would find the paved road leading to the bunkers, where I could hide for the time being. The smell of piss would throw everyone off the track. If only I could feel hard ground under my feet, I would be able to go faster. My left leg hurt, and my boots made so much noise that I could hardly hear the sea. If I stood still, my heart beat too loudly in my throat. I was growing hot, the slicker scorched my chest . . . my heart, even my heart was weaker than my father's. My coat was smoldering, I had been holding the lamp too close to my body. I blew it out and let the white of the dunes lead me along.

The voices were coming nearer, the howling resumed. This was Eliza's flight, I was fleeing my master, and the white stretches of sand were my ice floes, the voices were chasing me, a dog growled. The earth dropped away under my boots, grass, wet grass, pools and low wind-blown dunes—this was where the waterworks began. I had walked in the right direction after all. One shot, then another, they were shooting in the air. "Stop!" they called. The dog barked. "Stop."

They would not catch me alive, one more shot, one jump, and I would reach the quicksand. I jumped . . . stumbled over my boots, and fell into a circle of light. A barking dog ran at me, he panted and reared, a leash pulled him back, and a flashlight shone above his head. I looked into the face of the man from the gas company, gun in hand, a full bag across his shoulder, a bushy tail sticking out of it. He would surely shoot me. Behind him stood the coast guard. They had caught the fox, mad as any-thing, his paw neatly in the trap, and did he ever howl, something terrible. Finally the murderer was caught, looked for him for half a year. Those shots were to finish him off, a bullet from each of them. But they had seen something unusual in the dune, a little lamp that wandered off toward the quicksand, and just look, there was that little guy from the communal house. Almost in the piss, and even in a slicker and boots from the rescue team. What was he up to? The little thief, still up and about at this hour, yes, yes, now they knew who had left the stable door open. Come on, get back to your house.

The coast guard pulled off my boots and lifted me up on his shoulders. The moon shone through the clouds, the beautiful round sliver of the last quarter. I looked back and saw the quicksand, like a white ice floe, slip from sight. In front of us lay our house, lights burning in every window, a safe beacon in spite of everything. They were waiting for me.

And so I walked through the seasons of my youth, along the stable, the abandoned orphanage, through the dunes, over the untrodden terrain of the waterworks, where the rain pockmarked the sand and where you could hear a fox howl. For my mother I picked a sea thistle from her own garden, a survivor just like her, gray-green with a straw heart.

I had walked away my fury, let the wind blow away my temper. I could walk quietly with my father, relaxed, not in the ranks, no longer a child, but a man not afraid to be like his father.

That's what I thought then and, overconfident, decided to ask Aram whether he would like to come and live with me. He ought to come out from the shadow of a father who was fading away, I wished him to have a happier adolescence. I could handle it. I wanted to, and I would conquer my own weaknesses.

• • •

I drove to Aram's school and waited for him. He came spinning out, ahead of two girls who were clearly following him. Our eyes met, but he pretended not to see me and walked to the bicycle rack. Hanging out, making jokes, a cigarette hidden in his hand, he didn't come over to me until everyone else was gone. He was ashamed of being met.

"Hi, are we going moshing again?" he asked. His boots clattered on the pavement, he wore them every day. He hadn't forgotten the night of heavy metal, had I maybe seen the girl with the ring in her nose? No? "She sure went for you," he said.

"I've got a girlfriend, you know."

"But you're always alone, she didn't even come to the funeral."

"Can't I be alone?"

"You're too old for that."

"Then why don't you come and live with me?"

"But I live with my father."

I blushed and had to swallow hard to get up my courage. "A different atmosphere will be good for you, and in the summer we'll go on long trips."

Aram looked surprised. "With Maarten?"

"No, just with me. We'll find a home for Maarten where they'll take very good care of him."

"Never." Aram spoke sharply. "I want to take care of him. Papa has promised me that he will hold on until I've taken my final exams."

"And you believe him?"

"Of course. I'll even flunk, if necessary."

I was ashamed of my tactlessness. We had tea somewhere

and ate large slices of tart. Aram asked for a second slice and wrapped it in a napkin for his father.

"But he can hardly swallow. You have to feed him as it is."

"I mash it up, I look after him much better than the nurse does."

"If that's how you want to live . . . it's your choice."

"Yes," he said curtly. "You have no authority over me, you're not my father."

I apologized and told him that if the time ever came when he could no longer manage, I'd always have a bed for him.

What a fool I was, a dreamer of sons and fathers who would never find each other. I turned on the car radio, and all the long way home I drove with misty eyes. Perhaps I should give a dog another try.

6
REPEAT PERFORMANCE

═══════════

WE WOULD do it one more time: a funeral without a body but with music and words. Saskia lit a candle and placed a photograph of Ada on the table. My mother looked around, satisfied, at her assembled family . . . yes, I had been right to come! Listened to my inner voice after all, hadn't I, for be honest, didn't I love my family more than I let on? I read my eulogy, and violins oozed from the CD player. Jana had to go through it as well, whether she wanted to or not. The video froze, Mr. Korst's contribution didn't work in Canada, a different system. "Too bad, we all looked so well in it," said my mother.

So then we had to tell her, everything from the coffin to the rose garden . . . the announcement in the papers, the flowers, what we wore, the weather, Jana wasn't spared a single detail. "Did you all notice the double rainbows?" asked Saskia. "Just as the procession arrived at the funeral parlor, two rainbows appeared in the sky over the building. When we walked away after it was over, it disappeared all of a sudden."

Wasn't it amazing? I hadn't noticed, but Saskia happened to be acutely sensitive to whatever went on over our heads. My mother couldn't help looking outside, a gray polar light . . .

who knows, quite possible, didn't actually see it that day, but now that she was told, she did recognize the sign. In any case, it had been a sad but beautiful reunion, too bad Jana couldn't have been there. I too looked out the window, to hide my annoyance; would I really have to spend two weeks with these crazy women?

After the cake—surprise, surprise, baked with Dutch butter, good old Saskia, she thought of everything—the mourning bands, the letters, and the register of condolences were displayed on the table. Who had brought along those tasteless souvenirs? Saskia raised a modest finger. Today was about reliving the event together, it completed the experience. Jana leafed through the register, my, my, what a lot of names. Was it that easy to get the day off for a funeral in Holland? What a rich country we had become. Most of the names meant nothing to her . . . Aunt Nikki, Els, yes, she really should write her, but what could she say? On paper you always had a tendency to complain.

A few snapshots fell from the register—Ada laid out in her pajamas, the flashbulb had left a halo on the glass. "What a bag of bones," said Jana. "Poor thing, if only I could have fed you." No, this was not the way she was going to die. Jana did nothing but blow up. She took the last two slices of cake and stuffed them in her mouth. Her nylon wig moved to the rhythm of her chewing. At least eating still gave her some pleasure, for she no longer left the house except to go back and forth to the hospital, and even that was no longer necessary. They'd given up on her, they'd stopped the chemo. Now she just sat the whole day long, propped up on a pillow, her Pampers creaking.

Whatever she ingested stayed with her, in spite of my mother's urinary herbs. Her legs were pillars bloated with water, and the swelling in her groin pulsed like a toad. The cancer had spread through her whole body. In the mornings she was taken from her bed and seated at a table, at night her husband hoisted her upstairs on the stairlift. She was unable to walk, her hips were worn out, and she did not want to lie down, she had a need to look at living things, birds, clouds, and the last plants, the red trees, and the hills in the distance. At the back of the house Errol had put in a bay window especially for her, and there we sat—the patient with her mother, brother, and sister.

To sit and be bored and tell aloud what you see: "Goodness, a seagull, do they fly this far inland?"

"The lakes here are seas."

"But not salt water."

"No, not that."

And when the outside world had been exhausted, we began to retrieve memories. The communal house, the first years along the coast, and finally, slowly, unwillingly, the subject of the East Indies came up. The islands, the time in the outlying districts, the greenish light and the jungle, flying squirrels, wild cats and elephants on the grounds. Saskia kept asking about it, her sister had experienced a real colonial childhood, and Saskia really knew so little. How many times had they moved? What had it been like in Bali at the time, and the kubus, the aborigines, did you ever actually see any? Jana scratched at her wig, thinking tired her out. But working with her mother, Jana managed to recall quite a lot. Goodness, do you remember, gosh, do you remember, all day long. I heard nothing new I hadn't heard before, though I hadn't known the names of the regions and the vulcanoes and the taste of fruits and syrups.

Saskia wanted to go through the old photograph albums.

"Where did I put them?" Jana wondered. After searching through the closets, Saskia, grumbling, placed them on the table. How could her sister be so careless with them? They were heirlooms, photos that had been sent to Holland before the war, to reassure the Waldensians about the peaceful and exotic life in the colonies. Jana had been given the albums when she emigrated—she had swiped them, said Saskia—at first she had sometimes looked through them. "But it was upsetting, you know. We had to get on with things over here, looking back didn't do any good."

The first few pages Jana turned over roughly, the tissue paper, fragile as spiderwebs, tore between her fingers. She didn't seem pleased with what she saw: the houses on the outposts she found small and primitive, and she looked silly in all the pictures, in her memory everything had been bigger and more beautiful. But halfway through, her hand slowed and she grew dreamy at the sight of the black-and-white views of distant landscapes. It was true, a childhood in the tropics got under your skin, it affected your entire life, but what could you do with it in the end? Who would be able to share these memories after she was dead? In Canada people had never heard of the Dutch East Indies. Suddenly she realized that with her, the stories that went with the pictures would die as well. Errol was not interested in such things. Let's get the scissors. She would divide the whole batch up fairly. This would be her legacy. She groped for the scissors that lay on the pile of newspapers beside her and snipped the air. "Here you are, Sas, your father with the resident and a tiger with a stick under its jaw, shot by him personally. And this one, my raccoon that nibbled at your clothes, give it to Aram, he can show it off in school." She loudly laughed away her dreams and cut around the rectangular and oval edges, page after page.

"Stop it, Jana, stop it," cried my mother, unaware of mixing English into her speech, for wherever she happened to be she always adjusted to her surroundings. But Jana would not hear of stopping. "I don't want these pictures to end up in the garbage." Saskia pulled them from her hands and possessively picked the best ones.

"And how about your children?" asked my mother.

Them? Too young, not interested enough, no, they didn't want to know anything about the past, history, old stuff.

Oh, those children, they stood in frames on the dresser, fat and ugly. In school they failed, and at work they did too. Her son was in the army and was folding parachutes on a base somewhere, her daughter worked in a supermarket in the neighborhood. Hadn't finished college, not a degree between them, not children to be proud of. We hardly saw them, for Jana preferred to keep them in the background now that we were here. "They want to be Canadians, don't you see, the same as everyone else, they're a little bit ashamed of our background and everything."

But when her daughter dropped by after work, large with a child that was not due for another month, she did want to know everything about us. She hung on my mother's neck . . . Granny this and Granny that, she really, really wanted to be part of a large family . . . and looked jealously at the pictures that were piled up in front of us.

"Who's that black man?" she asked.

"Your grandfather," said my mother, "and he's not black, he's brown, a Menadonese." The young woman groped through the photos, well, she had never known that . . . tigers in Indonesia? A house on stilts? Her mother as a girl with a pig on a leash. And ooh, how creepy, those brown soldiers behind a canon, lieutenant van Cappellen observing them proudly.

"Natives," she said.

Saskia buried her face in her hands. How could ner niece be so ignorant, hadn't her mother told her anything? "How is it possible, the most important part of your life."

Jana went on snipping, impervious. My mother quietly pulled the cardboard from the back of the photographs.

"Mama and you are just alike," said Saskia. "You avoid confrontation. If you don't solve the problems from the past, you'll drag them along like a leaden weight."

"It won't last that much longer," said Jana.

"You'll suffer from it all the same."

"That's what pills are for."

"That's what I used to think, too." Saskia straightened her back and did her best to look superior. "And the camp? You must have told them something about the camp?"

"No, nothing," said Jana. "What good would it do them?"

"Look at your daughter," cried Saskia. "What does she look like? Half Chinese, did you explain that to her? You're robbing your children of their history." She swallowed her tears.

"This country is a mix of all colors, all kinds. That's what makes us Canadian."

We were beginning to repeat ourselves.

The scissors plowed through air, the past had been cut away. The thermostat for the central heating was turned up a little, and the last maple leaf had fallen. The world shrank around us. Ah well, what more could we do? A cup of tea, some fig Newtons, and staring out the window. And some more cutting, of course. We had acquired a taste for it. Sitting around cozily and cutting. There was so much to be cut out: stacks of newspapers full of coupons, great savings in the enclosed folders. Every wish within reach, save it with your scissors! "Garden chairs at a two-dollar discount." "Buy one box of laundry detergent, get one free with this coupon." Jana reached for her last chance at a bargain, and my mother cut.

The candle still burned. Ada's portrait was given a place of honor, and Saskia expressed her grief by playing the CD of the violin fantasy over and over. The Kleenex tissues flew from the box.

Every morning around eleven the nurse came by to wash, administer pills, change bandages, and then she was off. Jana's legs were slowly dying, her toes were black already. How much longer? No one could tell, even Saskia could not receive a clear message about an exact date. To hide her impatience, she threw herself into her former profession once more. She wrapped her sister in softer diapers, peeled away the rotting flesh, and bought lavender water to wash away the unpleasant odors. (At a discount, no lack of coupons.)

But diapers and love were not enough for her. Now that her sister was visibly weakening and was losing her resistance, she wanted to wash the wounds of the soul as well. The camp. Jana must be made to talk about it. Saskia said she felt so guilty, those worn-out hips, wasn't that a result of the camp? Jana had always had to carry Saskia. She had not spared herself, cooking, carrying water, keeping the little ones busy, nursing her mother. Jana had been the strongest then, and now she must face the consequences.

"Do you remember the time we had to walk from the prison to the train?" Saskia asked. "We could bring only what we could carry, I was given the canister, but it was so heavy. You helped me, you took the handle, I held on to the bottom, and so I did my share. 'Mama, I really have to pee,' I said. 'Do it in your pants.' We had to keep going, the wet fabric chafed my legs. You lifted me up and perched me on your hip. And you were carrying such a lot already. After the train, in Sawahlunto, we had to go on in trucks. I couldn't find all of you anywhere, and I walked to the front. Mama was in a panic, but you found me playing between the wheels, almost crushed under an oncoming truck." How could she thank Jana for all this?

Talk, talk, until the last pus had been drained. My mother looked compassionately at her youngest daughter. She herself had told Saskia the story, and now she was being accused of not talking.

I watched the scene a whole week and was amazed that I hadn't murdered someone yet, surpassing myself in patience. During the first few days I sat distant and alone among my family, but my annoyance gradually waned, and I felt myself growing gentler and kinder. To sit, to listen, no resistance, perhaps this was a form of love.

My mother and Saskia clung to me, I had to drive them wherever they wanted to go, have breakfast with them, dine with them. We slept in the same motel, a fifteen-minute drive from Jana's house, which was too small to accommodate three guests, and we did not want to trouble her with meals. Besides, none of us was very fond of her husband. His few years in the merchant marine hadn't taught him subtlety. At present he was doing something with marine equipment, and he was used to shouting over the sound of machines. When he went to work in the morning, we relieved him; after six, we withdrew to our motel. He was suspicious of our presence, he thought we were just waiting for Jana's death. And because he did not know what to do with his anger, he began to curse our language. He refused to speak Dutch. "Dutch is useless. It doesn't get you anywhere in Canada." Sometimes we could not understand his English.

Jana had adjusted to her husband's crude ways. When the first child was born, they stopped speaking Dutch with each other. Jana had long ago given up correcting his accent. Strange, there were more and more gaps in her English, sometimes she forgot the simplest words, and she had had such a good ear for languages! Only the old, familiar sounds remained, and because of the tales about the East Indies her Malay, too, returned. She enjoyed teasing my mother by speaking the Indo dialect, which the Dutch looked down on but which my father spoke surprisingly well ("just for the fun of it, yes"): "Doctor feel me up. Belly still sick, bleedinge, *aduuu-uu*, the *obat* makes me *malu*. Haha haha, you laugh yourself *kriput*." She loved the singsong rhythms, and whenever she was tired, that melody colored her Dutch: stresses in a Saint Vitus' dance, coconut vowels just like my father's. Surely I'm exaggerating. I would ask myself when I imitated him, don't I blow up something that is minor, liar that I am? But now that I heard Jana I knew that my memory had not failed me, her accent had been preserved under a glass bell, the only thing about my sister that had not been touched. A voice that could recall amusing details—songs for doing the dishes and fairy tales for going to sleep—they gave me a past that did not burden me after all.

•   •   •

My family may have been pleased with my presence, but my motives were not pure, I had come not for a farewell but for a beginning. I wanted to have a serious conversation with my oldest sister for the first time in my life. But how? I didn't get a chance to speak to her alone. Mother, Saskia, and I got in each other's way, hanging around by that damned bay window. I caught myself actually cutting out coupons. When it comes to bargains, there's no place like Canada.

One evening my mother knocked on my door. "Saskia is driving me crazy, I can't get a minute alone with Jana." A little later, Saskia came to complain. I cut the Gordian knot: everyone would have a day alone with the patient. Saskia could go first.

Relieved, I took my mother on an outing to New Brunswick. On my flight here I had already noticed that Canada was not my kind of country. Mountains, lakes, wide expanses, nature offered an unspoiled horizon; but you had to share it with the inhabitants, and you'd be hard pressed to meet such ugly people anywhere else: fat, plaid shirts, hair thick in the nape of the neck, and ridiculous baseball caps on their heads. A worker's paradise, not a bookstore in sight, one literary magazine at the most, but thousands of magazines about outdoor life. Wildlife, that's what they loved, riding about in a muddy pickup truck, a canoe on the roof, a can of beer in the driver's hand, to be squeezed flat by a fist when it was empty, a small exercise in strength as preparation for chopping wood, fishing for salmon, or murdering Indians. If you stood longer than a minute in front of a painting in a museum, they assumed you must be a homosexual.

After a drive under a gray sky, with the heat on and casual talk that carefully avoided all painful subjects, my mother asked me to drop her at a hardware store, no, she felt no need to visit the whaling museum. What a chameleon, I thought, her way of honoring local culture, for there was a multitude of hardware stores in New Brunswick. Or perhaps she wanted to buy a present for my brother-in-law. I had to wait by the display window, but a little later she did call me in.

"I want to ask for a magnet and a file."

"What do you need it for?" I asked.

"To lie at the foot of Jana's bed. It draws the dampness out of the legs, makes it easier to get up." She'd seen it at home on television, had tried it at once, and how well she walked for her age. While the shopkeeper wrapped the items, she looked at me searchingly . . . no, I was not angry, I was smiling . . . a poke in the ribs, and giggling, we left the store together.

The sky became a dirty blackboard, gray-black, there was snow in the air and it was not long before the first flakes piled up under the windshield wipers. My mother could feel the winter tingling in her toes, the view outside Jana's window would be changing.

Back in the motel, the red light blinked on my telephone. Message from the front desk. "Your sister called. Urgent."

I telephoned, and Jana answered. Screams and sobs in the background.

"What's going on?"

"Oh, it's terrible," Jana wept, but before she could tell me her side of the story, the phone was pulled out of her hand.

It was Saskia. "Please, come and get me."

"Why, what's the matter?"

"I won't stay here a moment longer, come and take me away, take me away!" She slammed down the receiver.

I put on a pair of dry shoes, went to my mother's room, and knocked at her door. I heard her talking to someone and went in. She signaled for me to sit down on the bed across from her.

"Yes, yes," she listened, worried, to a voice at the other end of the line. "Oh my God. . . . In this weather? . . . Oh, oh, yes, yes." She hung up and looked at me in despair. Jana had just told her that Saskia had run out of the house, without a coat, into the snow. "Did I do everything wrong?"

"Doesn't matter."

She wanted to cry, her shoulders shook, but no tears came. I sat down beside her and put my arm around her. "Mustn't feel guilty," I said. "You did all you could." And I rocked her like a child, patted her back, stroked her head. "Your children are old enough to take care of themselves."

"We should never have left those two alone."

"What happened exactly?"

"She kept after Jana all day long about the camp, full of reproaches and questions. Jana didn't want to talk, and then they had a fight. I don't know, she tore up the photographs. Errol came home early from work and found them both in tears. He blew up and read Saskia the riot act. She said it was all his fault, and then I think she scratched him and called him every name under the sun. Now what should we do?" she asked in despair.

I called Jana and got an outraged Errol on the line. He was very sorry, but my whole damned family was to blame, we were rushing his wife to her death, she was terribly upset. Couldn't I hear her crying?

I tried to explain Saskia's problem to him. "She's upset by the war."

"Which one?" he asked, so surprised that he lapsed into Dutch.

"The Japanese camp, she's in therapy."

"That sort of thing could happen only in your country."

"Where is she now?"

"No idea, she went for a walk, I don't know where. Take Grand Falls Road."

The parking lot lay under three inches of snow, and it was a while before I found my rented car. Large, dry flakes were falling, the wheels slipped, and I drove onto the road at walking speed, with both side windows open so as not to miss the curb; snow coating the seat.

Not another soul was venturing forth, there were no road sanders in sight, even tire tracks were wiped out in no time. The staff of the Burger King was trying to keep the entrance and drive-ways clear with a small snowplow and my headlights sucked in the snow on all sides. I was approaching the edge of the suburbs, fallow fields, the shoulder and the road merging with each other. How often had I driven this stretch? If Saskia was walking back to the motel, she should be coming this way; perhaps I had already passed her.

At the highest point I got out of the car, stepped to the side of the road, and peered downward between the large sheds and upward into the hills. Silence, the only sound my creaking shoes.

A steely calm overcame me. Everyone was crazy, but they wouldn't get the better of me. The big Eskimo was looking for his sister.

At Jana's house, too, we could not find a clue. Perhaps Saskia was hiding in the garden. I walked outside and looked in through the bay window. Jana, arms outstretched, was bent over the table, bald, the wig crumpled in her hands. Her pregnant daughter had come to the rescue and was trying to help her mother sit up straight in her chair. Errol was raging right through the glass. They were startled when I knocked on the window. Hadn't I found that madwoman yet? The daughter pointed accusingly at a pile of torn photographs.

Inside, standing on a newspaper because of the snow melting on my shoes, I saw that Jana was unable to speak. She gasped, her swollen cheeks bright red, her breath whistling painfully. The daughter tried to put her wig back on, but Jana kept shaking it off. "Now do you people have what you came for?" she said. Her cash-register fingers were shaking with emotion.

"Oh what a mess," wailed Jana after I had calmed her a little with a few hugs. Yes, Errol was moody and not always friendly, but I must remember that they lived very much on their own. And Saskia had been terribly mean. "She called Errol a '*schoft*.' I almost lost my temper."

"And *schoft* means bastard, doesn't it?" asked Errol. There were two red scratches across his cheek and his shirt was torn at the collar. Saskia was a banshee. "I'll kill her if she comes back." Granny would still be welcome, but that's all. "Those crazies ought to be locked up."

The daughter rubbed her big belly. She looked at me as if her water might break any minute.

I borrowed Errol's binoculars and drove out onto the Grand Falls Road once more. Sister, where are you?

The snow reduced visibility to zero, and I realized that I was not as calm as I had thought when I began my search. The flakes dove at me like white ghosts, I almost fell over backward with fright. Calling, blowing the horn, no matter where I drove, I got no answer. I was becoming really worried, and I hurried to the motel to alert the police.

A little white heap was sitting under the signboard in the parking lot: Saskia, the hysterical snowwoman, her hair clotted with snow, soaked to the skin, and inconsolable. I tried to brush the snow from her hair, but she cowered, afraid that I was going to hit her. "I did come back, didn't I?" she said. "I never get lost."

I took her to my room, and while she lay on my bed recovering, I emptied a couple of the little cognac bottles from the minibar into a glass for her. I felt a great need to lie beside her, to throw my arm around her, and to whisper in her ear that I loved her, that I would be nicer to her from now on, that she was brave, my one and only dearest sister. But I couldn't bring myself to do it, and I put the glass down roughly on the bedside table. "Here. Makes you feel better. And tomorrow I'm taking you home."

The desk clerk had taken it upon himself to call a doctor who gave Saskia an injection and wrote out a prescription. Saskia fell asleep at once.

My mother knew none of this, but when I came to her room, her suitcase lay open on the bed.

"Let's just pack," she said after I had filled her in. Her face was ashen and she suppressed a deep sigh. "Always running away."

"Isn't that what we're all doing?"

"In the camp, too. She is so restless."

"Why not just say crazy?"

She looked at me chidingly.

"She is mixed up, Mama, seriously mixed up," I said.

"Do you think she can travel?"

"I'll look after her."

"Don't even think of it, you just make her more nervous. She's going back with me. We left together, we'll go back together. Didn't you want to go to New York?"

"But what about Jana?"

"I've already said good-bye." She went to her chest of drawers and began to fold her underwear. "I don't have to anymore. I'm through."

"Don't give up."

She used a stocking to wipe away a tear. "A very old tear," she said with a painful little laugh. "A tear from a previous life." We patted each other affectionately on the back. I had never before been so physically close to my family.

It was quite a business to get my mother and Saskia on an earlier flight. The computer was not very accommodating, and it looked as if we'd have to pay the full overseas fare. But after endless telephoning, it turned out that a charter would be leaving the following day after all. I couldn't get them on the waiting list with the excuse of mental illness, but an invented death in the family did wonders. Mother and daughter would be able to leave in the afternoon.

"Do you realize that your father never told me about the camp during the first few years I knew him?" said my mother as she waved the steam away from her spaghetti. "That only started after 1950, when a man who recognized him from the transport from Java to Sumatra spoke to him at an anthroposophic gathering." She picked up a forkful of food and spilled it on her sweater.

"But you did know that he had been on the railway?" I asked.

"From people I knew in Palembang, yes. He didn't talk. I could tell from his eyes that he'd gone through some bad times. But that man told him about the torpedoing and about the British officer who saved your father's life. Only then did he remember. Odd, isn't it? Completely forgotten."

Saskia lay on my bed sound asleep, and I sat with my mother under a clothesline from which hung small Italian flags. The motel was having pasta week. My clams tasted like cod-liver oil. We drank wine; my mother recklessly ordered a second glass. It was almost as if we were secretly celebrating some bond between us two, the strong ones. Quite right that I had taken things in hand, I was the competent son she could lean on. When she died, I should be the one to make the funeral arrangements. Ordinarily Ada would have been the one, because she was so painstaking and thrifty, but now I was given the honor. "According to the stars, I still have a few years left." She giggled. "And please find some more suitable music. You have good taste, at least." She was really appeasing me, disowning her mad daughter and laughing at her own superstitious nature because she knew this attitude would appeal to me. Mimicry. She would adapt herself until the grave.

"Whatever did Daddy see in anthroposophy?"

"The education, the idea that you could teach a child anything. You mustn't forget that he himself never had any advantages. He was so anxious for you to go far."

"Beatings should not be part of this."

"Come now, it wasn't so bad."

"He beat me every day."

"Not every day."

"Oh, come on!"

"We always spent such cozy Sundays, the day of the rijsttafel. He was always in his element then. . . ."

Nonsense, that's not what I was after, I was dying to ask her a more hurtful question: Why did you leave the room whenever he beat me? For days I had been waiting for the moment when I could level this reproach at her. But I could not summon up the courage. Childish as I was, I began to calculate the number of times I had been beaten. During the writing lessons, at mealtimes, after dinner, every day if I was late coming home from school . . . I heard myself say the words and was ashamed of myself . . . 365 minus how many Sundays . . . my mother was visibly shocked at my calculations. After endless squabbling, we agreed: during the week but never on Sundays. "Don't be silly," I snarled at her. "Are six beatings more excusable than seven?"

She thought I was exaggerating.

"And the ruler?"

"Yes yes, goodness, yes," she said. My father happened to care about table manners.

"And the stick?"

"That didn't last very long." And hadn't that been for my own good? I hadn't had to live with any aftereffects of that paralysis.

No matter what painful memory I dredged up, my mother made it appear rosy. She tried to be honest, but she told lie after lie. To me it was not a question of one beating more or less, all I wanted to know was: Why did you walk away? I must have wondered even as child, but because later I had focused all my hatred on my father, the question had never come up.

I drank to give myself courage. I had played my role of capable son and sat across from her like a little boy, a contrite nui-

246 • ADRIAAN VAN DIS

sance, and that little boy wanted to spare her humiliation. If I resembled anyone at all, it was my mother.

So I changed the subject and blamed others, told her artfully and with great exaggeration about the unmentioned death of my father's first wife and the trickery of Daddy van Bennekom, the lawyer of dubious ethics. She hardly reacted, as if she had suspected the truth all along.

But my obsession did not leave me: Why did you abandon me? The answer had to come to the surface, my patience was at an end, I was in a hurry and restless. Tired of the trip and the emotion, with the bill already on the table, I changed my question into a statement: "I think you were afraid of him."

"Whatever gave you that idea?" she exclaimed. "I was a hot-head myself. When he was in one of his moods, I'd say, 'If you don't like it, there's the door.' Just like that." She gripped her fork, and made a face appropriate to her bold statement.

Inspired by her firm expression, I let her have it. "There was only one person who went out that door, and that was you."

My mother collapsed, closed her eyes tightly, and slowly rocked her whole body in denial. . . . I took her hand and tried to comfort her. The liberating feeling I had hoped for manifested itself in waves of regret. "No, no, no . . ." she moaned, pulling her hand away. "If I left, it was to go to another room to pray, to ask for peace to come to him, and to exorcize the spirits in his mind."

"The pope prayed the Jews out of the gas chambers."

"That's an outrageous thing to say." She jumped up, she did not know what to do with her anger. Excited, she spilled her glass of water. "You're making yourself so important," she said in a loud voice. "You're wallowing in self-pity. What in heaven's name did you have to go through? And to make fun of your sisters, how dare you, you self-indulgent baby!"

I hid my shame in a large snifter of cognac. My mother gathered up the spilled bits of ice with her hand. Outside, a polar snowstorm was raging, but here the waitresses kept pouring ice into your drinking water. Strange country.

"Your father was a good lover," said my mother when the last piece of ice had melted in the ashtray.

"Who's being immodest now?"

"I think it's important for you to know. Your father could be very tender and loving."

"Would Jana agree with that?"

Whack. She answered me with a slap, a good old-fashioned slap on my left cheek, delivered with an open hand. A Japanese slap. There was plenty of life left in her old fingers, her action set the little flags above our heads aflutter.

"That's what I did to your father, too, whenever he went too far."

Never noticed, I thought. She picked up her pocketbook and I took the bill. We walked through the sparsely lit halls and kept an uneasy silence.

"Never forget," she said at the door to her room. "You were very much wanted, we both longed for a boy." She gave me a maternal tap on the cheek.

It had stopped snowing. The sky was clear, full of stars, a yellowish light hung along the horizon. I walked out and washed my face with snow.

The desk clerk handed me a long fax from my girlfriend. "Darling man," was the address. "Later. . . ." She loved me, the farther

apart we were, the more she loved me in words. I really must tell
her one of these days that I was not a "man," never again someone's "man."

Saskia was breathing deeply. There was a second bed in my
room and I stretched out on it, fully dressed. Her presence
annoyed me, but why? Even her sleep drove me crazy. I must try
to like her, not to pity her. Stretch and relax the back muscles,
balance the imaginary stick on my chest, and try to find a spark
of tenderness . . . I'm in a room with my sister; the last time, we
were in the wooden bedstead on my grandfather's farm.

"I know a secret," she had said.

"What is it?"

"Can't tell."

"Oh, come on."

"If I tell, it will bring bad luck."

"I'll keep it to myself."

"Promise? Cross your heart and hope to die?"

"I swear."

"There was another little boy born before you."

"When?"

"In the camp."

"Oh," I said, dumbfounded. "Then where is he?"

"In the heaven of the East Indies. He was born dead."

"Is he in Grampa's photo album?"

"Mama named you for him."

"Did he look like me?"

"No, he was our real brother."

Memory is selective, everything is inscribed but much becomes
vague. I had never thought of this incident again, my mother
had never mentioned the baby, no diary or camp auntie had

said a word. Clean forgotten. And yet I missed my predecessor. Hadn't I felt his presence long ago? Perhaps I had tasted his memory in my mother's womb, and my longing for an imaginary brother had begun back there. I would not ask my mother anything further, but perhaps Jana could. . . .

Quebec was free of snow, the highways had been plowed. Nothing stood in the way of our departure. It was a five-hour drive to the airport. We had only the morning to say good-bye. I would go first, to stay behind alone did not appeal to me, there was no point in further waiting for Jana's life to end, her daughter's water did not seem ready to break, and it could still take quite a while before the actual death. Only bad doctors predict when you will die of cancer, the nurse had told us. My mother would come a little later. Saskia was not to be mollified, she never wanted to see her sister again, she was given a pill in her yogurt, and that's how we kept her quietly in the motel. We could be amazingly practical if necessary.

Jana had found it difficult in such a short time: "Mama had looked forward to the visit so much, and I did too, of course." She had done everything wrong. Too much tension. She and Errol were not talkative enough. "I'm guilty of that too, and I have no excuse." So much had happened at once, and she was ashamed at the way she had entertained us. "Our life here is not that grand."

We drank weak tea and I let her do the talking. "Great that we could be with Ada, your eulogy really captured her, her own way, her own life, but oh, so tired of all the caring. It makes you realize that you're isolated, alone, but this is the life I chose. Probably the way of least resistance, something you do when you're very young, but when you get older, you wonder whether it was an improvement. Perhaps it was inevitable." She bravely bit her lower lip.

"Why did you go to Canada?"

"The opportunities, you know, jobs were there for the asking."

"Els Groeneweg said that you fled."

"Goodness, Els. How is she?"

"Did something happen?"

"I was an innocent, inexperienced."

"Did he . . ."

"Ah well, you know . . ."

"No."

"I was the strong one at home, he leaned on me."

"His weak heart."

"Yes, sort of, you wouldn't understand." She pointed out the window. "Hey, what are those? Hand me the binoculars, please." She turned around in her chair and followed the black trail that flew against the snowy hills. "Swans, wild swans, we rarely see those here, they must be the last ones."

Something else flew away. She looked in every direction except at me. "So that's life, little brother," she said.

And so it was, no skeletons brought out of the closet, no more cross-examination and nagging insinuations. I got up and stood at the window with my hands in my pockets. Hadn't she told me the story of the princess who freed her seven brothers bewitched into swans, by throwing over their wings a web made of nettles? "Thank you for all the stories you used to read to me," I said.

A car horn honked, my mother's taxi. Because I did not know how to say good-bye, I moistened my finger with saliva and drew a cross on her forehead. According to my mother, that gesture conferred peace. "She used to do that in the camp all the time." Jana laughed.

I opened the door to my mother, and when she walked on my arm into the hothouse, Jana exclaimed from her chair, "You walk just like your father. Toes pointed out, swinging like an elephant." And then I bit my lower lip, I blushed, even though she had not meant to be mean. I was ashamed, no matter how much my mind resisted this emotion. My father was my mahout, my elephant boy. I had tried to shake him off, but Jana placed him back on my neck.

Saskia was waiting in the hall with the suitcases, we had decided merely to stop at the front door, pick up Mama, and off we'd go. No more farewells. But Jana could not bear to let her sister go without some last word. She stood at the window, leaning on her fat daughter, her face distorted with pain. Saskia looked the other way.

"Did you talk about anything else?" I asked on the highway headed for Quebec.

"No," said Mother, "we had nothing more to say."

"Then what did you do?"

"We cut out coupons."

On my way to New York I spent the night in Albany, was revived by a breakfast of pancakes and maple syrup, and decided to leave the south on my right for the time being and to drive East, just like that, on a whim, for a pleasant ride along the Atlantic Ocean, I had seen enough ugliness. A few hours later, I drove over the last of the coastal hills and passed a sign with an arrow

252 • ADRIAAN VAN DIS

pointing to Cape Cod. This was my sign! The name was the sound that went with a famous photograph: young Kennedy walking along the broad dunes of Cape Cod.

Dunes . . . I would be able to let the wind blow through me, regain my peace of mind, and wash away the smell of diapers and death. The sea wind pushed impatiently through the side window, and in the distance a promontory glistened in the bay, yachts and sailboats bobbed at wooden piers. I took the turnoff and rattled over an iron bridge. Cape Cod turned out to be an island.

On the map it had the shape of an arm with a raised fist, Pop-eye after a can of spinach. The wide road led past woods, rocks, pools, and creeks. I saw no dunes. Not until I had past the elbow, as the landscape flattened out, a promise of sand and clay was outlined on the eroded hills—stripes of rust, lead and ivory waved alongside; here the sea wind turned the earth into a flag. The white fences of the cottages were closed, the shutters of the old fishermen's houses were shiny with paint. The fashionable summer crowds had left, an old-timer sauntered by in pink plaid pants.

An osprey streaked over a marsh and flew off into the pine trees, its prey in its claws. The sun was shining, autumn was at its best that day, a soft southwesterly breeze passed over the island; the branches waved, heavy with pinecones.

Until finally the island grew more barren: bushes with crooked backs, tough grasses, barns, and wharves weathered by salt and wind, poor as is proper along the coast. I was approaching the fist, the road narrowed, I took my chances and drove down some smaller side roads, looking for the dunes and a clap-board hotel with a view of the sea. But the streets dead-ended or circled around and around, to end up back on the main road. Were there actually dunes here? Perhaps I had just imagined that photograph, and where was the sea? I could hear it, I could smell it, but I could not see it anywhere. It was getting late, the sun disappeared behind the bushes and the first lighthouses turned on their beacons, three fingers sweeping across the sky. I drove to the nearest lighthouse—Do Not Enter—jumped over the gate, and walked up the slope. The sea was rising, and not until I reached the highest point could I see it break, deep below me; the Atlantic Ocean, wild and foamy. I had driven around in a hollow, the sides of the island were higher than the middle, and only at this point did I discover that the island also had a low-lying edge of dunes, wide, full of whimsical notches and bays, dark and menacing in the afterglow of the setting sun. Everything was large and fierce, here the sea was master, and storms hacked cliffs into the wall. Tomorrow this would be my beach.

The sand was hard and untrodden, I walked with a high wind at my back. The autumn cold whistled through my clothes. The tide was pulling back, flakes of foam rolled toward me. Behind every curve I discovered a new view.

Suddenly a brown cloud rose from the dunes, the cloud shrieked, rode out to sea, rose and fell apart above the breakers. Thousands of birds dropped down at my feet. Whole regiments flocking together, snipes on their way south, came to earth for a meal and a resting place. There was order in their chaos, thousands of tiny brains deciding to spend a few hours here, and they did not make way for me. The front ranks, somewhat frightened, rose and landed behind me, but after a few yards the snipes' courage returned, and they closed ranks. Some of them stood on one leg and stared at me dreamily. They waited, peaceful and small, and yet they frightened me. One single bird tried to land on my shoulder, to the snipe I was only a moving tree. I turned back and walked away on tiptoe.

"Keep walking," said my father. "The jungle is full of wild animals, isolate yourself, keep your eyes on the vanishing point." It was nesting time, and the seagulls flew ahead of us. We were walking with backpacks filled with sand. Back straight, muscles straining and raise that left leg. I want, I'll win—when the leg hurt, I had to say this ten times. Don't walk like a girl. A heavy tread makes the legs strong. My father's soles stamped on the beach.

This was also how he had walked on patrol, he'd had to keep going for days, a wounded soldier on his back. Not allowed to complain, the wounded had to be brought along, otherwise they would become an easy target for the enemy and would betray them. The sand on my back was the wounded. Stop, let's add a few more handfuls, wet sand that leaked a trail down your buttocks, sand that scratched the insides of your thighs. Blood, think of the blood of the wounded man on your back.

We walked into the dunes, the looser the sand, the better. Let the reeds swish, down into the hollows, up into the hills. The male gulls circled above our heads. I looked up fearfully. They screeched, skimmed past, and tried to peck at us. We were walking straight through a colony of gulls, they were everywhere, new squadrons came flying by, low and vicious in their attack. I had to duck and could hear their wings beating against my backpack. The wind created by their diving flight slapped my neck.

My father pulled some reeds from the ground and began to chase away the divers, waving and screaming. But they would not stop and pecked at the spears in his hand. "Those birds are the enemy," he called out above their screeching. "This is a diversion, we must keep going. They want to cause confusion." His lips looked purple.

We walked on, hands on our heads and eyes fixed on the vanishing point. I want, I'll win. My father, gasping, walked behind me. We climbed higher, back to the sea strip, away from the green that housed the nests. I heard his breath rasping in his throat, looked back, and saw that he was pulling himself up by the dune grass.

He held on to me, exhausted, and leaned against my backpack. I undid the strap around my waist and collapsed in the sand. "Up," he panted. "Don't rest. Kick away the fatigue! The moment you give in they'll attack. If I'd sat down back then with the baggage, I wouldn't be standing here by your side. Keep on going and you'll win."

I climbed up the dune. My father leaned on me, and the load became lighter. The wounded man was an angel floating above my back.

THE MOTHER had buried her daughter, in the snow, in a hole dug with pickaxes. The tulips from Holland lay waxlike on the coffin. She stood by the grave, numb with cold. The icy wind took her breath away, the love and warmth she longed to send along with her daughter congealed in her mind. She was unable to think or speak a single sentence. To think that she must take leave of her daughter while her toes were becoming frostbitten! She was leaving behind in the frozen ground a child born in the heat. Jana must have chosen the time on purpose, so that the frost would embalm her and nature would hold on to her that much longer.

Jana had died in the sunroom, her bed had been moved downstairs weeks ago. She lay between two electric heaters, it did feel just like a hothouse, the snow melting under the window and the birds warming their feet on the glass roof. The garden fascinated her to the very last. She lost consciousness while pointing at a squirrel that was stealing the strung-up peanuts. The nurse was just about to wash her. Errol was at the factory; it was lasting too long, he could no longer bear to sit and twiddle his thumbs as he waited for her to die.

It was to be a modest funeral, not worth her coming over for. The coffin had been closed already. "It's too cold for you," said Errol on the phone. Too cold? She would decide about that herself! She'd wear something warm, she had knitted enough sweaters in her lifetime. Besides, wasn't there a baby in the cradle, her first great-grandchild? No, she would not be kept away, some restitution must still be made. To hold her daughter's hand one more time—how could you refuse a mother that? And none of her children need accompany her, better not, in fact: if they felt guilty, they might pay her fare. Sorrow was best born alone.

She regretted not having taken leave of Jana in a more worthy manner. The oldest was always shortchanged. "When you go, I'll be there to hold you." This was the promise she'd made when she'd traveled to Canada the last time, the sentence kept droning through her mind. What else could you do but lead your child gently to the dark tunnel, to take away the fear, just as she had done at Jana's birth; to comfort a helpless creature, to help it toward the light, deliverance lay on the other side, at birth, too, you had to go through a tunnel, there was not that much difference between beginning and end. But fate had decided otherwise. Saskia needed all her attention, and the choice had been made quickly. Her youngest daughter must not be allowed to perish as well. Life came first.

Saskia was better now, although there had been a few bad weeks. A lot of reproaches and angry words. It was all Mother's fault. She had not defended herself, to help your child, you swallow a lot.

There were not many people at the graveside, perhaps ten, the nearest kin, a few neighbors. Jana's son read something from the Bible and stumbled over the words. His sister clung to her grandmother with all her weight—poor Granny! Not much longer and she would be delivered of this burden for good. She knew that on this day she was taking her leave not only of Jana . . . son-in-law, grandchildren, they had become total strangers. At first she had looked forward to the new baby, but when she held it in her arms, a colorless, anonymous little boy, it had meant nothing to her. She didn't even inquire about the hour of its birth; what need did such a creature have of a horoscope?

The following night she was back on the plane. She had asked for a window seat, so as to get another good look at the frozen lakes. The view was excellent, the wind had swept the sky clear, the previous time the cloud cover had been thick. She studied the flight route depicted in the in-flight magazine stored in the back of the seat in front of her, this would be her last flight.

She was practiced in farewells. Not that it no longer hurt, but it was so much a part of existence. Her mother had disappeared from her life when she was only four, dying at the birth of her brother. That boy could do nothing right in his father's eyes, he was raised on a steady diet of reproaches, and she stood between them. She had been mother, sister, and arbiter at once, there was no time for unhappiness. That experience had shaped her: you could love people all you wanted, but they could disappear from your life just like that. You had no control, this is how you were put to the test. Karma, it was your destiny, the main lines were predetermined. This she firmly believed, and didn't she have proof enough?

Take her first husband, for instance: just before the war broke out, he predicted that she and the girls would go back to Holland alone. A separation, she thought, he wants to get rid of me, and she did not contradict him, for their marriage was head-ing in that direction. Later, in the camp, when it gradually became obvious that the swelling in her womb was not a tumor but a baby, she knew at once that she was too weak to deliver a living child, and this knowledge certaintly made the loss more bearable.

And then Just II, another typical example. He was convinced that he would die in his forty-second year, a seer in the camp had predicted as much. That's why he was in such a hurry to educate his son. She would never forget that the day after his forty-second birthday he came home with a large box of envelopes and sat down at the table, that's how convinced he was of his own death. Coincidence? You don't call that coincidence. Another prediction had come true earlier in his life. Justin would have a car accident before his ninth birthday— well, everyone had been forewarned! He couldn't take a step without someone going with him, always brought to school and picked up afterward. On his ninth birthday the whole family heaved a sigh of relief. They took him to school, piloted him through the gate, and drove off. Justin turns around, slips out of the gate, crosses the street, and is scooped up by a car. That was where he had gotten those scars on his back!

The seat belts need no longer be buckled, the flight attendants were distributing drinks. Oh, gosh, now she had forgotten all about the lakes. She leaned toward the window and looked out into a black hole . . . no icy surfaces in sight, only that strange yellow light on the horizon, it couldn't possibly be the moon, or was she already traveling toward the sun?

How delightful it would be to float away out there . . . toward the light, delivered of her earthly task. . . . She closed her eyes and saw Ada float by, then Jana . . . they were calling to her, they waved. No, she mustn't let herself go. There was still Aram, her favorite grandchild, smart and sensitive. The boy counted on her. She decided to visit him every Wednesday evening, a good hug and see to his ears; very convenient, for on that day there was no charge on the senior citizens' bus.

She took a snapshot out of her purse, Jana had left it for her in an envelope, one of the few that had escaped Saskia's fury, only the tip of a corner was missing. She would find a frame for it and give it a place of honor at home. It showed on the family on top of a dune: herself, Justin, and the four children. Who could have snapped it? She didn't recognize this picture at all. Where was her magnifying glass? Must look at it carefully . . . sunset . . . you could tell from the soft shadows that nestled in the dunes, the father at the center, the son safely tucked between his legs, the girls with drawn-up knees next to their mother. All equally brown in the evening light, all alike, a morsel of happiness at the end of a summer day. Her arm was draped over Justin's shoulder. She thought of the little wisps of hair at the nape of his neck, the soft curls she loved to run her fingers through. How lethargic she had been in those days, she still could not understand what he had seen in her. Justin could have had any woman he wanted in Palembang, everyone thought him handsome and charming, but he had chosen her, a worn-out widow with loose teeth. She would always be grateful to him, he had given her back her pride . . . no other man had made her feel so feminine.

How could that boy possibly hate his father? They were crazy about each other, you could tell from the photo, they were both radiant! All those stories he told now, bothering everyone . . . the beatings, the stick. . . . Serious mistakes had been made, certainly, but when would he ever get over it? She should really tell him that after dinner he would fetch the stick himself—"How about doing the exercises, Dad?" He dragged his father along outside, he wanted to learn how to climb trees, even though his father was much too ill for such things. She often worried that all those dune walks were bad for his heart. If she took her son outside with the sled in winter, he would stamp his feet and throw a tantrum, he did not want to go with a woman, there was no one like his father. The hothead, that kind of temper was quite common in red-headed children. Sometimes she was afraid that he was in love with his own father, a kind of mixed-up Oedipus; who knows, perhaps that could happen. He was so attached to him. Perhaps that was what Justin was trying to prevent but had not known how to deal with so much devotion.

She put away her magnifying glass and stared at the picture. Her children were running through the dunes, she could hear crying, laughing, whispering voices, she comforted, tidied, carried, made her way through nameless faces . . . music, dancing under the stars, in wooden shoes in the meadow, in bare feet in the dessa, bowing to the Japanese, bowing at a grave. . . . She was leafing through her life like a crazy woman, and every image shattered before her eyes.

The flight attendant lowered her table and placed a tray with a lukewarm roll under her nose. "Were we dreaming?" she said as she poured the coffee. "And can I take this away?" She held up a handful of torn bits of paper. Dazed, the mother put them in her purse.

The captain announced that they were approaching the Netherlands, the airplane was starting its descent. Someone had closed the curtains, the morning light shone through the cracks on the sides. The mother wanted to see the coast. She lifted her curtain and looked down. She saw nothing but waves.